OTHER STORIES

KANA COLD
Case of the Shinigami

A young girl is haunted by a Death God. Her only hope is a rum-drinking, bar-fighting paranormal investigator with a bad attitude.

After dropping out of Harvard, Kana Cold started a business as a sarcastic, rum-drinking, bar-fighting paranormal investigator. Most of her cases are hoaxes, much to Kana's disappointment, until one case involving a little girl and her powerful demon—a *Death God*—opens the door to the real Paranormal Underground... changing Kana's life forever.

Available now on Amazon!

www.aoestudios.com

BOOK 1

THE REAPING OF THE
BLACK GRIMOIRES

KC HUNTER

AOE STUDIOS

Published by AOE Studios

Cover Design KC Hunter

AOE Studios publication: First Edition March 2019

ISBN: 978-0-9829533-2-7

CONTENTS

INTRODUCTION

The origins of Kana Cold are strange to say the least. On Sunday nights I usually watch YouTube, particularly the paranormal countdown channels. Content creators like *Matt Santoro, The Boo Review, Dark 5, Top 10 Archive, Beyond Science* and others entertain me with their presentation of urban legends, *creepypastas*, and general odd facts and figures compiled into countdown lists or single topic videos.

One night the idea struck me that there were plenty of stories here that could be turned into novels. In fact, there could be an *Indiana Jones* type of character who went on adventures. Instead of the Ark of the Covenant or the Holy Grail as the *McGuffin*, these novels would feature some of these more bizarre and unknown mysteries from around the world.

If no one else was going to do it then I should.

That started the idea and from there the rest flowed rather easily. Kana (or Kanna) is a name synonymous with a few Japanese female heroines I admire. I wanted her personality to be aloof—someone who has seen so many fake hauntings and prank ghosts that she's lost interest, but then something real comes across her plate and it changes everything. *Kana Cold* was born and the world around her soon followed.

However, I didn't want to just recreate these existing *creepypastas* and legends, nor did I want to redo *Indiana Jones*. Many of my readers know how much I abhor rehashing existing stories by swapping out gender, race, or name for key characters and presenting it as your own. Instead, I wanted to create my own mythology about the paranormal underworld as seen through the eyes of a fledgling investigator.

Beyond just the strange stories of cryptids and secret societies there's a greater tale about a young woman who is learning her path in the world, dealing with emotional baggage from her upbringing into her college years, and has a desperate need to prove herself—to show that just because you don't look like the typical "lead" it doesn't mean you can't be.

The Reaping of the Black Grimoires is the first full adventure for Kana and I hope you enjoy taking this step with her.

> • *KC Hunter*
> *February 2019*

FOR ALL THOSE WHO DESIRE TO BE MORE
THAN THEY ARE AND ARE BRAVE ENOUGH
TO REACH FOR IT

KANA COLD

THE REAPING OF THE BLACK GRIMOIRES

CASE 100

———— ~~/ ————

Ten days ago, it started. Ten days ago, Peter Riley had peace of mind in his own home. Ten days later, that peace perished.

As a widower, Peter struggled day after day, not only to raise his son, but to maintain a job as a security officer. Working for an art museum was ideal. The quiet of the chambers suited him, each filled with hundred-year-old canvases coated in oils, pottery handcrafted by artisans long since buried, and the complicated metal constructions of art students from the nearby college. It was a secret he kept to himself, his love of the arts, hidden from his peers who found such things boring.

Two weeks ago, his peace was broken when she came to visit. *The Wraith*, as he nicknamed her, pale and gaunt, her face always covered by a mop of dark stringy hair. From his post he watched her, holding his posture upright and crossing his arms as she meandered through the museum as if she was gliding across the marble floor.

By lunch he lost sight of her. Hours passed and by the end of the day she had yet to pass through the exit. *I must have missed her when she walked out*, he thought. But his grumbling stomach told him that he had more pressing issues. The museum closed at 4 p.m. and as the last few patrons left, Peter snacked on a few leftovers from lunch.

"Ten!" The voice was garbled and feminine, and he stumbled when the icy breath tickled the back of his ear.

The Wraith was standing behind him. Peter took a few shallow breaths before ushering the woman from the museum, and she repeated the number as she left.

The next day, she returned and pulled the same stunt, but this time she repeated the number "nine" while kneeling in front of him and ripping at her oily hair with her nails. It was enough for Peter to have her banned from the building for life, thinking that would end the woman's game.

Over the next week, she found him every day, whether at the grocery store, a gas station, or even his son's playground. Each day, the number changed, decreasing from eight to one.

After taking his concerns to the local police and getting nothing more than a report to fill out for his trouble, Peter sought less conventional means to stop this stalker, The Wraith, before she reached the number zero.

***

"It's just you and your son here, correct?" asked AJ Guiscard, sitting cross-legged on Peter's living room floor.

"Yes, it's just us. His mother passed two years ago. I've been trying to hold it together. You know, maintaining the house and everything with just my income. It's been tough."

"I can imagine." AJ scribbled a few words on his notepad. "No history of mental disorders in the family, I assume? Paranoia? Schizophrenia?"

"No, nothing like that." Peter shook his head.

"I have to ask, Mr. Riley. It's not an insult."

"Of course."

"And you've never experienced anything paranormal or otherworldly before this incident?"

Peter shifted his jaw from side to side. "I don't believe in ghosts or anything if that's what you're asking. I've never seen anything nor has my son."

"Are you sure about that?"

"Quite."

AJ scratched the side of his head with the end of his pen. "Well, I ask because usually no one calls us unless they think there's something paranormal going on. Did you know that's what we did?"

"Look, my cousin gave me this number and said I should call you guys. I've got a freaky woman coming to my job, following me to the supermarket, counting down numbers, and the police can't—or won't—do anything about it. He said you guys could help. I'm quite frankly out of options."

"We're going to figure this out." AJ put down his pen. "I wish we had more time, but from what you told me, we may be running out of it. I have to finish this questionnaire before we can get to the next step."

"Why?"

"It's procedure." The teenager shrugged his shoulders before gathering his pen and paper again.

Peter stared at the boy, wondering whether he was being serious about this or not. How old was this boy anyway? Twenty, maybe?

"Are you sure you don't want a seat?" Peter pointed to a chair.

"Oh, no. I feel more comfortable this way. It's better for my back too."

"Right." Peter fidgeted in his chair as he watched AJ scribble away on the notepad, crossing out a few lines and feverishly writing again. "I'm sorry, can I ask when this is going to start? As you said, we're running out of time. Do we really have to finish this interview?"

The boy turned his wrist over, checking his watch. "You said this usually happens around 4 p.m. no matter where you are?"

"Yes, and it's quarter till right now. I'm sure she's going to show up here. The cops won't do anything. To listen to them explain it, she'd have to literally stab me first before they'll act. 'No evidence that's she a threat', as they say."

"Yeah, they tend to do that."

A buzzing came from AJ's backpack. He read the message on his phone and quickly made his way toward the front door.

Peter followed AJ to the door. "Is that your partner?"

"Yeah, that's her." The boy stopped and turned, lifting his hand to Peter's chest. "Look, she's a very peculiar person. Not normal like you and me." Peter tried to hold back his grin and failed. "I know she can be off-putting, but she means well. Don't question her too much, she hates that. Oh, and don't try to offer up any theories. That'll make her roll her eyes. Oh, and absolutely don't stare at her."

"Stare? Why?"

AJ rubbed his hands together and grabbed the door handle. Peter straightened his back as the door opened and AJ's business partner made her entrance.

***

The woman entering peered at Peter, who already violated one of AJ's warnings: he was staring.

"You're Kana Cold?" Peter raised an eyebrow.

She didn't answer and walked past him without so much as a glance. His glare radiated over her shoulder while she observed the house, modest but spacious, the kind of home she expected from the neighborhood outside. This was a place where people ate at a dinner table, played backyard games of catch, and had celebrations on Sunday for God and goalposts.

Kana turned back to speak to Peter and caught him gawking at her. It wasn't the first time she'd startled a man out of his lustful thoughts, of which she had no desire to know the details of. *Yellow Fever*, as it was known, was etched all over Peter's slack-jawed face. Kana recoiled as the man approached her, his hand extended while hers was firmly stuck in the pockets of her black leather jacket.

"I'm Peter." He pulled his hand back. "Your business partner here was telling me about you. You're not quite what I expected."

He may as well have been speaking to the wall. Kana scanned the sunlit living room. "Is your son still in the house?"

"He's asleep upstairs. I thought this might be a little much for him."

"He's alone?"

Peter flicked his tongue against his upper lip. "Well, yeah, there's no one else here."

That was the first mistake Kana noticed, and with a nod, instructed AJ to head upstairs to look in on the boy. Peter opened his mouth to speak now that they were alone, but Kana turned her back to him again to investigate the kitchen.

"I just have to ask..." he started but stopped when Kana began searching through his trash can. "Excuse me." He cleared his throat. "I just have to ask you a question."

Kana finished with the trash can and moved to the counter. "Go ahead and ask."

"What exactly is it that you're doing? I need help with this woman who is stalking me. You two seem to be more interested in my home."

Kana stopped her investigation of the mail on the countertop and sat on one of the kitchen stools, patting the seat of its sister. Peter took the second stool for himself, now eye to eye with Kana.

"You called my office. We are here to help. Now, you say this woman has been counting down for the last ten days, she always knows where you are, but you have no idea who she is or what she intends to do today when she hits the number zero. Is that right?"

"In a nutshell."

"And that doesn't seem extremely strange to you? Like, metaphysically strange?"

Peter's forehead wrinkled. "Metaphysically?"

"Yes, like metaphysics?"

He stared at her with an open mouth and wide eyes. She could have been speaking German right now and have a better chance of him understanding her.

Kana pushed a few strands of her black hair behind her ear.. "Well, as the word suggests, it's beyond physics to sum it up quickly for you."

"You mean, supernatural ghosts and stuff?"

"That can be part of it."

"I don't believe in any of that." Peter's scowl turned into a mocking grin. "That's why AJ was asking all of those weird questions. Look, I don't have anything against you people"—

"You people," Kana repeated under her breath.

—"but if you expect me to believe that this is some kind of haunting, then you've come to the wrong house. I have a stalker. That's the problem I have. Some crazy woman who is following me around and harassing my family. Not some ghost. Not some spirit. I don't believe in any of that silliness."

"That's nice. They don't care if you do or don't."

Kana patted Peter on the hand the way a parent would a child who told them Santa Claus was real. She knew she was irritating him, but his staunch rejection of her abilities, without even knowing what they were, was unacceptable. In her experience, people like him abhorred the spiritual or the supernatural, and certainly didn't want anything—Christian, Islamic, or even Wiccan, if that was the case—to be brought into their home.

Peter pushed her hand away. "If you're trying to scare me, sweetheart, it's not going to work."

Kana slid as far back on the stool as she could without falling off. "*Sweetheart?* Oh no, no. Nah—no, no, no! Don't ever call me *sweetheart* again."

"Look, if you are going to try and create some light show or throw some smoke around and try to charge me that fee of yours—which, by the way, is pretty high—you might as well just leave now. I'll take my chances."

"Really? How are you going to do that?"

"I'm a security guard." Peter stood from the stool, reached

into the cabinet above the refrigerator, and pulled out a lockbox. Inside was a 9mm handgun. He took it from the box and laid it on the kitchen counter.

"Savvy?"

Kana tapped her fingernails on the table. "Yeah, that's not going to work."

"A bullet works on a lot."

Kana stood and walked back into the living room, leaving the man to marvel over his weapon. Ten steps later, she marched back to Peter.

"Against my better judgment, I'm going to help you out," she said.

"I don't want your—"

"I don't care. If it weren't for your kid, I would have walked out of here the second I caught you staring at me, *sweetheart*."

"I wasn't staring."

"Sure you weren't. Listen, what you've got is what we call a *Keter*. It's an aggressive spirit that's hard to deal with. They can be very dangerous—physically dangerous." She slapped the arm of her jacket, the sound of which made Peter jump back. "They can get inside your head—trust me, you don't want that—and torment you for as long as they want. Your gun isn't going to do anything. Leave this to someone who knows what to do."

"Of course. You ain't afraid of no ghost. "Peter bounced from side to side, that stupid grin back on his face. Kana glared at him, as still as a "Are you done?" She crossed her arms. He stopped bouncing. "Good. At this point, I've given you more information than anyone else has on what this woman is. If that's not enough to convince you, then I don't know what else to tell you."

"It's not enough. I get it now. You're not trying to scam me. You actually believe in this." Peter picked up the gun from the counter and placed it back into the lockbox. "At this point, I think this was just a bad idea. You and your friend should leave."

"Kana!" AJ's voice rained from upstairs.

Peter and Kana followed AJ's cry up the stairs to the boy's bedroom. The door was wide open, AJ backing out of it with his hands shaking. "He won't leave the room. I couldn't stay in there. I'm... I'm sorry."

Peter pushed him out of the way and ran into the bedroom. Kana stayed with AJ, who waved off her concern and pointed to the boy. She followed Peter inside, seeing The Wraith for herself.

Just beyond the door frame stood Peter, frozen in place, and his son, Dallas, no more than five feet from him. The woman who had terrorized them for days stood behind the boy, her hands on his shoulders.

"This is her?" Kana asked Peter, who couldn't manage more than a nod.

The Wraith's oily hair concealed most her head, the mop

allowing only a glimpse of her sickly pale face, ashen and gray even in the light of day.

"I don't understand why I can't move. I can't get close to him," Peter whispered.In a full voice, he addressed his son. "Dallas! Come over here. It's okay. Just come over here."

The child sniffled as he swayed back and forth, his knees locked together.

"Do you recognize her?" Kana asked Peter.

"No. I don't... Well, I can't tell."

"Are you related? Is that your dead wife?"

"No. Of course not! But she's... there is something familiar there."

"Peter, be honest with me," Kana said, her voice stern. "Did you wrong anyone? Would anyone have a grudge against you?"

"No! I don't... I mean, years ago I..." he turned his head to Kana and lowered his voice. "I had an affair, okay? Then I ended it. She didn't take it well."

"Why am I not surprised?" Kana rolled her eyes before stepping farther into the room. "What was her name? And please don't tell me you called her sweetheart."

"Nina. Her name was Nina."

The Wraith shrieked at the sound of the name, the force of her howl causing the boy's bladder to release its contents, wetting the front of his pants. Nina exposed her scarred face, the oily strands pushed aside by her bluish gray fingers, her wrist showing the wounds of her suicide.

Kana inched to The Wraith. "Nina," she said softly, raising her hand.

Whatever invisible force that held Dallas and Peter in its grasp had no power over Kana. She took another cautious step to the boy, her black boots pressing into the carpet, kicking toy trucks from her path.

"You don't need the boy. Whatever it is that Peter did to you, it's not the kid's fault."

Peter scrunched his nose. "How come you can move?"

Kana threw her answer over her shoulder, her attention still on Nina. "She knows you. She doesn't know me. They have to know you to have that kind of power."

Nina's head shook wildly, her hair whipping around her. She staggered to Dallas, her body contorting as her bones popped and clicked.

Kana's raised hand turned into a fist. "Nina! Leave this child alone. There is no reason to harm him."

"Ten!" The Wraith grumbled, placing her hand on the boy's shoulder.

Kana shook her fist. "No, no. Nah—no, no, no."

"Nine!"

"Nina!"

The Wraith dug her fingers into Dallas's shoulder. "Eight!"

Peter's neck tightened, the veins pressing against the skin. "Leave my boy alone! Leave him alone, Nina!"

"AJ, I need you to hurry up," Kana called out.

Her assistant stumbled back to the bedroom and searched through his backpack, flinging its contents onto the carpet until he found what he was looking for: a hand mirror wrapped in several layers of bubble wrap and cloth. "I've got it."

"Hurry up, AJ!"

The counting grew louder, faster. "Seven, six, five—"

AJ handed the mirror to Kana. "Here!"

"—four, three, two, one—"

The counting stopped. Nina's emerald eyes flashed over to the mirror: a wooden frame with runic symbols carved along its side, the glass reflecting the sunlight from the window.

"I warned you." Kana pushed the face of the mirror at Nina, and the sunlight flooded the phantom. "Leave the boy alone."

Kana was close enough to reach Dallas, so she patted the boy on the shoulder before freeing him from the phantom's grip. He rushed into his father's waiting arms.

"No," Nina cried, her hands shielding her from the oppressive light, twitching as Kana closed in on her. "He must pay! He must pay!"

"You've done enough." Kana stopped her advance. "You've scared the hell out of him. Quite frankly, he's not worth being around with the living, let alone coming back from the grave for. Let it go, Nina. It's time to pass on."

"No!"

The Wraith spread her arms wide as an earsplitting scream erupted from her. The outburst sent a shockwave through the room that pushed Kana back a few feet, but she kept the mirror's reflected light on Nina.

"Let. Him. Go!"

Nina's hair whipped around her shoulders. "No! No! No!"

"You asked for it."

Kana pulled the mirror across her left shoulder, reared back, and backhanded Nina with a loud crack. The mirror remained intact, not a single crack in the glass, but Nina crumpled into a heap on the floor and her howling turned to sobs.

A chill pricked Kana's hand from fingertips to wrist. She shook it off, holding the mirror tight and refocusing the sunlight on Nina as the spirit cowered and quivered. "It's time to go, Nina," said Kana in a soft voice. "It's time to *let* go."

Nina turned her head from the mirror, tugging at her greasy strands of hair. Another sob, another tear, and one final word before her fragile form dispersed into flecks of ash.

"Zero."

BEEN THERE, DONE THAT

S ince the job was completed, Kana and AJ left the Riley house. AJ scrolled through his phone to check the recent deposits and gave Kana a thumbs-up once Peter Riley's transfer was complete.

AJ winked. "Just another day on the job."

"It wasn't much of a job. Another low-level Keter causing problems for some jerk who screwed someone over and thought he could get away with it." Kana brushed her hand over the mirror before stuffing it into her backpack. "Sometimes I think we should just let them have their way."

"You don't mean that."

Kana gave AJ a blank stare.

"Nevermind," AJ said as he fumbled for his car keys. "Are you heading back to the office, or do you have other things to do?"

"I think I'll head home. I stayed up late last night." Kana yawned.

AJ rolled his eyes. "Why am I not surprised?"

"Tuesday is ladies' night. Two for one drinks."

"That bar will be shut down if anyone finds out you're only

twenty-two."

Kana shrugged. "That's the legal drinking age, AJ."

"You've been drinking there for three years."

"Which is why no one ever says anything. So what if my ID says I've been twenty-one for the last three years? You were the one who made it anyway, so I don't want any finger-wagging from you."

AJ shook his head as he pressed the unlock button on his key chain. His ecologically-correct small car echoed a chime in response. He opened the passenger door and dropped his backpack on the front seat.

"How do you drive this thing?" Kana scrunched her nose. "Can it go above fifty-five?"

"Zero to sixty-five in twenty seconds if you must know."

"Twenty seconds. Wow, that's like so fast if this was 1933. Seriously, what is with you and these tiny little cars? I know you want to save the planet and all..."

He stood between her and his car, crossing his arms. "Don't make fun of *Dee Dee*."

"You call your car *Dee Dee*?"

"I said don't make fun of her." AJ didn't normally let her teasing rattle him, but his environmental crusade was one thing that would. "It's efficient, clean, doesn't need gas, and it spits out vapor. It's better than that harmful, bird-choking, fuming death trap you drive."

"It's a Dodge Challenger. A classic."

"It's obscene."

Kana threw her hands up. "Anyway, did you finish the interview this time?"

AJ reached into the car and pulled the notepad from his backpack. "Yes. He didn't want to do it, but I got most of the information you wanted."

Kana took the notepad from AJ and flipped through the pages, scanning the copious notes AJ took during the case. She then went back further, lining her finger alongside the numerous other cases they had taken on in the past few years. She stopped on Case #66, her finger pressing down on the word "Shinigami". The word chilled her spine, a pressure building up at the base of her neck, so she flipped back to the first page.

Kana looked up from the notepad. "This was case 100?"

"Yeah. A milestone for *Cold Fish Investigations*."

"I told you that's not the name of our business. Stop trying to make it happen." She handed him back the notepad.

"Okay, okay. I think it has a nice ring to it. It's also kind of quirky."

His insistence on this name over the last year was bordering on obsessive to Kana. "If someone handed me a business card, and it said, *Cold Fish Investigations*, I'd throw it back in their face."

AJ frowned and stuffed the notepad back into his backpack. "We should celebrate our hundredth case."

"Why?"

"It's a milestone, Kana. We've solved one hundred cases. Who would have thought two dropouts from Harvard would have a hundred cases to solve, let alone to do it in less than a few years?"

"First, you're the one who thinks this is a big deal, not me. Second, our methods of celebration are different. All you'll want to do is play some video game."

"Probably."

"Yeah, no thanks. I can find other things to do." A pair of squirrels scurried up the side of a nearby tree, drawing Kana's attention. "Besides, it's not that big a deal. This is all minor stuff. Most of our cases are hoaxes or someone with a leaky pipe in their house. This one was different. There was a Keter in the house, but any serious investigator who wasn't full of crap could have figured that out."

AJ's shoulders drooped as she talked. He was the more optimistic one, and her constant downplaying of their work disappointed him. But he needed to hear it. She was the realist, the one who had her eyes on the larger world that they weren't allowed in, the world of the *important* paranormal cases beyond weak phantoms and creaking noises in the basement. They barely ranked above amateurs, as she saw it.

And it bored her.

"I don't know how you can think what we just witnessed wasn't extraordinary, Kana. That thing in there freaked me out."

"That wasn't anything. Just some lost soul wandering around stuck in a loop that was created when she killed herself. All it takes is letting them know what they're doing and a little bitch-slap against the head, and they usually move on. It's tedious."

AJ tapped his lower lip. "If you say so. What about that cryptid we found in the basement of that house in Chicago?"

She rolled her eyes. "Nothing special either. There are all kinds of little mutant animals running around. Its only crime was trying to make a home in someone's basement."

AJ snapped his fingers. "The shipwreck case in Florida then? That had to be a highlight."

"Yeah, a piece of junk with some sad old man's ghost attached to it. All he wanted to do was sit in a rocking chair. Who is afraid of a chair rocking back and forth?"

He laughed. "When there's no one in it? That tends to unnerve most normal people."

They both looked at the ground for a moment as a gust of wind kicked up the fallen leaves nearby. The silence between them lingered for a few moments. AJ kicked at a pebble on the ground while Kana scratched at a speck of dirt on the door handle of her car. She suspected he was thinking about the same case he was, the Shinigami, and hoped he wasn't going to bring it up. She needed to change the topic.

"I'll stop by the office around six this even so we can catch up on whatever we have for the rest of the week." She stopped scratching at the dirt mark and wiped her hands on her jeans. "And yes, maybe we'll celebrate this stupid milestone you find so important."

"Don't forget we have a client meeting at 6:30. I have a feeling this is government work, and you know I hate talking to them."

"I'll be there at 5:45 then. Is that okay?"

AJ's raised an eyebrow.

"I'll be there, AJ. For God's sake!" Kana sucked her teeth as he smirked.

"I didn't say anything. But you do tend to be late."

Kana put on a pair of sunglasses and opened the door to her Dodge Challenger. She settled into the seat, turned the engine over, and pressed down on the gas a few times. The car roared, and the ground vibrated so much it shook the frame of AJ's *Dee Dee*.

She shouted to him over the growling engine. "Hear that? That's what a car sounds like."

"That's what pollution sounds like," AJ shouted.

"You're no fun, AJ. No fun at all! See you at 5:45."

"On the dot."

"On the dot."

Kana sped off down the quiet suburban street, the wheels of her car squealing against the asphalt as she rocketed away from the Riley home, leaving AJ to putter behind her in *Dee Dee* with a trail of water vapor following him.

THE MAN FROM ROME

I t was 4:45, and Kana had yet to arrive at the office. Other issues required her attention, and the most pressing was a series of text messages left on her phone. Mitchell—she thought his name was Mike—waited at a restaurant for their lunch date while she was on the Riley case. He was older, worked at a local marketing agency, and had the charm of a toad. The only thing going for him was his generosity when it came to buying Kana drinks. She entertained his advances the night before with zero intention of meeting later despite promising to do so.

Kana thought the least she could do was call him, a decision she immediately regretted after he answered the phone. Mitchell gave her an earful of chatter about respecting his time, being responsible, and taking advantage of him. After thirty minutes of defending herself, she hung up and blocked his number.

Mitchell was another in a long line of disappointing men. They were too easy, and she was too smart to fall for their games. Mitchell and Peter Riley had the same trait: middle-aged men with *Yellow Fever*. Her ethnicity was a fetish for them. No big loss.

A glass of wine would wash away the sourness of the phone call. It was now 5:30 p.m. which gave her enough time to relax before heading to the office to meet her new client. *Sure, I'll be late, but AJ won't mind.*

Before she knew it, Kana found herself wrapped up in some ridiculous reality show. She stared at the clock on the wall after finishing the bottle of wine and read the time. 6:30 p.m.

***

"I don't want to hear it, AJ, I know I'm late," Kana said as she entered the office. "I had some things to deal with."

AJ gave her a confused look, not sure where all of Kana's venom was coming from, but this wasn't the first time he had seen her like this. "I didn't say anything."

"I saw your look when I walked in. I know that look."

Their office was previously a satellite cell phone store that sat at the far end of a strip mall. Between Kana's lack of concern for aesthetics, and her refusal to let AJ name the company, the front of the shop looked abandoned. No sign overhead. No label on the glass door. Just a simple partition separating the front from the back. Remnants of the cell phone store remained intact: empty shelves, half-ripped price stickers, and an outdated cash register.

The back of the office was a different story. AJ converted

what was previously a storage area into a sophisticated work zone. Drywall concealed a menagerie of wires, fiber optic cables, and homemade RFI disruptors that kept unwanted signals from entering the building. Four workstations lined the wall on his side of the warehouse, each with multiple monitors and a stack of custom-made PC towers. He called it *The Bridge*. Kana's side looked more like a bar than an office, with a variety of band posters plastered on the concrete walls, her own personal bar, and at the center of it all, a professional pool table.

"How did the meeting go?" Kana grabbed a bottle of Captain Morgan from the shelf behind her bar.

"We were waiting for you." AJ nodded to the man sitting on Kana's black leather couch.

She paused, shrugged, and filled her glass. "Do you drink rum?"

"I'm a whiskey man, to be honest," the stranger answered, his voice peppered with a European accent.

"Suit yourself." She downed the shot.

AJ cleared his throat before making the introductions. "Kana, this is Tomas Moretti. What he's proposing is quite interesting, so I wanted to wait for you before hearing the details."

Tomas stood from the sofa and shook Kana's hand. His palms were rough which matched his weathered face.

"Tomas Moretti." Kana's skin crawled. "From?"

"I'm from *them*," he said.

"Them?" AJ raised an eyebrow.

Kana's smile turned into a grimace. They knew his name, or at least an alias, and this coy act furthered her unease with the man. Kana turned his wrist as she shook his hand, taking notice of his ring: a large block of silver with a beveled cross lined with small diamonds at its center.

"Vatican," Kana said.

Tomas blinked as he continued to shake her hand. He didn't need to confirm it. Kana knew enough about how the Church worked to spot an agent of the Papacy outside the city's borders.

"I am pleased to make your acquaintance, Ms. Kana Cold. What a unique name you have." Tomas sat back on the couch. "Surely it is not your given one?"

"Oh, I'd say it's about as given as yours, Tomas." Kana flashed a sarcastic grin as she pulled up a chair.

AJ lowered himself on the couch next to Tomas. "So, you've come a long way I assume. Should we just talk business?"

Tomas nodded, his gaze still on Kana. "Yes, perhaps we should."

As the staring contest continued, Kana never wavered, rocking back and forth in her chair while Tomas brushed his palms against his pants.

"You two have been very busy trying to find cases involving the occult." He nodded once at Kana. "Your work with the Shinigami case drew a lot of attention in the paranormal community. Kana, you studied under Professor Granger at

Harvard for a time, yes?"

"Why do you ask?"

"He was a former associate of ours. Great man. That's why I'm coming to you now." Tomas inched to the edge of the sofa. "You were a student he held in high esteem."

"I haven't seen him for a long time."

"But you kept in touch with him over the years."

Kana hadn't shared her history with the professor to many people outside of AJ. Yes, she kept in touch with Granger, but a year had passed since their last correspondence.

She leaned forward. "Is he the one who told you to hire us for this project?"

"He can't. He's dead." Kana tightened her lip as he continued. "To be accurate, he disappeared some time ago. We then came across information from an archeologist claiming Professor Granger had passed on. I'm sorry this is the first you're hearing of this." Kana waved him off. "This led us to researching what it was this archeologist and Granger were working on. It turns out they made quite the find."

"Which was?" AJ leaned over his knees.

"I'm not quite sure. His last email mentioned something about Honorius. Does that mean anything to either of you?"

"You mean Pope Honorius III." Kana stood and walked to the edge of the pool table. "Son of Euclid as the legends go."

She turned to AJ, and he gave her blank stare in return. Tomas gave her the same blank look.

"How much research have you guys actually done on this stuff? Pope Honorius III was the author of *The Sworn Book of Honorius* as well as *The Grand Grimoire*, or *The Red Dragon* as some call it. These books supposedly contain spells, black magic, and alchemy."

"Black magic?" AJ's eyebrows shot up.

Kana shrugged. "Yeah, that's the sort of stuff people believed back then. They thought humans could somehow control demons with a bunch of runes and scribbles on paper. It's all fiction, of course. Both of those books are only known to people who care about the subject. *The Red Dragon* is in the Vatican Archives, as I'm sure Tomas knows."

"It appears you have me at a disadvantage." Tomas folded his hands over his waist. "I tend to ignore speculation and rumors and deal with facts. I've never been inside the Vatican Archives."

"Well, I'm sure it's a safe bet that it's there," Kana said.

Tomas stood from the sofa and pulled a thumb drive from his pocket. He handed it over to AJ who walked over to his workstations, booted up one of his laptops, and inserted the drive into the machine. Once he was sure the drive was clean of viruses, he opened the only item on it, a video file.

"You may have just unlocked the biggest clue in this mystery." Tomas "You see, this archaeologist—he goes by Octavius—attempted to break into the Vatican Archives recently. He was caught just before he was able to get inside.

The Swiss guard interrogated him for some time and came up with nothing. If what you say is true, then it explains why he was there."

Kana's eyes narrowed. "How in the hell did he get that close to the Archives?"

"That's another mystery we're investigating. This recording is rather strange though. We figured, since you seem to know the subject, that you can explain what happened."

AJ nodded at the screen. "It's coming up now."

The video was of a man in his late twenties sitting with his hands and feet bound in a dimly lit room. Behind him, one of the Swiss guards stood stoic, his weapon at the ready. Another man was off camera asking questions in Italian, speaking frantically while Octavius quivered in the chair. Sweat poured from his brow as he refused to answer his interrogator, who became increasingly agitated with each question.

The interrogator circled behind Octavius while berating him. AJ turned on the computer's language translator. "Where did you get it? Why are you here? Answer me now!"

Octavius shook his head and sweat drenched his shirt as he struggled to free himself from the bindings pressing into his flesh. The interrogator huffed before grabbing a leather bag from offscreen, shoving it in his prisoner's face. Octavius bounced up and down at the sight of the bag, clenching his jaw as flecks of spittle flew from his mouth.

As the interrogator pressed the issue, he pushed the bag

closer with each question. Suddenly, Octavius stopped squirming. His jaw came unhinged as his lips and skin stretched like melted plastic, the gaping hole of his maw open to his captor. An otherworldly voice escaped the opening, spewing a string of words in a language the translator couldn't decipher, a line of dashes appearing at the bottom of the video. A sharp snap sounded before another and another. Octavius rose from his chair, his bindings broken, as the veins in his shoulder and neck pulsed against his flesh.

The Swiss guardsman rushed to take hold of the prisoner, wrapping his arms around Octavius only to have his neck snapped for his troubles. The interrogator trembled d, begging for his life as he dropped the bag to the floor. The confidence he had when his prisoner was subdued disappeared as he slouched, his hands shivering as he raised them in defense. His pleas would do him no good. Octavius snatched the interrogator by his neck, squinted at the security camera and, with one smooth motion, hurled the interrogator at it. Static filled the screen, and the video ended. AJ stared blankly while Kana turned away, thumbing her lower lip.

"Now, you can see our dilemma." Tomas turned the ring on his finger. "We're trying to find out why this man was at the Vatican and why he was trying to steal this grimoire you mentioned."

AJ fiddled with the computer mouse. "Hold on. I don't think he was trying to steal it. He already had it." He pointed to the bottom of the screen. "Look at that."

AJ rewound the video back to the moment of the attack and slowed its speed so the footage was broken down into a series of frames. He paused the video just as the interrogator dropped the bag. Captured in this single frame was the outline of a book falling from the bag to the floor.

Tomas squinted at the screen. "Is that the book you're speaking of? This *Red Dragon*?"

Kana moved closer to the screen. The video was not the best quality, but it was clear enough to make out the markings on the cover. She hummed as she backed away. "No, it's not. But that's a grimoire. I know a few of the symbols but... it can't be what I think it is."

Tomas followed her as she walked to her side of the warehouse. "Well, what do you think it is?"

"Pope Honorius III was known for writing *The Red Dragon*. Some also wondered if he had written other grimoires."

"So, you think this is one of those other grimoires, not *The Red Dragon*?"

"The symbols don't match what we know *The Red Dragon* to have, but they are related symbols. It's possible..." She pressed her fist against her lower lip. "Maybe he did write more. It was supposed to be a myth, no one actually believed any of it."

"Maybe there's some information here." AJ grabbed a second laptop and opened a new window. A list of files filled the screen, each one representing an email belonging to the departed Professor Granger.

"You just hacked into a dead man's account in front of a complete stranger, AJ," Kana whispered over his shoulder.

AJ shrugged. "He doesn't care. Do you, Tomas?"

Tomas shook his head, and Kana frowned at them both as AJ continued his investigation.

"These are from Octavius. And these mention a grimoire." He scrolled farther down the screen. "Sorry, grimoires."

Kana leaned over the AJ's shoulder. "Open it."

AJ clicked on the first email, uncovering a chain of correspondence between Professor Granger and Octavius. After a few pleasantries, the conversation turned into an excited discussion about an abandoned dig site. Octavius went on to detail his discovery at the Basilica of Santa Sabina in Rome. The timestamp on the email showed that Granger didn't respond for nearly four hours.

When he did, he asked a simple question. *All three?*

To which Octavius answered, *No, it just tells us where one is. The other two I think I can find from the clues here.*

Tomas leaned over AJ's shoulder. "Is there anything else?"

AJ opened a few more emails but nothing else was written about the grimoires. Kana left AJ's workstation for her pool table. She picked up the eight ball and placed it in the center, grabbed a pool stick, and lined up the cue ball at the other end.

Tomas stood at the other end of the table as she racked the

rest of the balls. "Three? There are three grimoires that are unaccounted for?"

"It appears so," Kana answered in a flat voice and narrowed her eyes as she pointed the end of her cue stick at him.

"So, will you take the job? All expenses paid, of course."

Kana cocked her head at Tomas and beamed before hitting the cue ball, knocking the eight ball into the corner pocket. "We'll call you."

Tomas nodded and placed a business card at the end of the pool table before leaving. AJ pocketed the card before turning to Kana, his hands crossed while she lined up shots. "You aren't seriously considering not taking this. Isn't this what you wanted, a real case after all this time?"

"Come on now, AJ. Haven't you learned anything from me about negotiating?" She picked another shot, the five ball this time, and ricocheted it off the six into the side pocket. "We'll take the job, no doubt, but he's got us at a disadvantage. I don't believe for a second he doesn't know anything about the grimoires. He wanted to see if we did."

"You caught that too?" AJ licked the corner of his mouth. "So, what do we do?"

"Make him wait. In the meantime, you have some research to do and I have somewhere to be. Meet me back here tomorrow morning at eight and we'll figure something out. And watch yourself leaving here tonight. I don't trust that guy."

"Okay, 8:00 a.m. And you'll be here on time, right?"

Kana took one more shot, splitting the seven and the eleven balls into the opposite corner pockets. "Oh, for this, I'll absolutely be on time."

THE ARCHENEMY IN HIGH HEELS

Not far from Kana's home was Orem Hill Apartments, a modest garden-style community for the working class, a few Section 8 families, and retirees. Five years ago, the neighborhood was a safe place where walking after dark wasn't considered a risky move.

The gawking of the local hoodlums echoed in the dark as she parked her Dodge Challenger next to the last set of buildings on the street. Their tactless taunting and cat calls, laced with racial stereotypes of "Five dollars, anything you want, Joe," and "sucky sucky" was nothing new or clever. She had heard far worse before. Instead of trading insults with them, she entered the apartment building at the end of the street, climbed two flights of stairs to apartment number 302, and entered using a spare key.

"What are you hiding in here, David?" Kana said to herself as she flicked the light switch on the wall.

The smell of mold and dust rushed at her once she entered the apartment. No one had lived here for years. The dim lights from the freestanding lamps brightened the living room, the bulbs struggling to hold their florescence. Time had not been kind to the place. Cobwebs clung to the walls. A thin layer of dust coated the furniture and television. This was a place of memories now.

Kana stared at the rocking chair in the corner, Professor Granger's chair. This was where she and several of his students sat and listened to him spin tales about his travels. His students were known as *The Prestige Club*—a collection of the more imaginative and gifted young minds at Harvard. They held weekly meetings inside this rented apartment that served as their secret getaway from the judgmental eyes of the Ivy League. Professor Granger hosted the meetings—without the university's knowledge, on Tuesday evenings for his most prized students.

To Kana, it was a refuge. Being gifted with early admission to Harvard, years younger than any of her peers, this weekly meetup was the only time during her brief stint in academia where she felt at home. It wasn't formal, it wasn't subject to rules or expectations, it was just a colloquium of thoughts and knowledge. Professor Granger pegged her from the first day as special, an outsider who had a knack for understanding the underworld. She was perfect for his group of misfits.

The club existed for years before Kana joined, but her brief time as a member was cherished time. She learned the truth about a range of subjects from alchemy to the limits of science to the corruption of the world's religions. She held artifacts that were thought to have either been lost to time or hadn't existed at all. She saw the reality of the metaphysical and the supernatural, the merger of science and magic, all while forging friendships she thought would last a lifetime. Under this tree of knowledge, she devoured every tasty bit of fruit that fell from it. That was, until it all ended abruptly one day—one sad day—over four years ago.

"It's probably in his bedroom." She made her way through the empty hallway and opened the door at the end.

The master bedroom was decorated with more furniture than the tiny space could comfortably hold. Beyond the door was a king-size bed, a large dresser, and two night stands crammed between the four walls with barely enough room for Kana, as slender as she was, to squeeze between. It also made finding anything difficult. The night stands were too close to the wall for her to open them fully, the dresser too close to the bed to pull out the bottom drawers, and the closet was stacked with boxes and old clothes.

Kana pulled a box down from the top shelf of the closet, but others followed, covering her in a cloud of dust and dirt. After cursing a few times, she cleaned herself off with a towel she found in the bathroom. As she washed away the last bit of dust from her face, a slow mocking clap sounded from the hallway. The clicking of heels on the hardwood floor let her know the other intruder's identity. "Anastasia," she murmured.

The statuesque blonde stopped in the doorway of the

bathroom. Her condescending applause continued as she leaned against the doorframe. A former member of *The Prestige Club* herself, Anastasia Dubois looked just as Kana remembered her, including her long legs, her flawless face, and her svelte body that was better suited for a magazine cover than a paranormal investigator. She hadn't aged much, her damned lightly tanned skin captured in the bathroom mirror's reflection.

Anastasia stopped clapping. "*Kinda Cold*. They still call you that back at Harvard, you know. 'Whatever happened to *Kinda Cold*?'" She tittered. "Oh, if they could see you now."

Kana threw the towel in the sink. "Their choice of nicknames is about as original as anything else that gang of self-appointed masters of the universe could come up with. Are you still sleeping with all of them, or have you taken a break?" Kana took one look at Anastasia's expensive high heels. "Apparently not. Were those a gift from a student or a faculty member?"

Anastasia pursed her lips. "I can afford my own heels, Kana. Still the petty little jealous girl I knew from college."

Anastasia pushed the smaller woman aside to check her makeup. Kana's hand itched to grab the woman by the back of the head and smash her pretty face in the mirror. "I guess you've already found Granger's flash drive."

"Of course I did." Anastasia licked her finger and ran it across her eyebrows. "But you can be thankful that you're not taking the job. It's actual work, not low-level haunted house nonsense or whatever it is you and AJ are doing."

"Why are you taking this job? You can have anything you want." A closed-lip smile spread across Kana's face. "Or is this the rich girl who needs excitement in her life because the senior citizens she's shacking up with don't quite cut it for her?"

Anastasia chuckled before she stopped stroking her eyebrows. "Honestly, you don't want to be a part of this, Kana. You're not ready. You don't have the resources to do this. Leave this to the professionals, okay?"

"Professionals? Oh, you mean *you*. Right. Just because you're five years older and your daddy pays for all your adventures doesn't make you a professional."

"Think whatever you want, but I'm serious. This isn't something you want to be involved with. I'm actually doing you a favor, believe it or not."

Kana huffed. "Not."

Anastasia brushed past Kana on her way to the front door. *God, I so want to throw something at her head.*

"Good luck with your next Bigfoot case or your hunt for Slenderman." Anastasia laughed on her way out the front door.

There was too much truth to what Anastasia said, exaggerated as it was, for Kana to have a comeback. The blonde was well funded and had experience in the paranormal underworld. Kana and AJ's operation was bush league by comparison. As much as she wanted to belittle the woman for her cliched appearance and questionable dating history, there was no doubting Anastasia's abilities and resources.

Kana kicked the living room sofa which pushed against the rocking chair, its slow sway calling her attention. Professor Granger would not approve of her giving up so easily. She felt his presence coming from the chair as it creaked back and forth. Anastasia may have been the most accomplished member of *The Prestige Club*, but Kana was Professor Granger's favorite. She knew it, and Anastasia knew it as well. He saw promise in her then, and if he was still alive, he would tell her to push on.

There had to be another way.

***

AJ arrived at the office just before 8:00 a.m. to find Kana waiting for him at the front door. She leaped from her seat on the bench just outside the entrance as AJ exited his car.

"Did you bring doughnuts?" he asked as he closed the door of his beloved *Dee Dee*.

Kana crowded AJ, barely allowing him room enough to carry his bags to the office. "Right. Yeah, I thought about it. But, you know, I'm not used to being up this early. My brain wasn't totally working."

"Well, tell me what's wrong, because you being here on time and awake before 8:00 a.m. is freaking me out a little bit."

He passed by her to the front door and insert his key into the lock it while she explained what happened the night before.

When she got to the part about Anastasia, she had AJ's full attention.

"She was there?" AJ stopped turning the key.

Kana rolled her eyes. "Put your boner away, she's not coming here. She took the flash drive, and now we have no way of getting whatever information Granger kept on it."

AJ grinned as the door to the office opened and the two entered. Kana pointed to the suitcases he carried inside. "What is all that for?"

"It's a suitcase, Kana. People use it to put clothes in when they travel." Kana sucked her teeth while he set the suitcases down and folded his arms. "So, that's what you had to do last night? You went to that old apartment looking for a flash drive?"

Kana leaned against the doorframe. "I knew he kept most of his stuff there. I figured it'd be the best chance of us getting any information on what he and Octavius were working on. But she's got it now, so I need you to get to work. Maybe you can check his social media accounts, old blog posts, anything that might tell us something."

AJ handed her one of the envelopes. "If I knew that's where you were going, I would have told you not to go."

"What? Why? And what is this?" She opened the envelope. Inside was a plane ticket for Bucharest with her name on it.

AJ went to his workstation. "I already found a ghosted copy of his flash drive. Granger wasn't very good at securing his files. He connected that drive to a lot of computers he used at the university. It wasn't too hard to track it down."

Kana blinked a few times at the ticket, pocketed it, and stood behind AJ as he packed his gear. "So, why Bucharest?"

"The two of them had a third contact who knew quite a bit about Honorius, the grimoires, everything. They called him Stefan. His name kept popping up on the emails too. I figured that's the best place to start. I already called that Tomas guy and told him that we were taking the job. He gave us an advance, so we're all set."

Kana nodded and went to her side of the office to pack a few clothes, a few notebooks, her passport, and a wad of cash. At the back of the locker was a necklace, gifted to her in secret by a little girl named Melody after saving the child's life from the Shinigami. She lingered on it, forced back to the memories of that case, and the consequences of it that followed her to this day. It had been months since she'd seen it last.

"Yeah, you keep losing that," AJ said over her shoulder. "I found it the other day and put a tracker on the thing, so you can't lose it again. I know it means a lot to you."

Kana nervously smiled at him, thanking him with a nod, and continued to pack her bags.

AJ lifted his bags and walked to the front door. "We have to be at the airport by 9:30."

She finished packing and followed him through the glass doors. Her mouth opened to speak and froze before the words left her lips. No, she thought, it was better to continue the way they had been. *If I start giving him compliments, he'll expect them anytime he does something right, and I'm not about to start doing that.*

By 10 a.m. their plane left the runway, heading nonstop to Bucharest. Kana and AJ spent the first few hours of their flight figuring out a plan for how to track down Stefan. After that, Kana caught a few hours of sleep while AJ researched Black Grimoires, typing away on his keyboard next to her. The noise he made was distracting at first, but she blocked it out over time. She yawned as her eyelids fluttered closed, hoping that when she woke, they'd be in Bucharest and the case could begin.

NOT WHAT WAS EXPECTED

"Not what I expected," AJ said as he and Kana settled in a taxi to their hotel in Bucharest.

Buildings and cars whisked by while Kana stared out the cab's window, absorbing the foreign sights of the city. "What did you expect?"

"I don't know, honestly. Just not this. It's all so... modern."

"So, you thought this place would be all rotting castles and gargoyle statues?"

AJ nodded. "Kind of, yeah."

Kana shook her head. "You spend way too much time on the internet, AJ."

Once at the hotel, the pair put away their clothes and equipment before sorting out a plan to find the archeologist. AJ searched all known addresses for Stefan while Kana spent her time at one of the many rooftop bars in the city, claiming she operated better with a glass of rum in her hand.

Bars were different here, not like back in Massachusetts where five minutes barely passed without someone trying to take her home with a cheesy line. She wasn't against a rendezvous, but it was best to stay professional on this trip. This wasn't a vacation, and fortunately the lack of suitable single men helped her keep to this guideline. Her arrival coincided with tourist season, so everyone in the city was either with their significant other or too preoccupied with sightseeing to notice her.

While hopping from bar to bar and enjoying the crisp night air, Kana noticed the same trio of men at every bar. A few times she caught one of them staring at her from across the room. At first, she thought nothing of it, but by the fourth bar it was clear they were following her. Maybe it was the CIA, MI6, or some organization she didn't know about. Any of those options were troubling. She had a tail, and she had to lose them quick.

Kana left the last bar and disappeared into the nearby alleyway to wait for her pursuers from the shadows. Sure enough, the same three men followed her out. They spoke in whispers to one another, checked their cell phones, and headed off in separate directions.

This was the stuff of *a cloak-and-dagger operation*, not a paranormal investigation. The hotel was probably monitored too. From here on out she would keep one eye open for the mysterious trio in black suits.

***

"Wake up." AJ shook Kana's shoulder.

She blinked a few times before rising out of bed. The

morning sun beamed through the window so harsh that Kana put her hand over her eyes to block the sunlight, but the instant she rolled over on her back, her stomach turned, and her head spun. Romanian bars were heavy on the liquor, and she was feeling it today.

"Drink some of this." AJ handed Kana a glass of orange juice. "And try to eat something. We've got about an hour before we need to get going."

She sipped the juice, wrinkled her nose, and put it aside. Pulp. She hated pulp, and this glass was full of it. *You would think he'd know better after all the years we've been friends.* "What time is it?"

"A little after seven. But from what I've learned, this Stefan is the early-to-rise type, so if we're going to talk to him, now is the time."

Stefan's name triggered a sense of purpose in Kana. They were here for a job. It was time to focus, put aside this nasty glass of orange juice, and hop in the shower. In the future, Kana would have to make it a point for AJ not to have a key to her hotel room. Fortunately, she slept in her clothes, but she certainly didn't want him walking in if she had a visitor over for the evening.

She gave AJ a half smile. "Thanks for the juice. Let's meet in the lobby in about ten minutes. I want to get a quick shower."

"That's fine." He closed his laptop. "Those men you texted me about last night never came to the hotel. Or at least, I didn't see anyone suspicious hanging around."

"That doesn't mean they're not here."

AJ stared at the nearly full glass of orange juice. "True. But no one has come to my door or anything. No bugs in either room. I did two sweeps this morning."

"Good to know." Kana groaned as she pushed herself off the bed and staggered to the bathroom. "Ten minutes." AJ raised an eyebrow. "Make it fifteen."

***

After Kana had two cups of coffee and a bagel, the pair rented a car and left the city for Ilfov County. The cobblestone roadways and tall city buildings city gave way to the rolling hills and green valleys of the countryside. An hour into their drive the vistas changed dramatically. The rural areas were vast but undergoing their own change, including a reconstruction project where the wealthy were establishing new communities beyond the city's borders. There wasn't much else to see except pastures and farm houses.

AJ marked a few locations where Stefan might be found. The first two attempts proved incorrect, abandoned homes in such a state of decay that the only occupants were mice and spiders. The third location was set far off the beaten path, the roads in this part of the countryside barely passable, littered with rocks and potholes. AJ directed them to a path that led up a hill, into the woods, far away from prying eyes. This seemed right, Kana thought. Their rental car had difficulty making it up the steep pathway, jostling back and forth as the suspension squeaked and groaned.

AJ pointed to the cabin ahead as the car reached the clearing. "Well, someone's home."

White smoke billowed from the cabin's chimney. They parked the vehicle next to a pile of freshly cut firewood, an ax lodged into one of the thicker pieces.

Kana turned off the ignition. "Did you find out anything else about this guy?"

"Not much. Just that he's worked with many people in Professor Granger's circle. He also speaks five languages and taught Ancient History for a few years at Stanford. Other than that, there isn't much information."

"I don't think this old man is much of a danger to us but still..." Kana pulled her Glock 19 from the pocket of her leather jacket and ejected the clip, confirming it was filled with bullets. "...you can never be too safe."

AJ turned his nose up at the weapon. "Is that really necessary?"

"You know I go by that saying, it's better to have a gun and not need one..."

"...than need a gun and not have one," AJ finished her quote. "Yeah, I get it. But seriously, with this guy? He's probably sitting in a rocking chair by the fireplace reading Dickens or something like that."

"Let me worry about it. You just follow the plan and ask the right questions. I'll hang back, you do the interview."

It was a quaint little place. Kana see why someone would retire out here away from everything, especially if they had spent years digging up relics out of the earth. With any luck, Stefan would prove to be a kindhearted father figure just like Professor Granger.

AJ knocked on the front door and waited. A few moments passed without a response, so he tried again. Still, no one came to the door. Kana cupped her hands and pressed her face against the windows. The curtains were drawn, making it hard to see, but the fireplace was lit, its orange flames dancing in the dark.

"Should I try again?" AJ asked.

Kana backed away from the window and squared up to the door. "Let me."

She pounded the wooden slats. A few seconds passed, and there was no answer. Again, she pounded the door, and again, there was no answer.

"This is ridiculous. We know someone's in there." When she raised her fist to knock again, the door swung open, and her fist landed on a bare chest instead of hard wood.

Kana backed up. The chest she hit was thick, bronze, and toned. Her eyes followed up from there to the broad shoulders, the square jaw, and the chiseled face of the man who stood in the doorway.

"Can I help you?" Bronze Chest asked, a hint of an Italian accent in his voice.

AJ stepped beside Kana, who was lost for words. "My name is AJ, and this is Kana. We were hoping to meet up with Stefan. We're not bill collectors." AJ waited for the man to laugh at his joke and was disappointed. "Can we speak to him? It's important."

Bronze Chest raised his hand to the top corner of the doorway, Kana bit her lower lip as the musculature of his body shifted. His abs were near perfect ripples. Her eyes followed down to the hint of his hips that peaked over a pair of rust-colored jeans. *No, it wasn't time for that.* Kana forced her eyes back to his. That may have been worse. His eyes had the blue of the sea in them with a few flecks of green.

"It's important, is it? Well, don't stand out there. Come on inside and have a seat." Bronze Chest waved them into the cabin.

AJ walked inside, but Kana needed a nudge, still marveling over the man's physique as he walked away.

"We need to talk to Stefan. Is he here?" AJ asked.

Bronze Chest entered the kitchen on the other side of the living room and lifted a steaming pot from the stove as he turned down the flame. "Yeah, he's here. You're talking to him."

Kana cut a look over to AJ. In her mind, Kana imagined someone with Stefan's resume to be well into retirement age, but Bronze Chest looked to be barely over thirty.

While Stefan was preoccupied, AJ examined the living room. "I thought you were an archaeologist."

"I am," Stefan shouted from the kitchen. "I've seen quite a few things in my lifetime, friends. I can only assume you are students of Granger."

Stefan stirred a pot of scrambled eggs before snatching a pepper grinder from the shelf above the stove and adding a little to the pot, followed by a pinch of salt and a handful of chopped chives. Again, he stirred, tilting the pot every so often.

AJ stood at the edge of the kitchen now, watching the cook at work. "Yes. Well, not exactly. I wasn't a student of his, but my colleague was."

Stefan smiled at them as he exited the kitchen, the pot held with one hand while his other continued stirring. He emptied the contents onto three plates and motioned for his guests to sit down.

He wiped the corners of Kana's plate with a napkin as she sat at the table. "You must be Kana, right?"

Those damn blue eyes. She needed to keep her giddiness from bubbling up to the surface, taking a seat at the table, doing everything in her power not to look at him.

"*Kinda Cold.* Yes, it fits. I can see that now." He flashed a set of perfectly straight teeth.

She wasn't fond of the nickname, even coming from this bare-chested Italian. It showed he knew Professor Granger, or at least had done his homework.

"Thanks for the food." AJ sat at the table. "It looks good."

"Yes, it does." Kana hoped no one else caught the double meaning.

AJ squinted at her before asking Bronze Chest, "Do you want to put on a shirt?"

The host looked down at his chest before he apologized and left the table, heading to the bedroom on the other side of the cabin. "I saw you coming from down the road. Sorry I made you wait," Stefan said, his voice carrying from the bedroom. "I wanted to get eggs for my guests. Fresh eggs. I had a feeling sooner or later Granger would send someone. How is my old friend?"

AJ looked to Kana for permission to break the news to Stefan. She nodded in agreement. There was no sense in hiding this from him.

AJ slumped in his seat. "I'm afraid he passed away."

Stefan's rustling in the bedroom ceased for a few moments. "It pains me to hear that. He was a good friend. One of the best, truly."

Stefan returned to the main room, now wearing a gray sweatshirt and carrying gifts in each hand. One was a journal, and in the other was a bottle of tuica—a native liquor of Romania. Not only was he handsome, he also offered alcohol for breakfast.

AJ swallowed a forkful of eggs. "We have a couple of

questions we'd like to ask about something you worked on with Professor Granger and another man known as Octavius."

"Octavius..." Stefan let the last letter trail. He poured a drink for himself and Kana, but AJ declined by putting his hand over the glass in front of him. "You are here about the Black Grimoires, yes?"

Kana lifted the cup to examine the liquor. "That is why we are here. Octavius broke into the Vatican archives. They thought he was after *The Red Dragon,* but now they think he was after the Black Grimoires."

"Impossible." Stefan sat down across from the pair. "The Vatican never had the Black Grimoires. If Octavius had one, he brought it with him."

"Why would he bring the grimoire there?"

"That, my beautiful lady, is the question." Stefan sipped his drink. "But I have a hard time believing my brother was involved in such a thing."

"Your brother?" AJ and Kana asked simultaneously.

"Yes. He's the oldest. We were among Professor Granger's earliest students and part of *The Prestige Club.* We took up archeology after we graduated. One of the projects we worked on for years was this notion that Pope Honorius III had written more grimoires. Over time they had become lost, not just in Europe, but around the world. Unfortunately, my brother and I had a falling out right before he made a breakthrough."

Kana leaned over the table. "What caused you two to stop

talking?"

"He worked with some rather nasty people." He turned his gaze to the window while his finger swirled around the rim of the glass. "Such a sad thing that it broke us apart. Those damn grimoires. He became obsessed."

AJ opened his laptop and played the video of Octavius's interrogation by the Swiss Guard. Stefan sat back and shook his head at what he saw on the screen.

"How could he do something like that?" Kana asked.

Stefan stroked his chin. "Not only has he found a Black Grimoire, but it appears he's read quite a bit of it. You see, they're not just books, and it's not just a myth. Those books contain information, rituals, rites, and spells that weren't meant for man. It's something beyond just metaphysics and ghosts and hauntings. They are a means of communicating with things locked away from this world."

When the video ended, AJ closed his laptop. "Our job is to find them before he does. Or at least stop him from finding them."

"You cannot stop him. If he is reading and practicing from a Black Grimoire, your best bet is to stay away from him." Stefan finished his drink and collected the empty plates from the table. "But I, on the other hand, need to help my brother."

Kana sat back in her seat and threw her napkin on the table. "No offense, Stefan, but this is our case. They came to us for a reason."

"Who came to you? Who hired you?"

Before Kana could answer, a loud buzzer went off. Stefan set the plates down on the table and rushed to the back rooms. Kana and AJ followed him to a security station setup of three monitors sitting on top of one another on a metal rack. Stefan pressed a few keys on the keyboard to turn off the buzzer before pointing to the center monitor and the two white vans pushing up the rocky path to the cabin.

AJ leaned against the doorframe. "So, that's how you knew we were coming,"

"Yes, and it appears you've brought me more guests."

Kana put her hands to her hips as the passengers exited the vans. "I recognize them. It's the three from last night. They found us somehow."

Stefan turned off the monitors and unplugged them. "I guess we are in business with one another for the time being. If they are who I think they are, I hope you have more than a laptop and some questions to defend yourselves with."

A THIRD PARTY

While Stefan rushed to stuff his backpack, he kept one eye on the front door to his cabin and another on his guests. AJ and Kana suggested they leave, but he explained there was no exit from his cabin aside from the front door.

"If you leave now, you'll be blocked in the driveway," Stefan said, stuffing the journal into a backpack. "We'll be forced to go on foot through the woods, and there's nobody else out here for miles. It's best to sit tight. Let me handle this."

The three men opened the door of Stefan's cabin and strolled into his living room. The word *Aryan* ran through Kana's mind as the three tall, blonde, and seemingly soulless figures lined up shoulder to shoulder. They wore the same dark suit, white dress shirts buttoned to the top, stuffed into a darker pair of slacks, black leather boots, their hair parted in the middle and slicked down against their skulls. They weren't identical though. The man in the middle was shorter than those at his sides, and his hair was dirty blonde as opposed to the bright platinum of his cohorts.

"Good morning." The middle man nodded once at them. "I hope we have not interrupted your breakfast, Stefan. We see you have company."

Stefan, AJ, and Kana sat on the couch facing the intruders.

"No, not at all. I would like to say it was pleasant to see you here, but it is bad manners to lie," Stefan said. "However, I must ask you kindly to leave."

The middle man took off his leather gloves and put them in his coat pocket before stepping to the couch. His companions put their hands in their coat pockets, the outline of their handguns pressing against the fabric.

"I should introduce myself. My name is Dieter. It is a pleasure to make your acquaintance." He extended his hand to Kana, who pursed her lips and glowered at him in return.. "Americans. Always so rude."

Stefan crossed his arms. "Perhaps you should get to the point, Dieter."

Dieter slapped his gloves against his palm. "Yes, yes. The point is that you have been a very hard man to find, but your services are needed by the society. It was requested from on-high. Let's not waste any more time. Please pack up your things and we can be on our way."

AJ wrinkled his forehead. "The society?"

Kana leaned forward on the couch . "The Thule Society."

"Good, you know of us." Dieter smiled. In a louder voice, he said, "Then you should know that we will not be made to wait.

Come now, grab your belongings."

Kana tapped her fingertips together. "And you think he's just going to go and we're going to stay behind?"

"No, Fraulein. We don't expect you to stay behind. Well, not in the way you are thinking."

"Why do I think I'm not going to like the way *you* are thinking?" AJ asked.

The two subordinates removed their pistols from their coats and aimed the muzzles at AJ and Kana. Stefan put his hand on Kana's leg as she reached for her gun before standing and approaching Dieter, his muscular physique dwarfing The Thule Society agent.

Stefan spoke in a low voice and emphasized each word. "Do not insult my guests. What you really want is the information I have. Isn't it?"

Dieter cocked his head. "Yes, what does that matter?"

Stefan leaned in to Dieter's ear. "It matters, because without my information you have nothing to take your superiors. I will agree to go with you, but I'm calling the shots." He straightened himself and backed away from the agents. "The first thing I am asking is that your men put their guns away. They don't need them, and you don't need to kill these kids. What harm could they do?"

The short agent laughed. "We have our orders."

"Then you have a tough decision to make. I'm not going to ask again. Put the guns away or I will not help you."

Dieter cleared his throat and glanced over his shoulder to his men before closing his eyes and waving his hand at his men. "Hans. Victor. Put away your weapons."

As the two henchmen holstered their guns, Stefan walked over to the dinner table and stuffed the journal into his backpack. There were a few other items he needed to grab from the kitchen, which Dieter allowed, all while standing over his shoulder.

As Stefan walked to the front door with his bag over his shoulder, he gave Kana the slightest of nods. She waited for the henchmen to turn their backs before pulling her gun and firing at the henchmen's legs. She missed, but the henchmen scampered through the front door.

When Dieter reached for his own weapon, Stefan punched him the temple, which sent Dieter into the dirt, unconscious.

"Let's go!" Stefan shouted.

Kana dragged AJ by the arm to their rental car, avoiding the two agents who were tending to their fallen leader. AJ was in no shape to drive, so she swiped the keys from his hand and jumped into the driver's seat. Stefan was close behind and leaped into the passenger seat. With no regard for who or what was behind them, Kana put the car in reverse, sped backward in a circle until the front of the car faced away from the cabin, shifted the car into drive, and sped off, leaving a cloud of dust and leaves in their wake.

A few gunshots rang out from behind them, but none of the

bullets coming close to hitting the car. The two henchmen grabbed Dieter, who used every German swear he could think of, and scrambled to the white vans.

AJ was hyperventilating in the backseat. "What the hell was that?"

Stefan looked past him at the pursuing vans. "That's what we're up against. Those are the kinds of people who got my brother involved in this."

"The Thule Society." Kana shook her head. "I thought they disbanded decades ago."

"This is a new, reenvisioned group. Octavius dealt with them from time to time, but I can see it went a lot deeper than I even knew. If they're after me, then that means they haven't found the other two grimoires."

AJ leaned back in the seat. "Which means?"

"You know what it means, AJ." Kana peered at AJ through the center rearview mirror. "We're going to find them first."

Stefan concentrated on the road ahead. "Well, right now we need to get out of Romania."

AJ hunkered down in the back seat, his knees folded against his chest. "Aren't they just going to follow us?"

"I have a few precautions set in place."

"I don't think I want to know." AJ turned to Kana. "I can't believe you shot them! I mean, you actually shot two people!"

"It was them or us, AJ. They would have killed us. Besides, I don't think it hit them."

"I noticed." Stefan snickered, patting Kana on the leg. "Have you ever shot a gun before, lady? I think there are more holes in my cabin than there are in those men."

That stung. She had no answer to his insulting observation of her marksman skills. With AJ, it was easy to make herself look like a stone-faced badass, but Stefan was different, he was an experienced man and could tell that she had never shot anyone or anything outside of a few coke bottles in a field. "I was nervous."

Stefan glanced at Kana. "That's fine. I didn't mean to upset you. Maybe I'll show you how to hold that thing sometime."

Kana's mind went immediately to an inappropriate joke. "I don't need your help, Stefan. What is your plan? They're going to catch up with us pretty soon."

Stefan reached into his bag and pulled out a handheld device that looked like a modified cellphone. From its lack of polish and style, Kana assumed it was something he made himself.

He pointed ahead. "When you get past those trees, slow down a little."

AJ sat up in his seat. "Slow down?"

Stefan turned in his seat. "Don't worry, my friend. It's going to be alright."

The two tall evergreen trees marked with stripes of white paint along the branches were ahead. She passed the imaginary goal line and reduced her speed, praying that Stefan knew what he was doing.

"Come on, you bastards," Stefan whispered as their pursuers rocketed down the hill. "Keep on coming. That's right. Come on."

Kana and AJ turned to see if his trap would work. The two vans behind bounced up and down as they neared the painted trees. Stefan put his hand on Kana's shoulder, signaling her to stop the car. Once their pursuers were close enough Stefan tapped a few buttons on the device. A rumble shook the ground beneath the path like a minor earthquake. Behind them a giant hole opened in the roadway, the pathway spilling into the chasm. The trees collapsed in response, blocking any attempt to navigate down the hill. The two vans screeched to a halt, the first not quick enough to keep its front wheels from dangling over the side, the second nearly rear-ending the first.

Stefan smirked, patted AJ on the head, and nodded to Kana. She had to admit his cockiness, his ingenuity, and the dimples that accented his devilish smirk, impressed her.

Stefan pointed to the intersection at the end of the road. "I have one stop to make before we leave. Trust me, it won't take long."

AJ sat up in the back seat. "I'm beginning to think maybe you could just tell us what you know, and we can be on our way. Separately."

"Are you kidding?" Stefan's eyes were wide. "You two wouldn't last a day by yourselves. You need my help."

AJ pushed his tongue against the inside of his cheek as he

turned away from Stefan. He wasn't going to like this job turning into a team endeavor. His ego would have to stay with him in the backseat. As good as they thought they were, this was their first time dealing with secret societies and ancient spell books. There was much more to learn than either of them had anticipated. Alone, she and AJ would be buried in a shallow grave before the week was over. Stefan was experienced. He knew Professor Granger. Most importantly, she trusted him.

She turned onto the main road, taking one last glance back to make sure they weren't being followed. "Let's get back to our hotel room and pack. After that, we'll start finding these grimoires. Together."

MOVING TARGETS

K ana and AJ hurried back to the hotel, fearing that their room had been ransacked while they were away. To their relief it wasn't, so they packed up their gear and checked out as fast as they could. After leaving the hotel, Stefan directed them to their next destination. Twenty minutes later, after driving around the backstreets of Bucharest, they found the a quaint coffee shop whose only patrons were an old man reading a newspaper and his dog sitting dutifully at his owner's feet. He made them wait, disappearing into the shop's backroom with the blessing of the young girl who let him through the kitchen doors. Several minutes later Stefan emerged from the store carrying a bag of bagels and a vanilla envelope. Without any explanation, he climbed back into the car, offered AJ one of the bagels, and stuffed the envelope on the floor between his feet.

Stefan pointed ahead. "We can go now. Our flights are arranged. We may have a few snags but nothing I can't deal with."

Trusting Stefan proved fruitful once they arrived at the

airport, because his connections proved useful. Purchasing tickets for their flight and passing through security with their fake ID's went without incident.

Within an hour, they were sitting in the waiting area for their next flight. AJ leaned over Kana's shoulder as she flipped through a magazine. "Why in the world do we have to go to Israel?"

"Can you keep it together for me, AJ?" Kana put her hand on his shoulder.

"I'm just saying that it's not necessarily the safest place in the world. I thought we could go somewhere and avoid gunfire and explosions after what we just went through. I was clearly wrong."

Stefan sat in the chair facing AJ, sipping a water from a bottle. "We won't be near the border if that's what you're worried about. It's not that bad. Besides, we'll be far away from all of that. Our hotel is one of the safest in the country."

"It's called the American Colony Hotel," AJ said mockingly. "You might as well just say 'Place bombs here'."

"What can I do to make you feel comfortable, my friend? There must be something."

AJ leaned over and placed his elbows on his knee. "How about you explain a little bit more about why we're going to Israel? You've been rather vague about details."

Kana's lips parted.. "Yes, that is a good point. Why don't you fill us in?"

Stefan scanned the immediate area. Their flight was not heavily booked, and most of the other passengers hadn't arrived yet. "The last time I discussed the Black Grimoires with my brother was about a year ago. The Catholic Church has been trying to claim them for some time, but there were other world leaders—or tyrants in many cases—who had an interest in them. The black market for real ancient objects, especially ones that are known to only a handful of people around the world, is quite substantial."

"And you and your brother had heavy dealings in that black market."

"Yes, but that's the cost of doing business to gain access to the true mysteries of the world, not the stuff of folklore or myth. Although, many times we found those to be true as well."

Kana glanced over her shoulder, eyeing the other airport patrons seated around them. "I'm not judging you. Go on with your story."

"Honorius wrote many things, but the grimoires were a way to warn humanity against the dark arts, not celebrate them. *The Grand Grimoire*, though it details many spells and incantations, is also a guide on what to avoid. His even darker visions went into the three Black Grimoires. Realizing what he wrote in those three tomes was more dangerous than informative, he hid them away. Over time, they changed many hands throughout Europe and Asia. We tracked down the likely locations of all three. The last time I spoke to Octavius he was in Germany where he suspected one of them was being held."

Kana closed her eyes, nodding. "Let me guess. By The Thule Society."

The Italian's mouth turned down into a frown. "It seems so."

"So, the second is in Israel. Where is the third?" AJ asked.

"Somewhere in Asia. I have an idea of who has it, but that is for later. We should get to the one we know about before they do."

The announcement that the flight to Israel was now boarding echoed through the waiting area. There were many more questions Kana wanted to ask, but for now, she had heard enough to know what they were dealing with. If The Thule Society was in possession of one of the black grimoires and were using Stefan's brother to find the other three, that meant they'd likely go to Israel too. What little she knew of The Thule Society, in its modern incarnation, told her that they were not an organization that shied away from murder to achieve their goals. Human life was expendable to them. Kana's trio would be outclassed in resources, but Stefan was their ace in the hole. Unlike his brother, Stefan wasn't possessed by whatever dark forces were attached to the relic, and his extensive knowledge of the Black Grimoires gave them the advantage.

As far as the occult powers these books held, Kana had little faith in the religious teachings of the Catholic Church and heavily doubted some pope from the eighteenth century could manufacture such instruments. Sure, she had seen ghosts, spirits, cryptids, and all manner of minor actors on the paranormal stage, but the nature of these books brushed on something entirely different. The halos of heaven and the horns of hell made her uncomfortable, and both pervaded this case. If any of this was real, they were stepping into territory that she wasn't comfortable with believing, much less confronting.

***

Even though Kana didn't share AJ's fear of being in Israel, she had her share of concern for their safety. Once they made it from the airport to their hotel, the anxiety about being in this war-torn land subsided. AJ still didn't trust that they wouldn't be blown to bits at any given moment, but once in Jerusalem, he softened.

Stefan's world experience and connections came in handy here just as they did in Bucharest, so she would stay close to him and observe how he operated—how he talked to people, what caught his eye in the city and what didn't, and even his body language when the hotel's front desk clerk told him only one room was available.

Using his charm on the female hotel manager, Stefan was able to secure two rooms. One he'd share with AJ while Kana was given a suite, something she hadn't expected. There wasn't much time for her to enjoy it though. Stefan had other plans for the afternoon.

"You're going to need to know how to shoot," he said to her while they waited for their room keys. "It's almost certain at some point in time we're going to run into trouble. I can't be the only one who can handle himself."

She crossed her arms, leaning away from him. "I can handle myself."

"You can fight, yes. But when it comes between your fists and a gun, your fists aren't going to win."

"Fair point. So, where are we doing this? Is there a shooting range nearby?"

He tipped the desk clerk and pocketed one keycard before handing the other to Kana. "So to speak."

***

Stefan rented a vehicle for their journey to this mystery shooting range. He preferred Audi's and took the newest model the rental agency offered: bold, silver, and expensive. Kana admired his specificity. He was almost too perfect, Maybe when this case was over, they could celebrate by getting hot and sweaty in some exotic suite he'd coerce another hotel manager into giving them. For now, this was about business.

The drive was long and boring, the beige horizon of the desert the only scenery this far outside of Jerusalem. Was it a mistake to go off with him? She never told AJ where they were going, just that she and Stefan were going to explore beyond the city limits. He protested of course, but she was going to do what she wanted to.

"We're almost there." Stefan flashed a wide smile. "It's a beautiful day for a drive anyway, no? This car was a good choice. It performs well on these roads."

Kana nodded, tilted her head, and gave him a tight grin. "A bright, shiny, silver car when we're trying to keep a low profile. A smart decision."

"You don't approve?"

"I like the car. Don't get me wrong. But it's just not what I'd choose for work."

He rolled down the window, letting the breeze blow through his well-groomed head of dark brown hair. "And what would you have chosen?"

She noticed how much he loved to question her. If it was anyone else, she'd take it as condescension. This man had a way of charming her even when he was toying with her. It must have been the dimples. "Just, something else. But it is a beautiful machine. I'm more into muscle cars though."

"What do you drive back in America?"

She raised her fist to the roof. "Dodge Challenger. The best car ever made."

Stefan started laughing but covered his mouth.

She pointed her fist at him. "What the hell is so funny? Oh, you think a girl can't handle that car?"

"No, no, my dear. It's not that. It's just... That car is so you.

When I asked the question, I immediately thought *she probably likes the Challenger*, and just like that, you proved me right."

"And I'm still asking, is there something wrong with that?"

"Not at all. You are everything Granger said you were. I can see now why you were one of his favorites."

Another mention of Granger, a reminder that Stefan knew more about her than she knew about him. "I think he cared more about my intelligence than my choice in cars."

"Absolutely. But your choice in cars, dress, attitude—everything—is what makes you such a delightfully difficult person, Kana. I think we'll have a lot of fun." He lifted his foot from the accelerator pedal. "We're here."

An abandoned amusement park was not Kana's first choice as a shooting range. "A water park?" She scanned the brightly colored, albeit faded, chutes and slides that peaked out above the overgrowth of weeds and palm trees.

Stefan put the car in park. "They called it Atraktzia, It was shut down in 2000. To be honest, most of Kalya is abandoned. No one comes out here except for people who don't want to be found."

"And it's the perfect place for target practice."

"Among other things Come on. Let's find a place. Did you bring your equipment?"

Kana showed him her handgun and a handful of magazine clips. He took the weapon from her hand, checked the iron sights, then the slider, and finally the trigger before handing it back to her. With a grunt of approval, he opened the car door and started to the center of the park.

The sun felt twice as hot out here than in the city, but a breeze blew from the east to counter it. They were close to the Dead Sea, which peppered the air with enough moisture to kick the humidity level up a few degrees.

Atrakzia held a special kind of creepiness to it. Any abandoned place did, but an abandoned water park in the middle of a desert upped the creep factor. Dozens upon dozens of water slides sat empty, as bone dry as the sandy landscape outside the gates. The desert's vegetation had broken through the concrete and mortar, now choking the flumes and covering playfully crafted signs. Every so often the wind blew through the tubes, creating a hauntingly subtle moan. Metal signposts squeaked, pebbles clattered across cracked sidewalks, and the din reinforced the fact that this complex was a skeleton of constructed happiness.

Ten minutes into their walk through the park, Stefan dropped his bag on the ground and pointed to a structure a few yards ahead. "Here we are. That's a good place to practice."

His choice of gun range was the base of one of the bigger slides, empty and filthy, with three tubes leading down into a massive empty pool. The inside of the empty pool was decorated with the artistic graffiti of drifters who once called this place home and long since moved on. Two broken chairs and a rusted table were propped up in a pile near the end of the pool. Stefan eagerly hopped down into the carved-out space and rearranged the furniture.

Kana stood at the edge of the pool with her hands on her hips. "You know, I've been to a firing range before. It's not like I don't know what I'm doing."

"Yes, you've shot a gun, but you've clearly never shot a person," he called back to her from the pool. "There's a big difference between hitting a person and hitting a paper cutout."

"So, we're shooting people here?"

She barely heard his answer her over the noise he made while rummaging through the pile of debris. "No, don't be silly. You'll see what I mean. I'm going to put some of those empty cans and bottles on the table, and we'll start there. I want to see how you shoot."

Kana shrugged. This was going to be any different than shooting at a range. Targets were targets. And while it was true that Bucharest was the first time she shot at a living person, it wasn't something she was afraid of doing if it came down to it. She'd make the decision to pull the trigger. But he was right, it was harder.

"Okay." He hopped out of the pool, brushed the dust and dirt from his jeans, and stood behind her. "Let me see what you can do, Kana."

She loaded the weapon, exhaled a deep breath, and pointed the gun at the four empty cans he placed on the table. There was something strange about having someone watch her, but she didn't want him to see her anxiety. Squinting, she eyed the first can and fired. Missed.

His voice tickled her ear. "Relax. Pretend I'm not here."

Again, she aimed and fired. This time she hit the can and sent it ricocheting off the side of the empty pool. Stefan gave her two slow claps. She ignored him and continued firing. Three shots rang out, and the three cans were hit, thank you very much.

She holstered the weapon and looked at him over her shoulder. "I told you, Stefan. I can shoot. It's not a problem."

"But those were cans. They were standing still. Let's see how you do with this next challenge. Just wait here for a minute."

He grabbed a few empty pieces of trash—bottles, boxes, and other debris—and marched off behind the slide, out of sight.

This was becoming tedious. It was hot, she was bored, and they were wasting time. They were supposed to be looking for the black grimoires, but instead, she was out here, sweating, on the strangest date she'd ever been on.

Stefan called to her from behind the slide. "Are you ready?"

"Ready for what?" Kana screamed back.

No response. She paced back and forth. This really wasn't the time for games. Did he want her to come find him?

Just as she was about to walk away, a bottle slid down one of the chutes and fell into the empty pool below and shattered. What the hell was he doing?

Stefan shouted from behind the slides again. "Here comes

some more. Try to hit them this time."

Another bottle slid down, Kana quickly raised her gun and fired. She didn't even come close. Two more bottles followed. He was testing her. She'd probably have done better if Stefan told her what she was shooting at, but he made his point. It was easy to hit static targets, not ones in motion. She aimed again as more bottles, boxes, and cans cascaded down the different slides. Despite her best efforts, she only hit one target: a plastic cup that she just barely nicked.

Of course, he had to let her know his observations, sauntering from behind the slides back to where she stood. "It doesn't sound like you hit anything."

"You do realize it's dangerous to walk in front of someone with a loaded gun. Especially someone you're making fun of."

He grinned from ear to ear. "I'm not making fun of you. I am making a point. Reload the gun, we've only got a few seconds maybe."

Kana ejected the spent magazine and loaded another. "A few seconds for what?"

"Hurry up. They're coming!"

He sprinted behind her and waited for whatever was coming down the slides. A chorus of squeals pierced the air, reverberating from the slide to Kana's ears.

Without warning, a writhing stream of mice scampered down the slide and into the empty pool. She lifted her hands. "What the hell, Stefan?"

Kana was no big animal rights advocate, and these were diseased feral mice by the looks of them, but she had no desire to shoot animals. She wouldn't.

He tapped her shoulder. "Wait, don't shoot yet."

A dirty stream of water rushed down the chutes and into the pool, the writhing mass of rodents now swimming among the refuse. Oh, he turned on the pumps. That was smart.

Kana lowered her gun. "This is stupid. I'm not doing this."

"Shoot the targets."

Kana clicked the safety on her gun and handed it to Stefan. "I'm not doing it!"

Stefan snatched the gun from her, clicked the safety off, and marched to the edge of the pool. "Watch and learn then." He aimed at the pool and pulled the trigger.

She couldn't believe he was shooting mice in a pool. This was sick. After a few shots, Kana stood by his shoulder, hoping to convince him to end this when he noticed what he was shooting at. He wasn't hitting the rats, he was hitting the floating debris around them.

"See?" He fired again. "Hit the targets."

He handed the gun back to Kana. Even though she was happy he wasn't shooting rats, nor wanted her to. This was going from zero to one hundred in a very short span. She had difficulty hitting cans sliding down into the pool, now he wanted her to shoot bottles bobbing up and down with live animals scurrying around them.

She squinted and aimed before relaxing and lowering the gun. "I can't do it. They're moving too fast."

"You have to focus. Lead the target, and when you're sure you have a clean shot—and I mean clean as in you won't also hit one of those mice—pull the trigger."

His instructions were sound. His logic made sense. But it didn't matter. She was way too afraid of hitting one of the rodents. He slid behind her, cupping his hands over hers to guide her aim.

"That bottle right there. It's a big enough target." His breath tickled her neck now, the small hairs raising on her nape and shoulder. "Now, keep the target in your sights. Do you see it?"

"Yes."

"Now, hold your hands steady. Don't try to push it, let the gun do what it does. See what direction it's going and move just slightly ahead of it. There you go. Mind the mice. Now, when you're ready..."

He moved his hands to her hips and held them there to hold her stance. Kana knew this game; dozens of men used the same trick to teach her how to play billiards. His fingertips kneaded at her hips, each digit pressing gently enough to let her know they were there. He finally succeeded in making her smile, and while beaming, she pulled the trigger.

Bang! A large bottle shattered into pieces, not one mouse was harmed, even though they squealed from the noise. It wasn't often that someone surprised Kana, but Stefan was as clever a seducer as he was a teacher.

He removed his hands from her hips and backed away from her. "Now, we practice here, yes? We do it until you get comfortable with it."

Kana closed one eye, grimacing as she aimed. "What if I miss? Won't I hit a mouse?"

"They're mice, Kana. The world won't miss them."

SECRETS IN THE DESERT

S tefan and Kana returned to the hotel to find AJ waiting for them in the lobby. Kana recognized the look on his face,

"Thanks for showing up you two." AJ lifted his arms to his sides then let them flap down against his legs. "While you've been off doing God-knows-what, I've been working on our case."

"I know, I know, AJ. I should have called."

"Where did you two go?"

"Target practice." She let a smile slip through, caught it, and returned to her usual scowl. "What have you found since we've been gone?"

AJ motioned for them to follow him into the hotel bar attached to the lobby where there were fewer people and fewer ears to overhear the conversation. They found a spot in the middle of the bar far enough away from the two other patrons.

"Based on the notes in Stefan's journal, I tracked down a few areas where the grimoire might be. They're loose threads, but it's something to go on."

Kana leaned back in her chair. "So, we still know very little."

"Well, I also dug around and found some information on The Thule Society. There are a few fragments about their involvement in Jerusalem." AJ scrolled through a series of documents on his electronic tablet. "Most of it is their backing of Palestine over the Israelis, but I did note that they were spending a lot of time in three of the places the grimoire is rumored to be."

"And you cross-referenced them of course. That's why I keep you around, AJ."

"Thanks." He glanced up at Kana and turned back to his tablet. "It looks like one of them was bombed to hell so I'm removing that from the equation. We're down to two possible areas."

He slid his finger across the tablet's screen, bringing up a map where he had pinpointed the two possible locations. One was to the north, the other was in the south, and choosing the wrong one would cost them a full day, enough time to give their rivals a chance to swipe the book for themselves.

"Both are dig sites." Stefan leaned over the tablet. "The West Bank in the north is dangerous. But then again, the south is no picnic either."

Kana extended her hand to AJ. "Give me those notes you have from Stefan's journal."

He swiped off the map and opened a document where he had transcribed various passages and notes from Stefan's journal.

Kana took the tablet for herself, turned away from both men and, squinted as she swiped through the various notes and screenshots. Occasionally, she would let loose an "uh-huh" or an "hmm", all culminating with one of her favorite phrases. "For the love of rum."

AJ tapped her on her shoulder. "You found something?"

"It's north of the West Bank." Kana placed the tablet back on the bar and pointed to a spot on the map. "Honorius insisted back in the early 11th century that King Frederick II reestablish the kingdom of Jerusalem, right? Frederick postponed it again and again. He didn't go there until after Honorius's death. For some reason, Frederick spent an odd amount of time in the West Bank. Some historians said it was a staging area, but there were parts of that initial camp where no one could go. The south he left alone. Barely touched it. If King Frederick had the grimoire and hid it, it's in the north."

AJ examined the map again. "Positive?"

"It makes the most sense."

Stefan nodded, pushing his lower lip out. "So, we head north."

"We'll leave in an hour. I need to change and take a shower. I'll meet you both back here at the bar."

As she left the bar for the elevator, AJ squirmed in his seat. He was growing less and less enamored with Stefan's presence on this case. It didn't matter how much his information helped, the man was disrupting his partnership with Kana.

Stefan turned back to the bar and motioned to the bartender. "She truly is amazing." At first, AJ was going to ignore the comment but changed his mind. What better time, with Kana gone, to address the elephant in the room?

AJ turned to the bar too, folding his arms. "I've known that for a long time, Stefan."

"Meaning?"

"Meaning, I know her strengths, and more importantly, I know her weaknesses."

The word *weaknesses* floated between the two of them.

"I think you're not giving her enough credit. That woman is extraordinary. Professor Granger always thought so. Weakness isn't a word I'd use to describe her."

"Yeah, well I know." AJ leaned closer to Stefan and lowered his voice. "I don't know who you are, not really. I don't need to know more than what I looked up about you."

Stefan sipped his drink, cleared his throat, and swirled the liquor in his glass. "Yeah, boy? What do you know?"

"I know enough. I know enough about you and women. I know about you and your brother."

The last statement might have been out of line, and AJ knew it. Stefan finished his drink, tilting his head back while cutting his eyes sideways at AJ. He emptied the glass, wiped the small drops of alcohol from his lips, and leaned in to AJ.

"That's what you do. Investigate other people's lives, yes?

You investigate them, categorize them, judge them, all from the safety of your little keyboard." Stefan mimicked typing on a keyboard, his fingers just inches from AJ's face. "All while having no life of your own. But the truth about me isn't going to be found on a laptop or in a database. We'll be working together for the foreseeable future. It's best not to make this an issue."

"As long as you don't make it one, neither will I."

Stefan's dimples formed on either side of his face. He ordered another drink, swallowed half of it, and set the glass down on the bar. "And here I thought you were the gay friend." He patted AJ on the shoulder. "If you've been around a woman like that for this long and haven't made a move, it's not going to happen. It would be childish to be angry at me for doing what you are incapable of doing yourself."

AJ knew it was the truth, and as uncomfortable as it made him, he had to consider Stefan's words. If there was meant to be anything more than a business relationship between the him and Kana, it would have happened already. There wasn't. And yes, it was childish of him to pout because she was looking at another man the way he wished she looked at him. While all of this was true, it didn't lessen the hole he felt in his stomach while Stefan seduced her right in front of his face.

Stefan waved to the bartender. "Have a drink, my friend. It's going to be a long night."

He finished his own and left AJ at the bar. The bartender went to pour AJ's drink, but he shook his head as Stefan headed to the elevator.

***

Checkpoints, private roadways, militias traversing the area, all added to the difficulty of leaving the tenuous borders of Jerusalem to the outright minefield north of the city. Every so often gunfire was heard off in the distance, a disturbing soundtrack on their trek to the dig site.

They needed to ditch the car in a few miles away from the danger zone and go on foot under cover of darkness. AJ, although he wouldn't admit it, was terrified He swallowed his pride and prayed that they wouldn't be caught by forces looking for foreigners to use as hostages.

A ten-mile journey in the pitch-black night ended in a trench created by Israeli forces for strategic purposes, but now lay dormant. Although it was tough to navigate, the trio trudged over rocky ground, through tunnels teaming with spiderwebs, around spent shells and discarded live warheads, ending up at the dig site where it was rumored the Black Grimoire was buried. The place looked like no one had been there in long time. Pickaxes, shovels, industrial-sized lamps, and all manner of digging materials were scattered around the makeshift pit.

"It's so quiet out here." AJ examined one of the gas-powered generators. It had power, so he turned it on, illuminating the entire area.

Stefan hunched down at the center of the site, examining the broken machinery covered in sand. "No one has been out here for a while. They made the tunnels and left in a hurry."

"I can only imagine the reason why," Kana lifted a crumpled glove from the dirt, shaking the dirt off its thick leather padding. "Let's get this over with. I don't want to know the reason."

"Right." Stefan dusted off a pickax and slung it over his shoulder. "In case they haven't finished the tunnels."

Kana snatched the tool from him. "No, you two stay out here. I'm going in there. There's no sense in all of us going down there and getting trapped. If something goes wrong, someone should be out here."

Before either man could argue with her, she stormed off into the tunnel alone. Stefan accepted, reluctantly handing Kana a flask of water.

AJ pressed a few buttons on his phone and lifted it to his mouth. "Turn your phone to hands-free. We can use them like walkie-talkies."

Her voice came back through the phone. "Good idea. I've got a full battery."

Stefan hovered over AJ's shoulder. "We'll be here. You be careful."

"What's the fun in that?"

***

Even with a flashlight, it was hard to see more than a few feet ahead inside the tunnel. There were power lines running along the ceiling, and Kana followed them to a generator. After a few cranks, it started up. The lanterns bolted to the walls lit the way ahead. The flickering golden lights made the passage feel less claustrophobic, yet the skittering sounds within the walls and a low hum from somewhere up ahead unnerved her. The farther she descended, the tighter the air became. A stale wind blew past her every so often, suggesting that there was a greater opening ahead. The stench of rot and mold clogged her nostrils almost to the point of choking. What was causing that smell?

The stench increased with every step, so bad that Kana put her hand over her mouth to keep out the nidorous fumes. She soon found the source of the odor. The tunnel ending at the mouth of a massive hole in the ground, a putrid howling air erupting from the pit. There was something else shifting and moving around her here in the dark from all sides. No, not around her, but behind her.

Kana slid her hand around the grip of her gun. It was getting close. Sucking in a deep breath she turned, raised her gun, squinted to see her target clearly through the sights, and prepared for the worse.

"You're really going to shoot me?"

For a split second, Kana entertained the thought, but no, her target didn't deserve a bullet. At least not yet. It was Anastasia, her blonde hair tied in a bun and her face smudged with dirt and grease.

Kana grunted, waving the gun at her. "What the hell are you doing here? You know what, I shouldn't be surprised. At least I know I'm in the right place."

"You wanna stop pointing that gun at me?"

Kana stretched her lips in a sly grin before holstering the weapon as Anastasia blew past Kana to the open pit.

"I think you enjoyed that too much for my liking," she said while looking into the dark expanse below.

"Don't tempt me. So, are we working together here or is this still a competition?"

Anastasia flicked her open hand at her.. "I don't care what you do, Kana. I'm here to find the grimoire. Just don't get in my way."

As Kana surveyed the giant pit, she had no idea what was down at the bottom of this hole in the ground. Having another pair of eyes down here might be a blessing in disguise.

***

AJ and Stefan didn't speak while they waited for Kana's return. AJ tinkered with his equipment, their function foreign to anyone else but him, attempting to rewire a box that looked like a cross between a handheld radio and a battery. Stefan opened the cases left behind by prior expedition crew. He wanted to know what made them evacuate the space so suddenly, and that answer could be stashed away in a journal or a piece of paper hidden among the debris.

After twenty minutes, Stefan sat next to AJ on a large utility crate as he undid his wiring work.

Stefan scratched at his beard stubble. "Do you mind me asking what that is?"

AJ concentrated on the box. "Yes, I do mind."

Stefan crossed his ankles. "Oh, come on, AJ. Don't be like that."

"You wouldn't understand, and I don't really feel like explaining."

Stefan stood and strolled toward the open tunnel, whistled to himself, and then spun back around. "Look, I'm sorry if I hurt your feelings earlier. If I crossed a line, then that was wrong."

AJ continued to tinker with the box. "You don't know Kana like I know her. She seems really tough on the outside, but there are a few things she can't handle."

"She seems pretty capable to me."

AJ shook his head, still avoiding eye contact. "Thank you for proving my point."

"No, don't shut down. What do you mean? She's smart, she's physically tough, she's mentally tough. I don't see where she's weak anywhere."

"It's not really a weakness. I guess what I'm trying to say is that she's sensitive to certain things, and I don't want to see her get hurt."

"And you think I'm going to hurt her?"

"Not intentionally." AJ put the box down on his lap before raising his head. "But to put it bluntly, she doesn't make good decisions when it comes to men."

Stefan laughed. It was simple. AJ was jealous. "Listen, I will not lie about my intentions for Kana. She's a very beautiful woman. Exquisite, I would say. It would be wrong of me to say that I was not interested in her, but you have to get beyond your jealousy, AJ."

"Jealousy," AJ mumbled to himself.

Stefan winked at him. "That's the best word I can use to describe how you're acting."

AJ returned to his tinkering. "Think what you will."

Stefan put his hands on his hips and lowered his head. "It's best for all of us if you don't make this a big deal."

"She's twenty-two years old."

"She's a woman."

The box fell from AJ's lap. "You know what, I'm not having this conversation with you anymore. Do what you want. She's not a piece of meat."

"I never said she was."

"You look at her like she is. I'm not..." AJ shook his head and focused on the box.

Stefan pursed his lips and raised his finger while motioning with his other hand to the ground. AJ didn't know why until Stefan pointed behind him. Too late. AJ was now staring at the business end of a rifle. His hands shot up as he backed away from the gun-wielding mercenary stepping from the shadows.

Six more men surrounded AJ and Stefan, all wearing the same paramilitary black outfit, all carrying AK-47s, and all prepared to fire on their targets. The only two exits out of the pit were blocked by the gunmen. The strands of platinum blonde hair sticking out of the masks and the white skin glowing from under their black masks proved these weren't Israeli or Palestinian military. These were agents of The Thule Society who had come to claim the prize hidden under the earth and who would possibly bury the duo in the process.

THE SILENT GUARDIANS

Anastasia and Kana were a mile beneath the Earth's surface and no closer to the bottom of this pit. The path into the earth wound around the sides of the massive hole and proved treacherous to navigate. Both women slipped at one point or another but managed to regain their footing, avoiding certain death by falling into the abyss.

After a long stretch of silence between the two, Anastasia cleared her throat. "Is AJ with you?"

"He is. You plan on playing him for a fool again?"

Anastasia huffed. "Who said I played him for a fool?"

"Come on, Anastasia. How many times have you gotten him to do work for you by simply sending him some suggestive pictures to his phone?"

Anastasia stumbled over an uneven part of the path and placed her hand against the slick walls of the cavern to steady herself. "Who said they were suggestive?"

Kana rolled her eyes. The way AJ drooled over this buxom blonde was annoying but knowing that she was using him in such an obvious way turned her stomach. But who was she to judge? If the situation called for it, she used her own looks to get her way when the time called for it. There was something about the way Anastasia did it,

Feeling that her temporary partner was upset by her answer, Anastasia tried to ease the tension. "I really don't have anything against you, Kana. I hope you know that. This is all friendly."

Kana scratched the side of her nose. "So you say."

"What I said back in Granger's apartment was the truth, though. You shouldn't be involved in this. Neither of you. That's why I asked about AJ. I hoped you didn't dragged him along with you. He's not cut out for this kind of thing."

Kana aimed her flashlight into the pit. Nothing but blackness below. "He might surprise you."

"You're not cut out for it either." Anastasia stopped walking put her hand on Kana's shoulder.. "We're dealing with serious people here and some freaky next level power. This isn't some scam case or using a charm to force a spirit away. What is down there, what you're about to walk into, are things from beyond this world you don't want to know about."

Kana pushed her hand away. "Are you trying to scare me away, Anastasia? You really need to get off this whole I'm-looking-out-for-you act. I studied the same as you did, and I followed the same path. I've faced things beyond this world already, far worse than you'll ever know."

Anastasia placed her hand against the wall, bracing herself as she continued down the path. "Like what?"

The tingle of the Shinigami tickled the back of her head. This wasn't the time to talk it up, even as proof to Anastasia. "It doesn't matter. What does matter is that Professor Granger had the same confidence in me that he had in you."

"And he knew you weren't ready. He told me. It was one of the last things he told me." With a sigh, Anastasia lowered the flashlight.

It was Kana now who took the lead, forcing her way past Anastasia. When she was a member of *The Prestige Club*, Kana always believed she was the special one, the one that Granger had so much hope in. And he did. Stefan verified that days ago. But here was Anastasia telling her that he didn't think she was ready. She was punching holes in this perception that Kana had of herself, and they were sharp jabs. This couldn't be true. She was playing a game again, trying to knock her confidence.

Kana faced Anastasia again. "You're full of it. Are we doing this or what?"

"No, Kana. You're not—"

"Yeah, yeah, I'm not ready. I'm only twenty-two. Right now, whether the professor thought that or not, it doesn't matter. I'm here. It's time to see whether or not I am ready." Enough of being questioned. She huffed and pushed past Anastasia, continuing down the stairwell without her.

As far as Kana was concerned, this was her show, and Anastasia just happened to be along for the ride. She had to think of it that way. Beyond the pride involved, she needed to prove herself. It may have been foolhardy, but she was determined to get to the bottom of this hole and take charge once they found the book. If Anastasia wanted to fight her for it, she would welcome the challenge. Kana excelled at combat, and she was happy to prove it to the buxom blonde.

Without warning, the bottom of the pit appeared in a sudden flash of light. Anastasia wasn't far behind and hit the ground with the same surprised suddenness.

They weren't alone in the pit. Kana stretched her arms out, looking side to side. "I assume this is what happened to the survey team that dug this hole."

Furniture from a variety of time periods filled the chamber. A grandfather clock from the mid-twentieth century, two reclining chairs, a long, massive dining room table, and a cluster of other antiques were scattered everywhere. Both women waved their flashlights around, uncovering more relics covered in a film of filth and rot, decaying in this forgotten museum flooded by sewage. The stench was intense, the same putrid smell that stunned Kana's senses in the passageway above. What was most disturbing was not the slime nor the out-of-place furniture, but the humanoid figures—caked in the same corrosive brown substance—standing around the room.

"Well, you wanted in on this. What would you classify this?" Anastasia asked.

Kana kicked at a pile of debris next to her foot, burned pieces of paper and shreds of clothing balled together on the floor. "It depends on if they're hostile or not. They look like they're from the Foundation."

The blonde laughed. "You know that's just a game. The SCP Foundation is no more than a listing of creepy pastas and supernatural anomalies on a website, like an interactive urban legend database. Those people made all that stuff up."

"Oh really?" Kana knelt near one of the piles of filth and pointed to a patch on the floor.

The letters "SCP" were bold and blatant on the pentagon-shaped vinyl patch, torn and discarded, covered in the same brown filth.

"And you're supposed to be the expert?" Kana stood from the debris and flung the patch at Anastasia. "Don't touch any of them. It's a trap."

"Wait, you know what this is?" the blonde said, flipping the patch over before tossing it back to the floor.

"Not for sure." Kana waved her flashlight at the other filth-covered bodies in the pit. "But AJ reads that website enough and tells me about it any chance he gets. I have an idea. We even based our classifications of cases on that website. These are probably *Euclid*."

"Euclid?"

"Something unpredictable but not necessarily dangerous. I'd put on gloves and a mask."

Neither had the proper equipment they would need for such an environment, so the paper face masks and rubber gloves would have to do.

As they prepared to examine the area, several of the SCP workers shuffled randomly around the room and stopped, frozen in place. There was no pattern to their activity, they weren't trying to get anywhere, nor was there any task they were attempting to complete. Two dozen of these bodies, faceless and emotionless thanks to the heavy coat of sludge encasing them, continued this eerie cycle of movement and stillness. The women let the cycle continue a few times, trying to decipher any pattern.

"There's some sort of ticking in here," Anastasia whispered to Kana. "Can you hear it?"

"It's faint but yes, I hear it. I can't really tell where it's coming from either. Maybe we should just focus on finding the grimoire."

One of the workers, or *Silent Guardians* as Anastasia called them, twitched to life and headed in their direction. Kana didn't move, hoping if she remained silent the creature would not notice her. Five steps before it would have collided with her, the body stopped and titled its head at an angle that should have broken its neck. Kana let out a sigh of relief and redirected her energy to finding the location of the grimoire.

Anastasia waved her flashlight to get Kana's attention. "It's the ticking. They can't hear anything but the ticking. You hear how it gets faster and slower? There's some sort of rhythm to it. Probably tied to when they start and stop moving."

"Maybe it's coming from that one over there." Kana jabbed her flashlight at the guardian sitting in a rocking chair, a black book in its hands, clean of the brown sludge encasing everything else.

There was one problem. A cluster of the guardians stood between them and the rocking chair, there wasn't much room for them to maneuver around, and they didn't have all night to wait for these humanoids to shuffle away. The only choice was to navigate between the bodies, grab the book, and squeeze their way back out.

Anastasia moved to the left of the sofa between them and the book holder while Kana crept around the other side. As Kana neared the first guardian, she felt her muscles tense up, her stomach churning as the stink of the pit intensified. Five feet was all the room she had to move between the sofa and the mannequin-like guardian ahead of her. There was enough space that she didn't worry too much about accidentally touching the thing. In her mind, of course, she had nerves of steel, but in practice, she didn't know how she'd react if one of these things grabbed her. This was foreign territory. Ghosts were one thing, shambling bags of meat were another.

Kana turned her back to the sofa to keep her eyes on the guardian. Slipping past the poor soul gave her an up close and personal look at it, and beneath the shell was the distorted face of a young man. His mouth was elongated into a frozen scream, his eyes solid white, and purple veins pressed against the flesh of his face.

The trio of guardians beyond the sofa would be a bigger obstacle. One was nestled at the end of the sofa with its right arm extended. The other was a taller male who took up so much space, Kana would have to duck below its outstretched arms to pass through. It wouldn't have been so bad if there wasn't a chair to the right of him and another guardian next to that. She'd have to squat, slide underneath his arms, and pray to God she didn't move the chair, make a sound, or even worse, stumble into one of the bodies.

On the other side of the sofa, Anastasia was far ahead of her, doing her own gymnastics routine to weave between two guardians and an oversized dresser. There was no time to worry about what would happen if Anastasia reached the grimoire first. Kana needed to get through this obstacle or none of that would matter. The ticking increased the closer she got to the book, the sound affecting her in ways she hadn't anticipated. A pressure pushed down on her head while sweat poured from her brow. Whatever spell bewitched the guardians had taken hold of her.

She had to move faster.

Down on both knees, she squeezed under the tall guardian's arm. So far, so good, but the nauseous fetor of feces and urine filled her nostrils, causing her to shift so she could cover her mouth. The motion nicked the side of the chair enough for the legs to screech against the floor.

Anastasia heard the sound. She pursed her lips and raised her eyebrows at Kana. Both held their breath as the back of the chair stopped a few inches from the third guardian. A few moments passed, and with no movement from the guardians, Kana slowly unhooked her jacket from the leg of the chair and reached back with her right hand and shifted her shoulders to free herself, taking great care not to bump into the guardian.

It was done. After a few more feet she stood. "I hate this place."

Only one guardian remained between Kana and the grimoire. Without warning, it jerked its head jerking and shook from side to side before it headed in Anastasia's direction. Now the path was clear between Kana and the guardian in the chair who held the Black Grimoire. As she thought, the ticking was emanated from the book clutched between the guardian's two deformed hands. Was there a trick to removing it?

"Kana, hold on." Anastasia whispered as quietly as she could without disturbing the other guardians, the shambling body blocking her path. "Don't touch it just yet. We don't know what that thing does."

It was good advice. Or, was it? It was entirely possible that Anastasia wanted Kana to hold back so she could claim the book for herself. They weren't partners; they were rivals who were temporarily on the same team. That time had passed.

The ticking intensified, making Kana's head throb. Her hands itched, and a thick film was coating her skin. No time to debate this. If she didn't do something to stop this ticking, she and Anastasia would wind up like the SCP investigators. Kana reached out with both hands to grab the book. The guardian holding the grimoire was still paralyzed in place, but she doubted it would stay that way. Maybe it would sit up when she got too close to the grimoire, or it was just waiting for her to get close enough to react. She had no way of knowing. The warnings in her head began to overwhelm her. Just a few more inches to go. No, she stopped and retracted, then shook her hands to rid herself of the nerves.

Just do it, she told herself.

Kana shut her eyes and lunged forward, snatching the book without thinking. The book came free without resistance, so easily she stumbled backward, almost bumping into one of the guardians. The former book holder hadn't moved an inch since the book was retrieved. *Maybe there's nothing to fear after all.* Kana flipped through the pages of the grimoire, each one as black as night and filled with Latin, unrecognizable symbols, and what she assumed was an extensive list of spells, all written in a bright red ink. AJ would have to examine this, but first, she had to end this ticking.

"Kana," Anastasia said softly.

"I'm trying to figure this out." She continued flipping through pages.

"Kana!"

"What?"

"We need to go, now!"

Kana looked up from the book to the rest of the room. All the guardians had turned their heads in her direction, some so twisted that their heads had completely spun around to their backs. When she slammed the book shut and put it in her bag, the ticking immediately stopped.

Both women sprinted to the exit. As they did, the heads of the guardians followed them as they climbed the spiral stairway to the tunnels above. The silent guardians broke their reticence, each one opening their mouths, howling a sour ghostly note, part human and part animal.

"Keep going!" Kana yelled at Anastasia.

Both women were highly athletic, so staying ahead of the horde that followed them wasn't too difficult, but the steepness of the stairwell made it hard on their legs. A burning set in their thighs. They couldn't let it slow them down, they had a mile to travel up.

As Kana turned back, the brown sludge fell from their bodies, revealing the fleshy wet meat beneath. With their shells falling away, the corpses degraded. Limbs detached, jaws dislodged, entrails spilled onto the steps and tumbled into the pit below.

The top of the stairs was ahead. "Come on! We're almost there," Kana shouted.

Anastasia needed to stop and catch her breath once they reached the top, unable to move. They'd have to make a stand here at the mouth of the tunnel. Both women pulled their firearms, standing shoulder to shoulder, waiting for the mutants to clear the top of the steps. The first guardian emerged, and Anastasia took it out with a single shot to the head, bursting a hole through the skull, the body collapsing in a heap.

She darted a look over at Kana who wasn't aiming her gun. "They can't be saved if that's what you are thinking. Get it out of your mind. Just pull the trigger."

"Not a problem." But were these people alive or the corpses used as pawns by some demonic spell from the grimoire? It was a question she couldn't answer.

Anastasia gripped her gun and braced herself. "Here comes some more. Are you ready?"

Kana pulled the trigger several times, slaying three of the walking corpses within a second. Anastasia smiled, and the two wiped out the horde of guardians. After the last body fell, they leaned against the tunnel wall to catch their breath before walking back through the tunnel, leaving a putrid pile of bullet-riddled bones and flesh behind.

ALWAYS HIRE THE LOCALS

Kana took her time walking back through the tunnel to the entrance. She was tired and filthy, but it was all worth it given her find, the same couldn't be said for her companion though. Anastasia tried every argument she could think of to convince Kana to share the discovery and it was a waste of breath. There was no amount of money, recognition, or assistance she could offer that would be good enough.

"How did you find this place?" Kana asked, wiping a chunk of brown sludge from her cheek.

"Granger's flash drive. How did you find it, Kana? I was shocked to see you here."

"AJ and I found someone who knows more about the black grimoires than anyone."

Anastasia tripped over a rock and grabbed Kana to keep herself from falling over. "Stefan. There's someone from the past. Is he still arrogant as hell?"

Kana shrugged. "No more than any of the rest of us."

"Well, AJ's not. He's probably the only good soul among us."

Kana had never thought about her partner that way. "I guess. He's a good hand to have around."

Anastasia nodded. "It'll be good to see him again."

"Don't lead him on. There's no reason to get his hopes up, and don't try to con him into giving you information. This is a job and I need him thinking clearly, not getting a chubby from looking at your giant fake breasts."

Anastasia raised her hands. "Hey, no need to go there. I just wanted to say hi. I have no desire to team up with you any more than we already have, Kana. You don't play well with others. It's always been your weakness."

"Weakness, huh? If playing well with others means doing what you do—"

"I thought it'd be beneath you to slut-shame me. It's something men say to women who get what they want." Anastasia lowered her voice. "I thought you were one of those women."

"Do what you like, Anastasia. I'm not judging you."

"You just did."

Kana raised her finger. "That was a joke. Let's not pretend you're trying to have a casual conversation here. You're trying to find a way to get your hands on this book. You're not doing it through AJ. So, I repeat: leave him alone. And for the record, I don't think you're a slut, but you certainly have used your looks to manipulate gullible boys like AJ. You've done it to him

Anastasia lifter her finger. "That was business and you know it. You'd do the same if you ever dressed in something other than a t-shirt and a leather jacket."

Kana brushed off a speck of dirt from that very jacket. "I don't need to. Remember, I have the grimoire. I didn't need to flaunt my body to some man to do so."

Anastasia balled her fist. "You're new to this, so I'll leave it be. All I'm saying is that in this world—that you so desperately want to get into—you'll eventually have to use more than a smart mouth and a few guns to survive."

"Whatever."

This conversation was over as far as Kana was concerned, so she took her phone from her pocket and used its walkie-talkie feature to radio AJ. It had been over an hour since she checked in with him.

"Are you there, AJ? AJ?"

"Is something wrong with the phone?" Anastasia asked.

"He's there." Kana shook the phone. "He probably just put the phone down." She tried again. "AJ, are you there? AJ?"

Still nothing.

Was there reason to worry? AJ wasn't the most capable person when it came to confrontations, but Stefan was with him. Any number of reasons could explain why Kana wasn't getting an answer from them right now. Instead of worrying herself, she put the phone away, they'd be out of the tunnel in a matter of minutes.

***

Kana and Anastasia exited the tunnel only to find a line of men standing shoulder to shoulder pointing guns at them. AJ and Stefan were between them and the mercenaries on their knees with their hands laced behind their heads.

"Well, now we know why he wasn't answering," Anastasia whispered.

The pained scowl on AJ's face turned into an awkward smile the moment Anastasia emerged from the tunnel, and in turn, she winked at him.

Kana wrinkled her nose. "Seriously?"

Another voice, thick with a German accent, cut through the silence. "You did quite well back in Bucharest. Since you managed to escape from down there, I'll assume you have the grimoire?"

Dieter strutted to the front of the line with his hands clasped behind his back, with the same smugness he had back in the cabin.

"The only thing he's missing is a mustache to twirl," Kana muttered.

Anastasia put her hands to her hips, ignoring Kana's joke. "So, you're Dieter? I'm surprised to see you get your hands dirty."

"For this, Fraulein, I will absolutely make sure it is done correctly. The other members of the society would not take kindly to any more failures in getting these books. But, in truth, it is you who dirtied your hands, not me. Anastasia, is it not? Another one of Granger's pet projects." Dieter approached the blonde and cupped her jaw with his index finger and thumb, turning her head from side to side gently. "He did have an eye for beautiful women, I must say."

Kana huffed loudly to get his attention. "Yes, yes, you know each other's backstory. I'm not impressed. Get on with whatever it is you need to do here."

Dieter dropped his hands from Anastasia's face and focused on Kana. "Such a hot temper on this one. Believe me, I don't want to spend any more time in this country of savages than I must. The very air makes me sick."

"Too bad you don't choke on it." Kana spat at his feet.

"You make it very hard for me to be polite about this." Dieter kicked the wad of phlegm soaking in the dirt while removing the bag from Kana's shoulder. "Three sides of the same triangle all in pursuit of the same thing. I assumed we would end up here eventually." He removed the grimoire from the bag. "All for this book."

Dieter's men surrounded the area with their jeeps, the headlights flooding the area with enough light that the grimoire could be seen clearly. To anyone else, it looked like any other old book, manufactured from a time where there was an art to handmade bookbinding. Time had not withered the tome. It was in pristine condition despite the muck of the cave and the six centuries that passed since its creation.

"One more to go." Dieter flipped through a few of the pages. "You all have been of a great help to me. We've kept your boyfriends entertained while we waited for you to come back to the surface. But I do believe it's time to wrap this up and go home."

Anastasia nudged her elbow against Kana's to get her attention. She nodded while Dieter rambled on about The Thule Society and how killing the four of them would be painful and so on and so forth.

"I'd give real money if he shut up," Kana whispered. How anyone took him seriously she didn't know, but he had followers, and from the looks of things, so did Anastasia.

"What is this?" Dieter shouted as his speech was cut short by the appearance of twenty Israeli soldiers on the hillside, their floodlights shining on the dig site.

Anastasia put her arms down, grinning from ear to ear. "This land of savages, as you call it, has a rather capable military if you didn't know. It helps to know the locals. I'll be taking that if you don't mind."

She held her hands out, waiting for Dieter to give her the book. He straightened his tie, swallowed hard, and reluctantly handed it over to Anastasia.

One of the Thule soldiers spoke up from under their mask.

"You're not honestly giving in to these dogs."

"There will be another time." Dieter raised an open palm, signaling for his troops to lower their weapons.

"That is unacceptable," said the dissident. "You three, take the ones on the far hill. We'll take the others. One of you gets the book. Fire on three. One!"

"Stop!" Dieter shouted. "That is an order!"

"Two!"

"I order you to—"

"Three!"

Kana grabbed her gun and ducked down. "No, no. Nah, no, no, no!"

Gunfire erupted in all directions. Dieter's men and Anastasia's hired Israeli soldiers started a mini war around the perimeter of the dig site, bullets flying in all directions, men screaming in either agony or exhilaration. Kana took cover behind a pile of discarded metal and rubble, mindful to keep out of the line of fire, especially from any of Dieter's men who wouldn't hesitate to fill her with holes.

Anastasia and Dieter engaged in a struggle on the ground, wrestling for ownership of the Black Grimoire. As the gunfire started to fade, the Israelis and the Thule troops took their war off into the hills. Dieter had Anastasia pinned down, his hand wrapped tightly around her throat. Kana leaped into the fray, kicking Dieter in the face and sending him tumbling off Anastasia.

"How dare you?"

Kana stepped between the two of them. "Get out of here, Anastasia."

As Dieter reached for the pistol strapped to his waist, Kana leaped on him and twisted his arm behind his back, causing so much pain that he dropped the weapon. He was a slow fighter, so Kana grabbed his other arm and flipped him to the ground.

"Get off of me mongrel!" Dieter stayed down for a few moments before standing up straight, his hands balled into fists, taking a 1940's carnival fighter's stance. That was fine, she wanted him to make another move. With every punch she landed his ego bruised more, and that ego wouldn't let him accept that a woman—an Asian woman at that—was getting the best of him in a fight. He charged her, his right hand cocked for a punch. It was another mistake.

Kana sidestepped him, took hold of his cocked fist, flipped him over her shoulder into the dirt, and locked her legs around his arm. Pulling with all her strength, she stretched him out and locked him in an armbar. She arched his back, the strain on her forearms burning through her skin, but she felt his elbow joint strain.

"Stop! Stop!" He wiggled in her grasp, his feet kicking wildly in vain. "Take the book. Take the damn thing! Just stop!"

Kana loosened her grip on his arm. "I'm not ever going to see you again, right? This is the end of this. Am I understood?"

"Yes! Yes! Just let me go!"

"If you come after us again, I won't be so easy on you next time."

Dieter nodded in compliance. Kana knew he had no intention of this being the end of it. He would come after her again and try to make her pay for humbling him. She needed to give him more incentive not to. One last tug would do it, increasing the pressure on his wrist, and within a split second it snapped. Dieter screamed as she let go, clasping his left hand around his broken arm, writhing on the ground screaming a litany of German curses at her.

"Jesus, Kana." Anastasia grabbed Kana's arm, pulling her away from the broken man. "You said you wouldn't be so easy on him *next* time."

"I just broke his arm. He doesn't know what I'll snap next."

The black grimoire lay in the dirt between the three of them, and as Kana was the only one standing, she casually lifted it off the ground and placed it back into her bag. Kana extended her hand, and Anastasia accepted before Kana hoisted Anastasia off the ground.

Anastasia brushed her backside. "I need to get back to my people. You did good today, Kana. I'm not going to take that away from you, but I intend on getting that back sooner than later."

Wiping the dirt from her jacket, Kana smirked. "You can try."

After Kana left, Anastasia turned back to Dieter and picked up the pistol he dropped earlier, but he was gone. She followed the trail of blood he left behind in the dirt, but it ended at a pair of footprints that trailed up the side of the hill and beyond. In the distance she heard a few cracks of gunfire. It wouldn't be long before more troops—those not on her payroll—investigated the source of the firefight. The last thing she wanted was the Israeli government to find out she paid their soldiers under the table to act as her own private army. It was time to leave but not quit. There'd be another way to get her hands on the Black Grimoire, even if it meant she was on the opposing side of a fight with Kana next time.

RUM ON THE WINDOWSILL

K ana found Stefan and AJ in the hollowed out tunnels that led away from the dig site; AJ's face pale and sweaty, Stefan's covered in dirt and streaks of blood.

"We ran into a few of them on the way here." He clutched at the deep gash on his right arm. "AJ held his own though. He's tougher than he looks."

"I'd say that was more panic than anything else," AJ added.

Stefan patted him on the shoulder. "We stopped here to wait for you. I don't think they're looking for us now with the Israelis on their backsides. We just have to keep moving and link up with my contacts."

Kana reached out to Stefan's wound, the blood flowing freely down his arm. "You need to see a doctor. Do you have some place we can stay? I don't want to be followed back to the hotel."

"No, the hotel is probably the safest place for us right now. It's far enough away from here and we're listed under assumed names. If we don't draw attention to ourselves leaving here, we should be fine." He glanced down at his arm. "I'll be okay, don't worry about this. Did you get the book?"

Kana lifted the top half of the Black Grimoire from her bag, enough for Stefan to get a glimpse before stuffing it back inside. "I also broke Dieter's arm."

AJ's hid his face in his hands. "You what?"

"Just to give him something to think about the next time he tries to mess with us."

Stefan ripped a piece of his shirt off and wrapped it around his wound. "You should have shot him."

"That's not who I am."

The Italian laughed, then winced as he tightened the knot. "It might have to be sooner or later."

"Why is everyone so desperate to try and get me to kill someone? I'd rather not have that on my conscience."

"It's fine for now. Like you said, you gave him something to think about, yes? With any luck, we can get to the next grimoire without killing anyone."

The conversation ended when AJ rose to his feet and tugged at Kana and Stefan's shoulders. "Let's just get back to the car. I've had enough violence and gunfire for one night, let alone have to talk about it."

***

It was 3 am by the time they returned to the hotel. They entered through the back of the building instead of the main lobby. It may have been excessive, but after running into not one, but two, opposing forces looking for the Black Grimoires, it was an inconvenience they all agreed to.

Kana went immediately to her suite without speaking to AJ or Stefan. Behind closed doors, she tore off her dirty clothes and put them in a plastic bag to be cleaned. It was time for a hot shower, warm towels, and a glass of chilled rum. Even though she wasn't injured, her body was sore, and she could still feel the film of mucus from the underground cavern all over her skin.

The hot water blasted her, the sludge and dirt sliding off her body, the scent of aloe replacing the stench of sweat and dirt. She luxuriated here, allowing the powerful streams of water pelt her head and shoulders. Her hands pressed against the wall as she dipped her head under the streams, allowing them to find their way through her hair, to caress her scalp, and trickle down her back.

After her shower, she wrapped herself in a fresh towel, its softness intoxicating. Tomorrow might not provide her the such amenities, so tonight she'd indulge in them. The king-sized bed looked like heaven, set between two arched windows that ran from floor to ceiling, overlooking a garden three stories down. The silver light of the new moon filtered through the curtains and onto the bed creating a spotlight over her as she lay on the plush sheets. Falling asleep with these windows open wasn't the smartest thing to do, but it's what she wanted. It's what she *needed*. She'd risk a bit of safety to have a few hours of peace.

Until a knock came at her door.

She groaned, the interruption coming halfway between waking and dreaming, and rolled out of the bed. Her handgun sat on the nightstand. She grabbed it, cocked the slider, and leaned her ear against the door, gripping the weapon with both hands. "Whoever it is, you're really picking the wrong time for this."

"It's Stefan," a muffled voice responded.

Kana rolled her eyes, feeling foolish now for grabbing her gun. She tucked it away in her travel bag and swung the door open. Stefan smiled at her, then doubled down on his grin as he looked her up and down. Kana forgot she was only in a bathrobe, groaned at his ogling, and left him standing in the open doorway. "If you say I look good in a bathrobe you can leave right now."

"I'm sorry. I'm a guy. It happens, you know." His explanation fell on deaf ears. "We were waiting for you to come plan our next move, but you never showed up."

She softened her tone. "I'm sorry. It slipped my mind. We can talk about it now. I'm sure you want to see the book."

Stefan took a seat on her bed and winced in pain. Kana noticed it but ignored his groans as she pulled the Black Grimoire from her bag, handing it over to Stefan.

He rubbed the textured leather cover with his fingertips. "In a strange way this is very exquisite, no? And in such fine condition." He flipped the book over as Kana sat down next to him. "I imagined it would be in far worse shape after all these years."

"Well, if it is a book of spells, that would make sense. Magical items, especially black magic, have a way of enduring."

Stefan let the book rest on his lap. "That is very, very true. It is something man should not meddle with, which is why I'm hesitant to even open this."

"So don't." Kana left the bed for the minibar in her suite and grabbed a glass. "We don't need to open them, we just need to collect them. Let others worry about what's inside."

"My curiosity though..." his words quieted to a whisper as his eyes lovingly scanned the book. "...you know what it did to the cat."

Kana filled her glass with ice cubes and rum. "Killed it stiffer than this shot."

"How about one of those for me?" Stefan asked, wetting his lips.

"Rum?"

"Absolutely."

Kana made a second drink for Stefan and joined him on the edge of the bed. He took a sip and winced again at the stabbing pain in his arm. Whether he was trying to win sympathy from her or he was truly in pain didn't matter to Kana, she took the grimoire for herself and inspected the spine while sipping from her own drink. Out of the corner of her eye she could see Stefan watching her, smiling, then turning away.

He sucked in a breath between his gnashed teeth. "So, the arrangements have been made. We have a flight out of here tomorrow heading for Japan."

"Yeah, that's kind of messing with me. That's where I was born."

"I thought you were American?"

She swirled the last sip of rum between her gums and swallowed. "I am, but I was born in Tokyo. We moved to the States when I was two-years-old. I don't remember much of Tokyo as a kid, but I've been there a few times since. Most of my family is still there."

"You never told me anything about your family."

"That's a topic for another time," Kana said coolly. He hadn't earned that level of trust yet and she was determined not to have this evening ruined by a therapy session about her childhood. "I'm not blowing you off, Stefan. It's just not something I want to talk about right now."

"I understand. Believe me, with what my brother is doing I know how sensitive family matters can be."

"Thank you."

He swirled his glass, the ice cubes rattling against each other. "We'll be heading to Shinjuku anyway. I doubt you'd want to let your family know why you're going there."

He had been coy about their plans in Japan and there wasn't a better time for Stefan to clarify them. Kana and AJ were in the dark about how all this tied together. They trusted Stefan to a point, but trust only went so far.

"What's in Shinjuku anyway?" Kana asked. "I mean, I doubt we'll be wandering through underground tunnels there."

Stefan set the glass down on his lap. "This is a much different task. There are a few powerful players in Shinjuku who deal in these things. My brother and I conducted plenty of business there in the past, enough to make me think the third grimoire was there. There's this woman, an old hag who calls herself Kuroi Majo, who runs the underground there. She'd know where it is or might even have it herself." Another grimace twisted his face as he rubbed at his shoulder. "This won't be easy. It's downright impossible to get anywhere near her."

"*Kuroi Majo*," Kana repeated the name, the syllables slowly leaving her lips. "Black Witch? That's a bit on the nose don't you think?"

"From what I hear, it's accurate. There are some twisted stories surrounding that woman. We'll have to be clever to find her and careful when we meet her, but I have a plan."

"Which is?"

"It's complicated. We should probably save it for tomorrow when all three of us are together. It's just you and me right now."

Kana took another sip of her drink and frowned. She didn't like secrets but for the time being, she'd give him the benefit of the doubt. Besides, she was tired and just wanted to enjoy the night. "Whatever it is, we'll be closer to finishing this job."

He was giving her that look again; that hungry, longing look with his piercing blue eyes that made her insides flutter. Kana let their eyes meet before blinking away the connection and chose to move to the windows. The rum, the moonlight, and the cityscape were perfect at this moment, her insides warm from shower, drink, and arousal. That's when the chill hit her, a skin-crawling frost that moved through her insides, snatching away a piece of that warmth. She knew this feeling. It haunted her for two years now, this sinister feeling, an incurable cancer that plagued her at the worst times.

Stefan was speaking to her, but his voice sounded like he was underwater. "You handled yourself well out there. But, I'm not that surprised."

She didn't respond to him. Her body stiffened as she tried to ignore the nasty chill that was spreading through her.

"Is everything alright?" Stefan rose from the bed and joined her at the window.

Kana stared up at his face and tried to speak, the words in her throat but not coming through her lips. She was slipping into someplace dark, deep within.

Stefan put his hands on her shoulders, his face distorted in a glossy haze. "Kana? Are you okay?"

His touch was like lightning surging down her back and arms. He was being protective while she couldn't help but indulge in more carnal thoughts. They were welcome. It was a pleasant distraction from the growing chill.

Stefan cringed, the touch of his hand softening as he rubbed his shoulder. She didn't ignore him this time, gently placing her hand over his, and in turn, he drew her closer. The touch stole her breath, his lips just inches away from hers. She hummed playfully and turned to face the window. Stefan slid both hands over her shoulders and pressed himself against her back. She could feel him through the cotton robe, this thin layer between his body and hers. It could fall so easily to the floor, and then he'd be able to touch her, to kiss her, to see her.

She whispered to him over her shoulder. "No, I can't."

His lips found her neck and she buckled. Where her professionalism ended and her desires began were lost in the contrasting sensations of cold and warmth, fear and lust, each from different sources and neither under her control. Stefan placed hands on her waist, and she reached down to meet them, tilting her neck so he could explore more of her with his lips. His kisses were so sweet on her skin, her body tingling every time they met her flesh. She knew his reputation, and there was a possibility that he was using her, yet she was also using him. The dark thoughts that were filling her head led to only one place and Stefan was effectively driving them out. They needed to stay out. It was a fair trade. If there were consequences, she'd deal with them tomorrow. Right now, he was just what she needed.

***

An hour later Kana sat in bed awake, staring at the ceiling, with her lover in bed beside her. Stefan had succumbed to his exhaustion and was fast asleep, his body hot beside her, his chiseled chest heaving while he slept. Making love to him was a pleasurable, if not temporary, distraction from the dark thoughts that were creeping into her mind. They returned with a vengeance. She sat up and pushed her upper body against the headboard, waiting.

A hissing, deep voice echoed from the only corner of the room moonlight couldn't find. *You should know that I will find a way in when I want.*

It was *him* again, the Shinigami, a lingering consequence of her sacrifice for a little girl nearly two years ago. The demon randomly visited her over the years, stalking in the deep shadows, coming out to taunt her at the most inopportune moments. Kana didn't fear the beast, it was an annoyance more than anything else, and persistent. She knew it wouldn't just disappear, she'd have to speak to it if there was any hope for a peaceful night's sleep.

"It figures you'd show up now," Kana said to the darkness. "My thoughts went to crap and crap then appears."

Mind your tongue, girl! the disembodied voice boomed.

The shadow's anger stiffened Kana's spine. She couldn't show fear; this thing had seen enough of it in the past. "What do you want now?"

The disembodied voice hissed over the air. *Oh, you know what I want. You know what I will get. But I've seen where you have been. I know what you are trying to do. Oh, there it is, isn't it?* There was nothing visible in the room, but Kana could feel the presence of this creature stretching itself from the shadows in the corner toward the nightstand. *A Black Grimoire. Those Catholics, always so eager to deal with the other side. Always so crafty in the way they try to control us. It never works. Honorius found that out.*

Kana's forehead wrinkled. "How do you mean?"

They tricked him. Honorius thought these last three grimoires would be a warning to mankind. Little did he know that he was writing his own doom. The brothers who guided his hand were quite clever.

Kana crossed her arms. "It sounds as if you admire it."

Not in the way you think, child. The potential of this is deliciously promising. But I have no desire to snatch it from you. It's valuable to others, but you are what's valuable to me.

"I don't think you can have either."

But I will. Do not try to insult me. Do you not remember what happened the first time?

Kana's mind shot back to the first time the Shinigami haunted her, a full week after she allowed it to attach itself to her. At the time, she thought she could fight back against it, but the beast destroyed her bedroom and choked her a few seconds from death. For months she and AJ tried over two dozen techniques, spells, and rituals to block the Shinigami and all failed except one. She peered at it now, a Japanese script, ancient and potent, tattooed on her wrist to keep the creature from harming her.

"I remember," Kana said. "I hope you remember that you cannot touch me."

Yes, yes, I know the little trap you and your whelp set for me. I cannot touch you, at least not for now. You found a spell that shields you from my touch. A temporary shield, I'll remind you of that too. But your lover here has no such protection. Perhaps I should slit his throat right in front of you.

Kana could feel the energy of the room shift, a great chill flowing over the bed near Stefan. He looked at peace, dreaming a wonderful dream, completely unaware of the terror that hovered over him. Kana clenched her fist around the bedsheets, watching for any sign that the Shinigami was near him.

That wasn't enough. She needed to be more forceful. "Leave."

Oh, but he's so attractive. Much better than the others you've fumbled around with.

"I said leave."

She heard it sniffing. It made her skin crawl. A few strands of Stefan's hair lifted from his head, held in the air by some invisible force. Another few sniffs, then a satisfied exhale, the foul breeze blowing against Kana's face.

Heh, I might be doing you a favor. This one I will leave alone. But I so love to see that look on your face. Trying so hard to be strong, but I know what fears swell in your heart, Kana. Just remember, one day, you will be mine.

"GET THE HELL OUT OF HERE!"

She felt the Shinigami's energy leave the room, its gargled cackle echoing into silence. It was gone. The encounter left her stomach empty, turning and twisting as she rubbed her palms against her cheeks.

Her screaming roused Stefan from his sleep. "Kana? What's going on? If you want me to go you just—"

"No, I wasn't talking to you, Stefan."

He waited for her to continue but she didn't. "A bad dream?"

"Yeah. It was just a bad dream. Sorry if I woke you."

"It's fine." He kissed her cheek and pulled her into his arms.

For a moment, she thought to confess. That moment passed. How would she explain to him that a spirit—a Shinigami, which he likely had never heard of—was about to slit his throat two minutes ago? Sure, Stefan had seen some weird things, but none of it so intimate, which made her night terror so different. It was attached to her and had been for some time. Any sensible man would run from a woman who had a stalker that could appear from the shadows any time it pleased, capable of slitting their throats while they slept as she sat helplessly.

A knock came at the door and Kana recoiled momentarily. The knock continued and Stefan, who himself was still groggy, pulled on his pants and shuffled to the door of the suite. He looked through the peephole and grunted before opening the door revealing AJ on the other side.

"Oh, uh..." is all AJ could muster while Stefan stood in the doorway, shirtless, his board chest and sculpted abs glistening in the moonlight.

"Is something wrong, AJ?" Stefan asked.

"I... I need to speak to Kana."

"I've got it." Kana took Stefan's place in the doorway, covering herself up with a bathrobe. "What is it, AJ?"

AJ couldn't look at her, trying to focus on anything else in the room. "It was... well, the alarm went off. And, well... uh... you now... well, I knew... the Shinigami... That *it* was here..."

"Not now, AJ. Can we talk about this in the morning?"

"Yeah, but it's just that I, uh..." AJ frowned, taking a step into the room. "I mean, this guy? Really Kana? I mean, he's handsome and everything, but really? Him?"

Kana's jaw tightened. She needed to set him straight. "It's really none of your business, now is it?"

"I know, Kana. It's just that... with everything... I'm just..."

"Good night, AJ." She slammed the door in his face, ending the conversation before he could say another word.

AJ finished his sentence of apology to the door, the last few words trailing off as he realized how silly he looked. The thought of Kana and this stranger was one thing, but to see it nearly tore his insides apart. His heart was beating so fast he felt as if he was having a heart attack.

The last thing AJ, or any man for that matter, wanted to witness was someone he loved touched by another man. And for AJ, who was a visual person, it was doubly painful. He walked down the hallway back to the elevator, trying his hardest to get the mental images out of his head, but it was no use. He had already seen it and he'd have to go back to his room tonight, alone, and find a way to flush those thoughts out of his head.

Instead of that, he went downstairs to the hotel bar and broke his sobriety, ordering one drink, then a three more after that. It didn't take much for his virgin system to feel the effects of alcohol. He'd regret it in the morning, he knew that. Even the bartender took pity on him and cut him off after his fourth drink. The alcohol was working its intoxicating magic, numbing the feeling of pain in his chest. It was a feeling he didn't want, didn't know he had, and desperately wanted to be rid of.

THE THULE SOCIETY

S uffering such an embarrassing failure because of two women, a computer hacker, and a pretty boy archeologist made it hard for Dieter to hold his head up high on the trip back to Germany. He'd also been physically bested by a woman—a mongrel in his eyes. It was unacceptable.

Word was already spreading among the troops, which meant the other members of the Society were aware as well. This was confirmed when he received a blunt text message on the way home:

Your presence is demanded at The Hex. Your failure will be dealt with.

The black words on the white screen burned him. Failure! It wasn't a word he was used to. While it was a fact that he did not retrieve the Black Grimoire, the circumstances surrounding the mission certainly hadn't been expressed to the rest of the Thule hierarchy, otherwise, they would not have sent him such a curt message. He'd explain it to them, in detail, and wash away this stain on his character.

As for the woman, that Kana Cold, his revenge would be long and calculated. Death would be too fast. For this embarrassment, he would concoct a very special form of punishment, one that would break her in a most convincing manner and reassert his status in the eyes of his peers. Even more importantly, he'd salvage his ego.

It was a two-hour drive from the airport to the safe house, also known as *The Hex*, nestled in the countryside of Germany. It was an unassuming building that resembled more of a cabin than a control center, but that was the intent. Despite its drab appearance, it was surrounded by high-tech surveillance: hidden guard bunkers, electronic sensors that scanned for biological and mechanical signatures, laser tripwires, and a variety of other defenses designed to keep away unwanted visitors.

Entering the main building required three scans of a person's biological data. Fingerprints were first, followed by a retinal scan, and then finally a voice recognition procedure that required Dieter to repeat the same phrase five times. He wasn't sure why five was the magic number here. He heard speculation that it was the number of times needed to detect whether someone was mimicking a voice. Although he understood why it was necessary the process was tedious to him.

On the other side of cabin's entrance was a large room with two desks on opposite sides of a pathway leading to a steel door that resembled a bank vault. A secretary sat at each desk, but their real function was as security. The Killaugh Sisters they were called, even though they weren't sisters, whose reputation was known in most circles of the underworld—a reputation coated in tales of bloodstained ballroom gowns and severed male body parts.

After the sisters verified his identity, Dieter was allowed through the door and into the hallway beyond. From here he traveled down two sets of stairs connected by a cold, white hallway, and finally into the meeting chamber where other members of the Thule Society were in the middle of a meeting.

He was greeted by the deep voice of one of the senior members, Marcus Godolphin. "Late again? Or should I say, late as always?"

Dieter didn't respond, passing by Godolphin to hang his overcoat on the rack next to the entrance. The guards, who escorted him to this room, left immediately, locking the door behind them.

"Please, have a seat at the table, Dieter. We'll get to your report in a moment," Timothy Luckless said, the oldest of the brotherhood in this meeting, who had the appearance and persona of a car salesman. "There are some other matters we need to finish discussing before we get to what happened in Israel."

Marcus Godolphin extended his hand, palm open, to the far end of the table where there were empty chairs. "On that end of the table if you don't mind."

Godolphin by far was the most intimidating member of the group physically. He was tall, bulky, brutish, and beastly with his thick brown beard and beady black eyes. Dieter referred to him as a "grizzly bear in a suit", a sentiment repeated by many behind Godolphin's back, but never to his face.

Andreas shuffled through a few papers, peering down at them through a pair of thick-rimmed glasses that hung off the end of his nose. "That's quite enough of that. Let's continue our conversation."

Sometimes seen as the leader of the group, although that distinction changed depending on the month, Andreas joined this incarnation of the society eleven years ago claiming that he was a descendant from one of the original members through DNA tests. While many had their doubts to his claims, they all suspected who he was, or at least who he wanted them to think he was. The truth lay somewhere hidden. His parentage was inconsequential when compared to the influence and power he held in China.

"So, what have I missed? I do apologize for being late by the way. But as you know, I've been rather busy," Dieter said.

"We were just going over the financials for this past month," said Luckless. "There is a considerable amount of inventory we are missing from the Eastern markets, Thailand in particular.

But that can be resolved with a little bit of a push. We're not hurting for money in that region, far from it, but there could be more coming in."

"Is that of the utmost importance right now?" Godolphin squeezed his bulk into a chair at the opposite end of the table from Dieter. "There's only so much value to be gained from that region of the world."

"It's worth it, believe me." Luckless flicked away the screen on his tablet, financial figures populating the flat screen monitor behind Dieter's head. "Either they're holding back on us or someone is stealing."

"What do you expect from them?" asked Theodoric Krauss, a young portly man with a pronounced receding hairline. "Thieves the lot of them. And they reproduce like damned rabbits."

Godolphin stroked his thick beard. "But they're good for labor so let's not get too pushy. We'll handle that later. We have elections to worry about next year. Our influence in Britain has decreased after Parliament passed that Inclusion Bill. It would serve us to have a few new sympathetic ears. That will necessitate some skillful work on our part. Andreas can help there."

"My connections in the British political class has never been stronger." Andreas wiggled the knot of his tie back-and-forth around his thin neck. "But these are strange times. Things have not gone quite as we would have liked."

Luckless chewed on his tongue. "Well, we can't do both at the same time. We need to focus on the best approach here."

Krauss pointed his finger at the screen, his lip curled. "There's much more to gain from Great Britain than the rice pickers in the Orient."

The conversation spilled into a chorus of raised voices, arguments, and accusations breaking out among many of the fifteen members. Dieter sat and watched as these men bickered; financial figures and social concerns being hurled back and forth. The spectacle was entertaining and leaned back in his chair to watch the drama unfold, the blue light of the monitor highlighting his face. The other members at the table who weren't contributing to the noise, Hannah Schmidt, the only female of the group, and her rumored lover Christopher Gallows, weren't focused on the arguments, they were focused on Dieter.

Hannah was luxurious in every sense of the word. A tall woman with flowing strawberry-blonde hair, porcelain pale skin, a narrow nose, and emerald eyes. The widow of Eckard Schmidt, who died due to mysterious circumstances some years ago, willed his spot in the Society to her in absence of any children. It was protested by most, but the legalities were concrete. She would be the first—and if the others had their way, last—female member of the Thule Society. Her beau, on the other hand, did not share any lineage, through blood or marriage, with the founders. Christopher Gallows was sponsored by Godolphin five years prior. The two had long since parted ways as Godolphin found Christopher's ambitions exotic and, in some respects, wasteful. His chief ambition was acquiring all three Black Grimoires.

"Enough!" Christopher bellowed as he slammed his fist on the table. "All of this bickering and fighting over money and product and petty claims on useless political figures. Enough! That is low-hanging fruit brothers... low-hanging fruit. This meeting wasn't called to discuss how you can further line your pockets or how to continue to waste the resources and capabilities the Society has afforded us all." He stood from his seat, tapping his fingertips together. "More pressing matters are at hand, right Dieter?"

Gallows didn't possess the great bulk of Godolphin or the authoritarian presence of Andreas. Instead, he exuded a primal, savage nature, encroaching upon Dieter like a panther stalking prey.

"Yes, we do," Dieter answered confidently. He was from a bloodline tied to the founders of The Thule Society whereas Gallows was not much more than Hannah's boy toy. There was nothing to fear from this upstart. And if he ever did get cocky enough to try and big boy Dieter, the rest of the brotherhood would take his side.

"As I come to understand it you were—unsuccessful, shall we say—in retrieving the Black Grimoire or Octavius' brother,

Stefan?" Christopher's words echoed through the darkened chamber, his proper British accent thick and confident.

Dieter sat upright in his chair as Christopher got closer. "A minor setback. I may have underestimated the girl. That will not happen again. I have special plans for her."

"Indeed." Christopher crossed his hands behind his back and walked away from Dieter. "And please tell me, what is this plan of yours?"

"Well, I figured you would have an idea of where they are going." Dieter cupped his chin in his palm. "After all, you are the one who wanted this. You are the one who planned all of this. You are the one who brought in Octavius, trying to get that shamble of a man to focus when it's clear his mind is gone."

"Not gone. Split would be a better word choice."

"Yes, sure. Split. Describe him how you will. The point is I am in the field. You are supposed to come up with the where and how. Don't profess to tell me how to do my job and I won't tell you how to do yours, Herr Gallows."

He expected anger from Gallows who instead answered in a calm, even tone. "No, I'd never imagined such a thing. I agree, you might need a little direction."

Godolphin cleared his throat. "Christopher, your pursuit of these objects has become somewhat obsessive, to be honest. The rest of us think you may have devoted too much time and too many resources to this project. The Black Grimoire was in our possession for generations, and yes, we give you credit for finding someone to unlock its potential. But the expenditures in trying to attain the other two might be more than it's worth."

"I have to agree," Andreas added. "A small fortune was spent between research, weapons, travel, manpower, and we have very little to show for it outside of that gibbering mess of a man, Octavius."

Christopher paced back and forth before the Society, his thumb tapping against his chin. "I wouldn't go that far and say we have nothing to show for it." Gallows paced until he reached the center of the room and lifted his chin from his thumb. "Dieter, you want to have your revenge on this girl, correct?"

Dieter rubbed the cast on his arm. "As I said before, I have special plans for her."

"Well, you won't realize those plans your current condition. Pain is your weakness. It's *our* weakness. And seeing as she is clearly the more skilled fighter between you two—"

"I wouldn't say that."

"—you need an edge when you meet her again. Now, I am no ally of yours nor are you mine. But we share a common goal. These irritants must be removed if we are to achieve our goal." He motioned to Helen who handed him two objects wrapped in a red cloth. "I think it is time to show you all what that gibbering mess of a man has unlocked for us. Your arm, Dieter. The one the girl broke."

Was he insane? Dieter was near the end of his patience with Christopher's theatrics. Was he going to perform some magic trick to try and convince the rest of the Society that the books were worth pursuing? Maybe he'd make his skin change color or manifest a strange tattoo on his arm. Best to get this over with so he could go back out into the field and regain his dignity by tracking down that woman.

Dieter rolled up his sleeve, the cast covering most of his forearm. "I'm always up for a good magic trick."

As a few members chuckled, Christopher placed the two items Hannah gave him on the table next to Dieter's arm. One was a small box that resembled a metal cigarette case while the other remained under the cloth. He gripped the meaty part of Dieter's forearm and flicked the latch on the small box. "I'm afraid this is going to hurt."

Without hesitation, Gallows unveiled a cleaver hidden in the folded cloth. Before Dieter could move the blade sliced through his arm just below the wrist. Half of the Society members gasped, some springing up from their chairs and protesting, but none of them were getting anywhere near Christopher and that cleaver. The blade needed to be worked free, but once it was, it left Dieter's hand severed from his arm. Christopher held the prize above his head before tossing it onto the floor, leaving Dieter to whimper and howl in agonizing pain.

"What in the hell?" Godolphin shouted.

Luckless grit his teeth. "Have you lost your mind?"

Unaffected by the screams and threats, Hannah took the metal box and pranced behind Dieter, who was literally shaking in his chair, and placed her hands at his temples. She whispered in his ear, repeating the word "relax" while Christopher opened the box. Inside were several vials, a combination of fluids, herbs, and some gelatinous material that defied explanation. The smell of this concoction was atrocious, filling the chamber with the stench of sulfur and the perfume of jasmine.

"Relax Dieter. My *magic trick* is almost done." Gallows poured the brew on the wound, bubbling the instant it hit the bloody stump. Flesh, bone, and sinew rearranged and reformed, discarding unneeded chunks of meat during the process. The brotherhood lost their prior fear and gave in to their curiosity, each member crowding near Dieter as the potion did its work. Flesh extended from the wound in stringy clusters, twitched, and then solidified into a new growth. It wasn't a new hand. In fact, it didn't resemble anything human. This was something else, grotesque and ancient. Dieter's eyes widened as his new appendage fully formed, ripping the cracked cast from his arm and tossing it to the floor. A series of tendrils, thick and fleshy, crawled over the edge of the table. He could feel every single one, an entirely different sensation from the fingers and hand he lost seconds ago.

"Such a beautiful thing." Christopher released his hold on Dieter's arm. "Not quite refined, but the ancient text has improved him beyond what any human could have naturally."

"That's insane!" Andreas pushed his way to the edge of the table, tipping his head forward to get a better look. "You've turned him into a monster. Look at his hand! It's not even a hand anymore, it's a useless string of flesh."

"No." Dieter lifted his tendrils to examine their movement. "This is strength. I feel... powerful."

"Preposterous!" Andreas waved off Dieter's claim. "Call the doctor. It is not natural. We'll have this abomination amputated—"

His instructions were cut short as three of Dieter's tendrils latched onto Andreas's throat, one of which morphed into a sharpened point, aimed at his windpipe.

"You'll do no such thing," Dieter said. "This is not an abomination. It is power, little man. Now take your seat and continue to squabble over Märkers and Manchurian candidates. Leave the real work of our forefathers to the only visionaries left in this Society."

Dieter released his grip on Andreas who fell on his backside with a thud. The strength of his grip was evident in the ring of bruises around Andreas's neck. Even Godolphin, who feared no one in the Society, recoiled from the scene.

Christopher took his place in the center of the room, raising his hands to the brotherhood. "I'm sorry for having to be so dramatic. I knew this was the best way to get your full attention and—if you have any sense—full loyalty. The Thule Society had long sought this kind of power. We were never able to fully tap into all the Black Grimoire contained. Then, we lost its knowledge to the Catholics. Octavius, although mad, retrieved the cipher from the Vatican, allowing us to unlock the grimoire's secrets. We are capable of so much more now, brothers. This is what we were meant for."

Christopher closed his eyes and inhaled deeply. Dieter watched him, his former dismissal of the man turned into awe. Such power had been within their house for decades and they never thought to use it.

"Perhaps..." Andreas swallowed hard, using the large meeting table to pull himself back to his feet. "I think maybe we should consider, for the time being, diverting more attention to your work, Christopher. If this is just an example of what can be done, then surely there is much to gain from having all three."

The other members murmured in secondary discussions, some agreeing to follow Gallows while others feared the unnatural and supernatural entering the brotherhood. It would take time, but Christopher knew he'd win most of them. Those that wouldn't comply would be cast out as The Thule Society had done throughout its history. The pursuits of the brotherhood were not for simple monetary power or the manipulation of the masses. It was in the harnessing of forces the world had long since forgotten or pretended didn't exist, and thus would have no ability to disobey. All three Black Grimoires would give them influence both in the physical world and dimensions unknown, a knowledge not meant for common man. It was only for the elite.

Only for The Thule Society.

Christopher took his seat beside Hannah, her arm snaking around his. "If there are no more objections we can proceed. There are preparations to be made and further research to be completed. While we take care of that here, Dieter, my new friend, you must find the other two grimoires. Put an end to this mission and put an end to the ones who are in the way. Granger's student, this woman—this Kana Cold—and her partner know too much. They tread on very thin ice. Make sure they fall through it."

SHINJUKU

AJ and Kana didn't speak to one another from the time they left the hotel in Israel through the plane ride to Japan. Ten hours of awkward silence and separation. AJ busied himself on his laptop with research while Kana spent most of her time with Stefan, who themselves were trying to find their own comfort zone.

Unspoken was the preferred course of action for AJ. He changed his seat to one in the back of the plane, far away from the couple. Anything was better than watching Stefan and Kana make lovey eyes to each other. AJ knew there was nothing he could say that would make it better. He'd be the third wheel in this triangle. Instead, he buried himself in work.

Whether he forced himself to swallow his jealousy or not, he couldn't see himself warming to Stefan. Yes, he saved his life in Israel, but there was something in how he looked at Kana that rubbed AJ the wrong way. Stefan's reputation with women wasn't a big secret. Dozens had been heartbroken after being seduced by his tall, dark and handsome features. When Stefan got bored with them, he'd chuck them aside without as much as a phone call or a goodbye. AJ knew Kana and her history with men, especially in relationships, that left a mark on her. Was this protectiveness he had for her morphing into this mis-aligned sense of attraction? It was a moot point. It wasn't his business. At least that's what his head told him. After a few more hours of travel, he'd convince his heart of the same.

***

Stefan used his connections in Japan, much as he did in Israel, to secure a place to stay. Hotels had become risky with The Thule Society and Anastasia tracking them. Instead, a private condo was the choice for lodging. With nearly 2 million residents, Shinjuku was an easy city to get lost in.

The trio entered the condo, Stefan taking the lead as Kana stood in the doorway waiting for AJ to bring up the rear. "This place belongs to an acquaintance of mine, Yujiro. He's away on business for the next few days so this is perfect for us."

There were four bedrooms in total, a massive kitchen, and an open-air living room with a loft above. Decorated by a bachelor with an eye for the modern, the apartment could have been featured in a magazine.

"Yujiro trades in commodities on the black market and in the public space, which not only made him a small fortune, but also required a level of anonymity." Stefan carried Kana's bags to the center of the room, a sunken square space that was the focal point of the room, two white leather sofas and a loveseat nestled next to one another. "He does have quite the eye for the finer things in life." Stefan set her bag down and ran his hand over a silver sphere sculpture placed in the center of the glass coffee table.

"Where will you be sleeping?" AJ asked Kana, the first words he had spoken to her since they left Israel.

She blinked twice and pointed at the room to her left. "I think I'll take that one with the big window."

AJ nodded quickly. "Then I'll be in the loft."

"What? Why are you—"

"I'm in the loft!" AJ took a breath. "Up there I can work late at night without hearing any..."

Kana frowned, realizing what he was implying after a few beats. She wanted to call him out on how childish this was being, but before she could even say a word, he was off up the stairs.

An hour later, AJ unpacked while Kana sat in the living room trying as hard as she could to ignore the cold shoulder he was giving her. Part of her wanted to deal with this. The other part understood that silence was the best course of action.

The third party in this conflict found that cooking was a better use of his time. Kana closed her laptop and walked to the kitchen to see what Stefan was conjuring up for lunch. "Tell me that's something good."

He stopped stirring the pot for a second to wink at her before lifting a steaming spoon of rice for her to sample. "Here. Come taste this. Be careful though. It's a little hot."

Kana wrapped her lips around the end of the spoon. "Risotto. It's good." She wiped her lower lip with her finger. "Leave it to you to make something Italian in the middle of Japan."

He sampled the rice himself before wiping off the spoon. "We can order takeout if you'd like. An American cheeseburger from that disgusting McDonald's down the street, maybe?"

"Um, no. I don't even eat McDonald's when I'm home. I'm certainly not going to do it here." She licked her fingers, smiling at him. "You're a pretty good cook."

"Eh, I dabble. I've been making risotto since I was a child. My mother taught us. Every Sunday she would cook over a steaming pot, pouring in the chicken stock, stirring and pouring, stirring and pouring. And when she finished, Octavius and I would sit at the kitchen table and eat as much as we could stuff in our faces."

"When was the last time you talked to Octavius?"

Stefan looked up at the ceiling for a few beats before answering. "Probably two years," he said, now stirring in a handful of parmesan cheese. "He and I had a conversation on the phone. It was brief. I had retired from the work we were doing, and he told me he was going to continue with his research on the Black Grimoires. He said he had a new partner. I always assumed it was Professor Granger."

"Turns out that was partially true." Kana folded the napkin on the kitchen countertop. "I've researched some of what you two were doing in the last twenty-four hours."

Stefan continued stirring. "Did you?"

"Yeah, well a girl's gotta know what she's getting herself into." She waited for him to say something and got nothing in return. "Well, let's just say I know you and Octavius weren't saints. You guys were trading illegal goods, allegedly, and made a small fortune. Did you have a crisis of conscience?"

"You mean, why did I quit? It wasn't anything like that. There was a better way to live without being in the field. This work, as you have seen, is dangerous. Laws don't apply in what we were doing. There would be no rescue if we were captured by criminals and no lawyers to get us out of trouble if we were caught by the government. There are other ways to live."

Stefan stirred the pot one final time before he scooped a heaping pile of risotto onto a plate for Kana. He handed it to her, added another spoonful to his own plate, and poured two glasses of wine. Kana waited for him to raise his glass, they toasted, and she dove her fork into the plate of rice.

Stefan beamed as he watched her eat. "It's good to see you like this. When we first met you were so serious and tough." He mocked her angry face, pushing his shoulders out and curling his arms beneath them.

"Keep cooking like this and I'll be smiling a lot more," she said.

A loud crash from the loft drew their attention. AJ had dropped his suitcase, cursing as he tried to pick it back up.

"Should we worry about that?" Stefan asked Kana. "Do you think he's going to be able to get over this or..."

"Give him time." Kana turned back to her plate and poked at the rice with her fork. "AJ's a good friend. He'll come around."

"And if he doesn't?"

Kana shot him a cold stare. Stefan was bordering on none-of-your-business territory, but she knew why it was an issue for him. If AJ's emotions blinded him, and he was as sloppy with work as he was with that suitcase, it could cost them their lives.

"I'll handle it. What's the plan for this party we're going to?"

Stefan flipped a towel over his shoulder. "It's a ball. The Black Lotus Ball to be exact. Tomorrow night we'll go mingle and try to get information."

"Information about this *yokai* called Kuroi Majo: The Black Witch."

Stefan pushed his lips together. "Yokai! You have been doing research. If the rumors are true, and she's the real thing, that's going to be the easy part. No one has ever seen her outside her inner circle and lived to tell about it."

"It would make sense for her to hide. If she's got a Black Grimoire, and the underworld knows about it, that makes her a target."

Stefan swallowed a mouthful of wine and cleared his throat. "Yes, but you see the problem with many of the Eastern legends is that they tend not to be all they're cracked up to be. Chances are this could just be some old woman who is putting out a false image to keep people away."

"From what you tell me it's working." Kana shrunk in her seat. "That's not what I'm worried about the most."

Stefan cocked his head and then smiled with realization. "You have to wear a dress."

"Don't remind me."

"I think you would look ravishing in a formal evening gown."

Kana fidgeted, pulled her arms in tight, and knocked her fists together. "I don't wear high heels. I don't like high heels. Now, not only do I have to put them on, but I have to pretend I'm used to wearing them."

"You'll do fine. We need to mingle at this event and talk to the right people. Nobody there is going to know who you are."

"I'm still not entirely sure how this works but if you say that's the plan then we'll go with it." Kana ate the last bit of risotto and dropped the fork on her plate, satisfied. "This was really good. Thanks for lunch."

"It was my pleasure." He pulled the towel from his shoulder and wiped his hands. "Now, seeing as we have some time to get things in order, I have some errands to run."

"Where are you going?"

"Preparations for tomorrow. I want to get it done well ahead of time."

She pouted at the thought of him leaving. "Do you always prepare for things ahead of time? That's not me at all. I'm more of a seat-of-the-pants type."

Stefan brushed a loose strand of hair from Kana's face. "Yes, I can tell. It's part of your charm."

"You're the one with all the charm, Stefan." His touch melted her pouting away. "Okay, don't let me keep you. Just keep your phone on in case something comes up."

"Of course. I won't be long," Stefan gently kissed her forehead.

Kana understood what this meant. *I'll have to spend the rest of the day with AJ in uncomfortable silence.* They'd have to hash out this issue between them. She needed him to be on top of his game since he'd be monitoring them from the apartment, using his tech skills to hack into a satellite feed of the building. The ball was in her court to find a solution to this, whether she liked it or not.

"Okay, I will see you later tonight." Stefan slipped on a hoodie and left to tend to his preparations.

With Stefan gone, the condo fell silent. Kana looked over at AJ, opened her mouth to speak, then just as quickly closed it. No, he still needed time, and she wanted to rest. Taking the second option, she pulled the risotto from the refrigerator and made herself another plate. With that and another glass of wine, she walked to the bedroom and shut the door behind her.

"He still needs time," she said to herself.

***

Kana took a long nap during the afternoon. By the time she woke, night had fallen over the city. The bed was so comfortable she didn't want to get out of it. With a stretch and a yawn, she glanced over at the alarm clock on the nightstand to see what time it was.

"It's 8:30 already?" She left the bedroom and entered the kitchen to find AJ fiddling with the coffee machine. He stopped when he caught sight of her, turned to her for a moment, and then moved back to the disagreeable kitchen appliance.

Kana took over for AJ, grabbing the machine. "Here, let me do it."

AJ backed away a few steps and let Kana have her way. She removed the dirty filter, replaced it with a new one, and then turned the machine on again.

"I thought I changed the filter already." AJ ran his fingers through his hair. "I've been working too hard."

"You should get some rest."

He shrugged. "I can't. These translators need to be up and running before you and Stefan go to that party tomorrow or you won't understand anything anyone is saying. That is unless your Mandarin, Russian, and Portuguese is any better."

Kana grabbed a coffee mug from the cupboard to pour herself a cup. How to start such an awkward conversation? "So, are we going to do this?"

AJ nodded. "Yes, we need to talk. I'm not as irritated now as I was earlier."

"That was irritated?"

"What would you call it?"

Kana spun the cup around on the countertop with her fingers. "I don't know, AJ. The way you've been acting for the last day or so is weird to me. You don't like Stefan but he's not that bad a guy."

AJ rubbed his hands across the countertop as the coffee machine dribbled a stream of its dark brew into the pot. "It's not necessarily about him. But you... you have this tendency to get involved with the absolute worst guy you can find."

"Is that so?"

"Come on, Kana. I've been there. This is me you're talking to. You may be smart, but I have the higher IQ."

She threw her hands up in the air. "Here we go with that again."

"You wanted someone there because of the Shinigami."

She hated that word. It made that dark spirit that visited her randomly at night sound too official, too real. "I'm not going to let it control me. I've been dealing with it for a long time now and I don't need a body in my bed to protect me if that's what you're thinking."

"Not at all. I think you wanted Stefan there because it drove the thoughts you get—those evil thoughts—out of your head. Am I right or wrong?"

She turned away from him, swirling the rim of the coffee cup with her finger.

AJ continued. "I get it. Alright. I know having that thing following you around anywhere you go has got to be a terrible burden. If I could find a way to get rid of it, I would. I still don't know what in the world possessed you to invite that thing to latch itself onto you."

She pounded her fist on the countertop. "You know damn well why, AJ. It was all we could do to save that girl. We didn't know what we were doing with an actual Keter. She needed our help, and it worked."

He peered down into his coffee mug. "But at what cost?"

Kana remembered that night nearly two years ago. It was one of their earlier cases. Up until that point they had mostly encountered people either faking a paranormal experience or pranksters who wanted to make fun of them. The McNeil's Shinigami case proved to be entirely different. Due to neither of them being familiar with how to deal with an actual Keter spirit, they were at a loss. All of AJ's technical knowledge proved useless and Kana didn't see any other way around it.

After several nights of trying everything they could come up with, while at the same time trying to convince the parents of the little girl who was being terrorized that they knew what they were doing, Kana grew desperate. She invited the Shinigami to take her instead and the monster didn't hesitate to take her up on the offer. Ever since that evening, Kana was condemned, but she learned how to deal with it. Eventually, it would claim her soul for eternity, according to what little material they could find on the subject. At this point, Kana could sense when the Shinigami was about to visit; her thoughts would turn dark and her mood would shift.

"There may be some truth to that," Kana confessed. "But that's not why you're mad. Let's not pussyfoot around it though. Do you have feelings for me?"

AJ didn't hesitate to answer. "No."

Kana arched an eyebrow. "AJ, if you do—"

"Kana, I'm not an idiot. Our relationship is purely professional. Well, I also consider you a friend, but romantically, no. Don't worry about that."

The machine chimed twice notifying them that their coffee was ready. AJ poured himself a cup and then filled Kana's. He motioned toward the balcony and she followed him.

She placed her mug on the railing and took in the sight of the sprawling city. "He isn't that bad, you know. Stefan is smart, he's strong, he's great at—"

AJ raised his palm. "Okay, I don't need to hear anymore. Just because I accept that you're screwing doesn't mean that I want to hear details."

"Understood." She let the moment linger, taking a sip of her coffee. "Besides, he lives in a cabin in Bucharest. I live in Massachusetts. This likely won't go anywhere beyond this job."

"How does that make you feel?"

Kana shrugged. She hadn't thought that far ahead. Now it was her who lied. She wanted to be casual about her romance with Stefan, but deep inside she was already growing attached. It wasn't overwhelming. She rationalized the entire affair as nothing more than a fling. Still, her heart wanted more. Her body wanted more. "I do appreciate you looking out for me, AJ. Don't think that I don't."

"I know you do, in your own way."

"So, we can get back to normal now? Well, normal for us."

AJ took another sip of his coffee. "I still don't entirely trust him. For now, I can deal with it."

That was good enough for Kana. She gave AJ a light jab to the shoulder to seal the deal. The pair spent the next few minutes drinking their coffee and watching the traffic go by beneath them.

Shinjuku was busy tonight. A stream of bodies and vehicles passed by beneath them, heading toward their own destinations, desires, and disagreements that weren't that much different from the ones AJ and Kana were experiencing now. As far removed as they felt at times from society at large this sight reminded them how they were, at the end of it all, just like everyone else.

"He probably would like that obnoxious car of yours," AJ said. "It's about as subtle as he is."

"With my luck, he'll like your water vapor toy car being he's European."

AJ scratched at his ear, grinning. "Well then, if he does, he might not be all that bad. I'm getting a Tesla with the money from this when we get back home."

"He knows Elon Musk."

"Really? Maybe he can teach you a thing or two after all."

Kana playfully jabbed him in the shoulder as she finished her cup of coffee. "Shut up, AJ."

THE RED DRESS

I t was nearly midnight before Stefan returned to the apartment. He found Kana and AJ working together on the earpieces they would be wearing at the Black Lotus Ball. The devices were so small that no one would notice them unless they looked directly into their ear. Having real-time language translation would be of great help with the variety of languages that would be spoken at the gala. Stefan was well versed in European languages, but his Japanese was rusty at best, let alone his familiarity with other Eastern languages.

AJ worked out the signal strength, crammed as much data as he could for different variations of dialect, and synced the earpieces with a hub he had built earlier in the day, allowing him to monitor everything from the condo. Kana tested the earpieces to make sure there weren't any hiccups with slang or different variations in the way someone spoke. She used the television in the spare bedroom and flipped through the different channels as a test.

"It's pretty much done then, yes?" Stefan asked AJ.

AJ looked up at Stefan, sans his earlier grimacing. "Yes. It's a two-way signal too. You can hear me, and I can hear you. If there's anything that's tough to translate I'll be able to adjust on the fly."

"Well it looks like you two have everything sorted out." He locked eyes with Kana. "I'm heading to bed then. It's been a long day."

Kana sprung from her seat. "How did it go?"

"Precisely how I planned."

"Are you gonna clue us in on what it is you were doing, or do we have to guess?"

Stefan walked over to Kana and placed his hands on her shoulders, staring at her with those eyes, melting away any concerns she had about him. "It's nothing, Kana. I just needed to make sure we had some backup if needed. It took a bit of time, but we have a few friends now who will be there."

Kana nodded and went back to work on the earpieces. His posture was out of sorts, his shoulders slumped as he dragged himself to one of the bedrooms.

"Poor guy looks exhausted," AJ said.

His words took a second to register with Kana. "Yes, I guess. It's been a long day for all of us."

"Well, at least I don't have to hear you two going at it tonight."

"AJ!"

He tapped a few keys on his laptop, his hand covering his mouth to hide his grin. "I'm just saying… not hearing grunts and groans will help me focus."

As much as Kana tried to fight against it she couldn't help but share in AJ's amusement. "I'm so glad you decided to stay in the loft."

***

Around six in the evening the next day the trio prepared for their clandestine operation at the Black Lotus Ball. Stefan was ready far ahead of schedule, as seemed to be a trait with him, while Kana was taking a lot longer to prepare herself. The main issue: fitting herself into a dress.

Two hours passed with no word from Kana on when she'd be ready. She tried to put it off most of the day, but there was no avoiding it.

A leather jacket, a white t-shirt, and a pair of good jeans worked for her since she was fifteen. This dress was something that Anastasia would be accustomed to. The woman walked around in high heels like they were sneakers. Kana wondered how in the world any woman felt comfortable in them or dresses that hugged her body so much that she felt like she was suffocating. And an off-the-shoulder dress at that. She felt exposed and uncomfortable wearing this getup. AJ offered to help her but was met with a flying shoe for his trouble.

That didn't stop him from trying again.

"Are you sure you couldn't use some help? I'm not trying to creep on you or anything but it's getting a bit late." He yelled into the room from a safe distance away, keeping himself outside of shoe throwing range.

"I've got it, AJ!" Kana yelled back, followed by an "ouch".

AJ gave up. This was not his area of expertise. Throwing his hands up, he retreated to the living room where Stefan was sitting on the couch, an amused grin on his face.

"You try to do something with her," AJ said. "I have a feeling she'll let you in there."

"You give me too much credit. But I will do my best." He turned over his wrist to glance at his watch. "It is getting late and we have a lot to do tonight."

AJ flopped down on the couch and exhaled. He motioned to Kana's room with both hands as if to say "have at it". Stefan cleared his throat, adjusted the tie on his tuxedo, and made his way to the bedroom. He stopped in the doorway, watching Kana spin around in a circle trying desperately to zip up the back of her dress. On the third spin he approached and zipped up the dress for her.

"Thank you." She plopped down on the bed with her head in her hands. "This is not a good idea."

"You look fine. You're just not used to wearing these kinds of clothes."

"I wish I didn't have to. Trust me! This isn't me. I don't look right."

Stefan took her hand gently and coaxed her up to her feet. He led her to the standing mirror on the other side of the room and made her face it. It wasn't working, she still frowned as she saw her reflection. In her mind, she wasn't the kind of *pretty* that could pull off such an ensemble. Her hair wasn't quite right even though she had spent hours on it. Her makeup didn't quite look like that of the models in the dozens of magazines that were scattered all over the bed. This wasn't working the way she thought it would.

Stefan braced her, putting his hands on both of her arms. "You are exquisite, Kana. Truly. What you have isn't found on the cover of a magazine with airbrushing, it's not even in this dress. You radiate something else entirely, something mysterious and powerful."

Mysterious and powerful, she liked the sound of that.

"If I hadn't just zipped this dress up, I'd be compelled to take it off of you right now," he whispered in her ear.

"Okay, you've convinced me." She fought her body against blushing and lost. "And thank you for that. I needed it."

She grabbed his hand and placed it against the middle of her chest. The two lingered there for a minute, admiring their reflection. This was exactly what she was afraid of though; growing attached to Stefan after one night. But that wasn't out of the question, was it? Love affairs were built from much less. At least tonight she could pretend that this was a life she could have with him, a man of the world who took her to exotic places.

It was the princess wish that she had as a small girl. A wish she discarded for the grit of reality, revisited now in this near-perfect image of the ideal relationship reflected in the mirror.

"It's time to go. Are you almost ready?" he asked.

"I am now. Just..." She glanced over at the crimson pair of high heel shoes in the corner, her frown returning. "...I have to put those things on. It might be a minute."

THE BLACK LOTUS BALL

S hinjuku breathed like a city with a pronounced underworld beneath its rather ordinary exterior. Its skin of concrete extended in all direction, traced with lanes of traffic bordered by cramped buildings, all adorned with bright neon images for the pedestrians who passed under the lights of blue, red, and orange. The air was thick between the buildings, the summer heat passing over the open streets and through the congested alleys filled with signs and sellers. Shinjuku's fame was not on the main roads but in the deeper parts, side streets where shop owners watched and waited for the unsuspecting foreigner, or *gaijin*, to stumble toward them like a fly into a spider web, suckering them into their shops to relieve them of as much money as they could. Bizarre advertising was everywhere from a King Kong replica wearing American flag boxers climbing on a wall to robotic geisha girls on a carousel in a window display, all designed to draw attention amongst a thousand other such decorations in the crowded cityscape. Only a few blocks would separate the more pedestrian areas from some of the unsavory side streets. Shinjuku was Tokyo's bad girl that didn't shy away from showing her legs to anyone willing to pay.

Even in a city like this, Kana found no comfort in her tight dress and high heel shoes. After Stefan parked in the garage across the street from the gala, she began shaking uncontrollably, her knees knocking against each other the moment he stopped out of the car. Stefan allayed her fears once again by opening the door for her, taking hold of her arm, and wrapping it around his. *Those damn dimples*. With a nod, he escorted her to the tallest building on the street.

Stefan drew Kana's attention to the spotters in the windows across the street. "Yakuza," he whispered to her.

The infamous mafia of Japan. It shouldn't have surprised Kana that they would be involved in this. Growing up, her parents told her stories of the Yakuza and how they were to be respected. Here in Shinjuku, not only did they hold the territory and conduct business here, but the police worked with them to maintain the way the city functioned, often overlooking their more criminal enterprises in return.

She was getting an earful from Stefan as they approached the building. "Don't look but there two above us, in the windows. Another two are probably stationed in the garage as well."

She kept her head straight, using her peripheral vision to spot the Yakuza. "That's a lot of underworld security for a party. What have you gotten me into here, Stefan?"

"Nothing you can't handle. After what I saw you do in Israel, they should be worried about you."

He was exaggerating but she took his point. She shouldn't be afraid but remain aware that they were not attending some high school prom. If the Yakuza had this much of a presence outside, and likely more inside, this Kuroi Majo had to be legitimate.

AJ's voice crackled over the earpieces. "They're everywhere. There's lots of chatter over their network. It's been that way for the last hour or so."

"You can hear their communications?" Stefan asked.

"Yes. I'm hacked into their network."

"Anything we should be concerned about?" Kana asked.

"As long as you're not armed it shouldn't be a problem. From what I can translate they've been having issues with people trying to smuggle guns into the Ball. Something about "dirty westerners" so I guess you won't be the only American there, Kana."

"How comforting."

Stefan rubbed the back of her hand. "Okay, we're getting close to the door. Time to put on our best faces. If we need help or you see anything on your side just alert us like we talked about, AJ."

"Will do. Or, roger that. Is that what we're supposed to say? Right... roger that!"

Stefan cocked an eyebrow, but Kana tightened her grip on his forearm to let him know that it was okay. Stefan would have to suck it up and trust them as much as they were trusting him.

Two plump men stood at the door dressed in tuxedos holding electronic tablets. Stefan presented their invitation to one of them who scanned it, confirmed its validity, and then took a photo of Kana and Stefan. After all of this, he opened the door and let the couple inside.

"Nice to see AJ's ID hack worked," Kana said as they passed into a dark corridor.

"And I'm swapping those images right now with some other faces so there's no record," AJ said.

The dark corridor led them to the back of a long line. From what they could tell there was a bottleneck up ahead of people trying to enter the main room. All Kana could see were the backs of people's heads. Up ahead the line turned toward the right, the muffled sound of acid jazz—an electronic variation of light jazz music—seeped through the black walls.

Kana felt an itch developing at her waist. The dress felt like it was tightening around her, and as much as she wanted to scratch, she knew there were eyes everywhere. Must keep up appearances. She squirmed just a bit to move the fabric around. Fortunately, that was enough to get a bit of relief. When this was all over the damn thing was coming off and would never be seen again if Kana had her way.

The line was starting to move now. As Stefan and Kana rounded the corner ahead the scope of the Black Lotus Ball became clear.

The ballroom was massive; a ceiling one hundred feet high with over a dozen hanging glass chandeliers. The walls were decorated with video screens the height of most buildings, each one running a video loop of demented images, straight from Japanese folklore, realized in graphic detail. A fanged dragon devouring a basketful of babies flashed on the screens and then dissolved into a new image of a blob-like creature with stringy long hair hovering over a graveyard. Dotted throughout the room were glass cases containing all manner of artifact from around the world, each one suspended by an unseen force. Kana recognized a few of the items, extending her hand to the glass enclosures but not touching them. The other cases held items she didn't recognize.

The couples were ushered to their assigned seats in the ballroom. It was split into four seating areas with guests tagged to a specific table, each one set with the finest dinnerware, candles set in holders molded to look like gargoyles, and custom place cards. Kana noticed a logo marking different objects in the room, some of the display cases, on the lapels of the security guards, and even on the napkins at each place setting. The design was simple and cryptic: a series of blood red lines that formed triangles, looped together to create the shape of a star on a black background. The top tip of the star was split, a gap running between the two joining sides.

AJ's voice crackled over the earpieces. "Never seen that symbol before. I'm searching for it now."

Stefan and Kana couldn't respond to him. They were surrounded by other guests. It was a valuable image, worth chronicling, so they made sure to keep the logo in view of their hidden cameras.

"These are nice." Stefan picked up a napkin with his left hand and turned his right wrist, the hidden camera embedded in his cufflink giving AJ a clear view of the logo.

"Scanned. Searching," AJ said.

Kana took this time to observe the other guests at this ball. She counted perhaps 250 people of various nationalities and ethnicities gathered here, but the majority were Asian. It was the most formal gathering she had attended since her first—and only—wedding at age twelve. This was far more sophisticated. No one had a hair out of place or a stitch of clothing that wasn't custom made. Every so often there'd be a burst of laughter coming from one of the tables over the tinkling of martini glasses. These were the elite of the East's underworld, and this was their night of celebration. They could revel in their excess and talk openly about their enterprises without the scrutiny of law enforcement or public perception.

One of the other guests at the table, a tall man with a narrow face and rotten teeth, inched closer to Kana. He was alone, content to sit at the dinner table and watch others. He spoke Mandarin, which neither Kana or Stefan understood.

"Hold." AJ could be heard typing on the other end of the earpieces. "And... it should be translating now."

The translator worked, Rotten Teeth's words coming through in English. "... yesterday was her birthday. She had five wild boars brought in from China and conducted the rite for everyone to see. It was a good day. Is this your first time?"

Kana responded in Mandarin, one of few phrases she knew. "Yes. We are from the West."

Rotten Teeth's eyes widened, looking them both over with greater interest. He spoke in English for the rest of the conversation. "So many Westerners here tonight. I am Jiang. I speak some English, not much. But you can understand me?"

"Enough," Stefan said. "I am Shane, and this is Eliza."

"Ah, Eliza," Jiang repeated, lingering on the syllables of her name with a creepy delight. "I hope you would do me the honor of a dance later?"

He took Kana's hand and lifted it gently to his lips. The last thing Kana wanted was for this man to touch her, let alone put his lips on her skin. She had to play the part though. Straining not to lose her composure, Kana nodded in agreement, bringing a wide smile from Jiang, his hideous teeth exposed. She gripped Stefan's arm, trying her best not to squeal as he pressed his lips on the back of her hand.

"I look forward to it, Eliza." Rotten Teeth stood and straightened his jacket. "I'll get us drinks. Something special."

Kana let out a heavy breath once he was gone. Stefan rubbed her shoulders and told her how well she was doing.

AJ had his own take on their new acquaintance. "You've got another boyfriend? Better watch out, Stefan. Jiang is worth two billion allegedly. He might sweep her off her feet with those chicklets of his."

Kana clenched her teeth. "Shut up, AJ."

The lighting in the ballroom started to dim and the other guests were taking their seats as the night's entertainment began. The host descended a spiral staircase in the middle of the hall, dressed in a pure white suit with a black tie. He carried a small box in his hands as if it was some sacred prize. It shimmered in the darkness, its lacquer sides bouncing reflections of light around the ballroom. His hair was a mess of curls, streaked with dyed blonde strands throughout.

Once he reached the bottom of the steps, he paused for a moment to look out at the room. "I welcome you all, my brothers and sisters, to the Black Lotus Ball!"

Raucous applause followed from the guests. Kana and Stefan joined the adulation late, remembering their role here. Jiang returned with their drinks. Kana smiled politely and grabbed the glass by the stem with her fingers, raising it to her lips.

Stefan grabbed her hand to kiss it before she could. "Don't drink it."

She set the glass back down on the table. Stefan had a point. She had no idea where this drink came from, and given Jiang's unsettling disposition, it wasn't the wisest thing to blindly put something he brought them into her body.

Meanwhile, the host continued his presentation. "We gather here every year to celebrate our achievements, make new connections, and enjoy the fruits of our labor. We know how the world sees us. We also know the world *needs* us. Without our efforts, there would be no avenues for them to release their stress or indulge in their deepest desires."

A line of figures gathered behind the host as he continued. Covered from head to toe in black outfits, they reminded Kana of a clan of ninjas. Their movements were stiff, not like a normal person's or a trained fighter, closer to that of a marionette. Their joints didn't bend properly, their heads wobbled as they formed a line behind the speaker.

"Now my friends, let us have tonight's offering!" the speaker shouted.

Powerful spotlights flooded the ballroom. Six female dancers sprung from seemingly out of nowhere to dazzle the crowd in vibrantly colored geisha robes, their arms swinging about as they moved with perfect synchronicity. Another row of performers, each carrying a flaming torch, leaped into a circle between the female dancers. They held the torches above their heads, arched backward, and spit fire to the heavens, the flames white hot and blue. Five more characters made their way into the fray wearing demonic masks of traditional Japanese oni— their costumes a craftwork of scales with tufts of wooly hair. Behind the entire cast was an instrumental ensemble, the Hayashi-Kata, made up of two men banging on hourglass-shaped drums, a flutist, and a solitary singer howling theatrical lyrics, a mix of Buddhist sutras delivered in a haunting voice, providing a rhythmic background to the spectacle.

Kana had never witnessed such a wild menagerie of sounds, colors, and motion. She caught a strange smell floating through the room; the scent of static in the air after a lightning storm mixed with a hint of lotus blossom. A man on stilts wandered into the center of it all, covered in blossoms and wearing a massive headdress in the shape of the same flower, the petals darkened, pulsing with red neon light.

AJ's voice crackled over the earpiece. "They certainly get an A for presentation."

"I've never seen anything like it," Kana added.

The line of black-clad marionettes clapped their hands in unison, abruptly ending the music and the dancing, the performers kneeling and bowing. They waited for the next act, and when it came, Kana squeezed Stefan's wrist. "What's going on?"

A woman's screams echoed from behind the line of performers, her cries bouncing off the walls.

Stefan leaned in to Kana's ear. "I've heard of this. Whatever you do, do not react. Remember, we have to act as if we're part of this society."

The host returned with his right hand clamped around the arm of a young woman who couldn't have been more than eighteen. He pushed her into the bright spotlight, kicking and screaming but unable to break herself free from his grasp. What made this doubly uncomfortable for Kana was the resemblance she had to this woman, from the structure of her face to the understated way in which she dressed.

With a disapproving grunt, the speaker tossed the woman down to the floor. The victim cowered there in the spotlight, searching the room for an escape. "Can you not see?" the woman's trembling voice filled the ballroom. "Are you not human? I just want to live. It is all I ask. You have everything. Why do you need me?" She sobbed, her shoulders shaking. "I want to see my mother again."

Under the table, Kana balled her fist.

The girl continued to cry out. "I just want to live. I just want to live!"

"She looks like me," Kana said under her breath.

AJ spoke up. "Hold it together, Kana. There's nothing you can do. You're outnumbered three hundred to two in there."

The black-clad marionettes circled the woman at the host's command. Each grabbed an arm or leg, hoisted her waist high off the ground, and stretched her for the room to see. She screamed again as the host casually approached her, opening the lacquered box and removing a decorative knife from inside. The metal gleamed in the spotlight as he toyed with her, flipping the blade between his hands over her body.

Were they really going to sacrifice this woman here? No one in this room was going to do anything about this? What kind of sick society was this where something this disgusting, this barbaric, this evil existed? Kana couldn't bear to watch this take place. She felt the Shinigami scratching at the back of her head. Oh, how it would love this torturous exhibition.

She whispered to Stefan. "Come here." She turned his head with her hand, kissing him.

He didn't reciprocate at first but eventually gave in. The two lost themselves in their embrace, their tongues and lips finding in each other a release from the tension in the room. Their ears were not so distracted, and the howls and screams of the heinous act being committed in the ballroom still found their way into Kana's head. *Just keep kissing him*, she told herself, *lose yourself in him*. Someday in the future, she'd make it her life's mission to make these bastards pay for this, but that would not be tonight.

Their kiss ended once the music returned, the ritual completed. Stefan held Kana's head for a moment to keep their foreheads together while she gasped for air. Her panting wasn't from the overwhelming passion of the kiss but relief that the butchering was over. After a few breaths, Kana wiped her lips and turned back to the room. The first thing she saw was Jiang starting at her, grotesquely satisfied. Their eyes locked for a moment. Her first instinct was to punch his rotten teeth down his throat, but she stuffed that down inside and forced a polite smile.

"You two are very good," said Jiang. "But I must go now. I have many people to talk to. We should speak again when dinner is served."

Thank God he was leaving. There was only so much more of this pervert's advances she could take. The rest of the guests at their table also noted the couple's actions during the ceremony. Two of them followed Kana and Stefan's lead, embracing without abandon over their dinnerware.

The smell of spilled body fluids hit Kana suddenly. "I need to go to the bathroom."

She didn't wait for Stefan, storming from the dinner table and down the adjacent hallway. It took him a few seconds to follow her.

The hallway leading to the bathroom was empty, except the wait staff, who used this part of the ballroom as a prep area. Stefan caught up with Kana who was hyperventilating, her hand clutching her stomach.

"Are you going to be okay?" Stefan put his hand to her back, keeping an eye out for anyone who may be watching them.

Taking another couple of breaths, she nodded and then lifted her head. "I think I know a way for us to get on the inside with these... people... and find this Kuroi Majo."

"I was going to suggest we start mingling after you took a few moments." Stefan let go of her and leaned his shoulders back, his arms crossed. "If you have another idea, I'm all ears."

Kana sneered as she stared back at the decadent ballroom. "Yeah, I have an idea. We're going to give these freaks something they value. A sacrifice. We're going to give them me."

INDECENT PROPOSAL

"Have you lost your mind?" AJ repeated three times over the earpieces. "No, seriously, have you completely checked out of reality? You're supposed to be smart, but this is something even a crackhead with brain damage, high on dope after falling on his head from a five-story window would think about and go 'nope'!"

Kana pulled the device out of her ear until AJ's rant was over. "That's the plan, AJ. You just worry about doing your part."

"Doing my part? There is no part to do if you wind up filleted like a fish!"

Kana closed her eyes, waving off AJ. "Calm down."

"Stefan, help me out here."

"I'm going to have to side with AJ on this one." Stefan lifted his arm and dropped hopelessly. "You don't know what these people are capable of. This isn't just something you can fight your way out of."

"I know what I'm doing, Stefan. I just need for the two of you to do your parts. Especially you. Use that silver tongue of yours for some good."

"Kana, I'm telling you that the instant they feel something is off they'll slit your throat. You are offering yourself up as bait... there are a thousand ways in which it can go wrong and only one in which it can go right."

Stefan was making sense. AJ was making sense. But this was something Kana felt she had to do. They didn't know her reasons and there wasn't enough time to explain them. Seeing another woman, let alone one who resembled her so closely, being used for the sick delight of the powerful touched something that neither one of them had the ability to understand. This den of criminally elite bastards needed a kick in the daddy bags in the worst way and she'd be the one to do it.

"Then you better be on your A-game. Let's go." Without waiting for a further debate, Kana walked back to the ballroom.

Stefan stood in place, staring blankly at the spot where Kana had been standing before she bolted off, his mouth stuck open at the beginning of a sentence he never got a chance to start. He closed his mouth, adjusted his tuxedo jacket, and cleared his throat. "Is she always like this?" he asked AJ.

"Disagreeable? Yes. Stubborn? Yes. Suicidal... that's a new one."

"I guess we'd better do our part then to keep her from getting herself killed."

"On this, we agree."

It didn't take long for him to find her among the mass of guests, the blood red dress didn't make it all that difficult. He caught her grabbing a glass of champagne, downing it like a shot, and then marching to the back of the ballroom where the ritual sacrifice had taken place. She made it to the very spot where the young girl had been dissected when Stefan caught up with her, gently taking hold of her arm.

She growled in his ear. "Don't try to stop me."

Stefan relaxed his grip. "If you're going to do this, my dear, then at least go about it smartly. The best way is for me to do the introduction, okay? You're the little piece of pretty flesh I'm offering them for access to the Black Witch. I'll do all the talking, use my *silver tongue*, as you call it."

"Now that sounds like an actual plan."

Together they walked toward the nearest security officer. It was the best way to make initial contact. Approaching anyone else in the room would likely be a waste of time. Along the way, Stefan stroked at his chin as he drew Kana closer to him. "You were just going to walk up to them and say, *here I am*?"

Kana pushed a few of the guests out of her way, politely smiling as she did so before answering him. "No, but I knew if you thought I was, you'd go along with it instead of trying to talk me out of it. You know, save the poor damsel in distress and all that."

Stefan couldn't help but laugh. "You are quite cunning. Cold, but brilliantly cunning."

"It's all in the name."

Jiang broke into the conversation, his face flush with alcohol. "Maybe I can help. You two seem to be lost."

"Not lost. I just have some business I'd like to discuss with Yoshi," said Stefan.

"You know Yoshi, do you?" Jiang cleared his throat. "What is it that you want with him?"

Stefan glanced at Kana and then turned back to Jiang. "I have an offering for him, for his boss."

Jiang put his hand over his mouth to cover his lustful smile. "You do indeed, my friend. A great gift." He wiped the spit from his chin. "Well, this isn't the way. Come. I show you."

Jiang pulled out his phone and made a call. He looked at Stefan and Kana while he spoke to whoever was on the other end of the line. With a thumbs up, he finished his call and then pulled Stefan close so only he could hear what was being said. It was brief, and Kana was left in the dark, still playing the ditsy girlfriend, twirling her finger in her hair. Jiang led them back to the front of the ballroom to the entrance of the building.

"Keep your eyes open. I'm seeing a few vehicles pulling up to the main entrance," AJ warned them.

When they reached the front door, Stefan tugged on Jiang's coat. "I thought we were going to meet Yoshi."

"He left some time ago." Jiang opened the door and led them outside. "We will have to take a car there. He is not one for mingling. But if what you're offering is what I think it is..." he looked Kana up and down with an appetite the made her skin crawl "...I'm sure he'll be interested."

The Yakuza outside had grown in numbers. They surrounded a caravan of Cadillacs and motorcycles, the door of the middle car open. Jiang offered his hand to Kana to help her inside.

Stefan pointed to the adjacent parking garage. "We're parked over there. We can follow if that's alright?"

"I must insist we provide transportation," Jiang countered. "It's for security reasons."

"Yes, but an additional part of what I'm offering is in the car. It's not something that I wish to have out in the open if you get what I mean."

Clever, Kana thought. Jiang clearly wanted Kana in the car with him—for whatever reason she didn't want to suspect—but the addition of another offering was likely something Jiang would bend the rules for.

Their greasy contact mulled over the idea for a moment before agreeing, flashing his yellow teeth in a demented smile. "Okay. Bring your car around and stay with the group. If what you have is that good, then I wish to see for myself."

Stefan and Kana brought their car around to join the caravan. The bikers formed a perimeter around them, revving their engines as a playful warning. None of these men were too shy about the firearms they carried under their leather jackets, making sure they were visible to Kana and Stefan.

Kana couldn't help but stare at them. "I thought guns were illegal in Japan."

"They're the Yakuza, they do what they want." Stefan glanced around at their escorts, putting the car into drive. "Well, we got this far. Are you sure you're ready for this?"

"Absolutely." There was no wavering in her position. "Sorry for messing up whatever plan you had though."

"Don't worry about that. I always think six steps ahead."

The way he said it made Kana believe him, but she could tell that he was out of his comfort zone, perhaps for the first time since she had met him. Good, she thought. He had been so confident for so long it was nice for her to be calling the shots for a change.

As the line of vehicles traveled through the bright streets of Shinjuku, it gave Kana time to think. Offering herself up as a doe-eyed sacrifice was one thing, and it had afforded them access deeper into the underworld than they likely would have just asking random people at the Black Lotus Ball, but now she had to go through with this and not wind up—as AJ so delicately put it—filleted like a fish. Much of this would depend on where they were going, if this Black Witch was as powerful as rumored, and most importantly, how they'd get their hands on the grimoire.

"They're messing with the GPS," AJ said over the earpieces. "I'm having lots of trouble keeping track of you two. They've got some sophisticated software. It's probably coming from a few of the vehicles in the caravan."

Stefan navigated the car down the next road, keeping pace with the rest of the caravan. "It's not surprising. The Kuroi Majo hasn't remained hidden by being sloppy."

"Well, don't worry about it too much. I'm able to keep up. We might just lose each other from time to time. I'm working on getting around whatever they've got that's jamming me. Once you get to where they're taking you it'll be easier."

"It feels like they're driving us in circles too," Kana added. "Getting out of here could be a problem without GPS. Neither of us know the city. We'll probably need you to figure that out before this is all over with."

"I'm on it, Kana. Don't worry. You just stay alive."

Stefan kept one eye on the car ahead of him and another on the motorcycles in tight formation around their car. It would be near impossible at this point know the route they were on. All the streets looked the same at the speed they were traveling. Without some sort of map or guidance, they'd be lost.

Kana noted as the brake lights of the vehicles ahead flashed bright red. "We're slowing down. It must be close."

The caravan turned down one of the side streets and stopped in a narrow alley between two buildings. This wasn't an abandoned area, a few pedestrians still wandered the streets, but the dimly lit alley didn't feel like the safest place to be. The shady atmosphere was offset by the brightly colored juice dispenser to the right of where they parked.

"We're here, AJ," Kana said.

Static crackled through the earpieces as AJ's voice faded in and out. "Something strange is going on now. Whoa, what in the world?"

"Are you alright, AJ?"

"I... that's weird... I'm going to have to—"

"AJ? AJ?"

He wasn't responding. Stefan tapped the side of his ear. "They may have jammed the signal for good. We're going to have to wing it." Stefan braced his hand on the car door. "But trust me, Kana. I'll be watching out for you."

"This doesn't change things. Remember, you're going to offer me in exchange for seeing the Black Grimoire."

"Well, about that." He reached into the back seat of the car. "Remember how I said I had something to sweeten the deal to Jiang? I've been thinking, we might as well use this, so they know we're serious."

He grabbed their Black Grimoire from the backseat, which Kana could have sworn was locked up in a safe back at the condo.

"You brought that with you? If you show that to them, they're not going to give a damn about me. They'll just kill both of us and take it."

Stefan patted the front of the book. "Trust me. This is a last resort. We'll still go with your plan."

She wondered why he had just brought this up now. "Is that what you had planned all along?"

"It was a backup plan. Don't worry, I have no intention of letting them get anywhere near it."

He placed the book in a Halliburton briefcase, locked it tight, and handed it to Kana. She took the case, squinting one eye at Stefan, and exited the car.

Jiang approached them and shook Stefan's hand. It wasn't until now that Kana realized how many people were in the entourage with them. She counted twelve men and two women with not a smile among any of them. The roar of a passing train echoed through the small alleyway. At least she knew they were near some sort of transportation which might come in handy as a point of reference.

One of the female bikers was chattering away, mocking Kana and the damn red dress. The others laughed at whatever she said. What she didn't know is that Kana understood every word, responding in Japanese with her own level of sass, earning a second round of laughter from the bikers to the displeasure of their female comrade.

"Wait, I didn't know you could speak Japanese," Stefan whispered to her as they followed Jiang into the adjacent building.

"How many times do I have to remind you: I'm Japanese."

"Then what did we need these earpieces for?" Stefan pushed his finger against it, his lips tightening. "Oh, you guys wanted to keep tabs on me. I'm a little hurt by that, Kana."

She patted his arm reassuringly. "It's not that we don't trust you, Stefan. It's that we don't know what you know. The more we learn, the better. Don't get upset about it." She looked down at the Haliburton containing the Black Grimoire. "Besides, it's not as if you didn't have your own secrets going into this, remember."

"Touché. Well, let's get into character. I have no idea what we're about to walk into."

THE WITCH SEES ALL

Once inside the building, Kana, Stefan, Jiang, and their escorts took a service elevator to the top floor. This was one of the older hotels in the area, evident by the drab interior, outdated magazine ads plastered on inside of the elevator car, and the stained water marks on the ceiling. Even the gears that pulled the car up the shaft knocked and shuttered from age. While it wasn't quite a slum, the hotel wasn't a proud monument to the city. It was the kind of place someone who didn't want to draw attention to themselves would live.

With a chime, the elevator doors opened, and Jiang led the company out into a sparsely decorated hallway. Two antique chairs with the stuffing spilling from the corners were all that sat between the elevator and the door to the only unit on this floor. The door sat singular at the end of a long hallway, beckoning visitors toward it.

"We must wait here for a moment. Yoshi will be with us soon," Jiang said.

As if on cue, the host from the Black Lotus Ball, known as Kensuke, approached the visitors flanked by two men, both in tuxedos.

Jiang greeted them, bowing. "Good evening Kensuke-san, Suzuki-san, Yoshi-san. It has been a while."

Yoshi was one of the men flanking the speaker who turned to Jiang with a stern, unforgiving glare. "We are only taking this meeting because I know you." He then turned to the host. "They can pass, Kensuke. He brings a great gift for the Madam."

Yoshi's eyes darted over to Kana. Again, she felt like a piece of meat being observed in a butcher's shop, the knot in her stomach growing and twisting with every passing moment.

Kensuke spoke in English to Stefan, brushing his dyed blonde bangs from his face. "Let us see what the gaijin has brought us."

"You will not be disappointed." Stefan shook Kensuke's hand. The host's grip was painful, matching the sadistic smile he wore, squeezing so hard that his own body started to shake. It was a test of Stefan's toughness—or fighting spirit—as he bit his lower lip to keep from wincing. After Kensuke was satisfied with his attempted torture, he allowed them to pass, gesturing to the end of the hall.

This was an awkward walk for Kana. Every step down this hallway felt as if the ceiling and walls were closing in on her. The corners of her vision darkened, a pressure pushed on her skull, like the onset of a migraine. She could feel the thirty eyeballs of the Yakuza fixed on her from behind. She worried that AJ's problems were more than a communication issue, he may have been discovered, meaning they were on their own. All she had to count on was Stefan and his ability to talk his way out of anything. Could he do that without giving up the Black Grimoire they already had or, even worse, her having to give up her life? She made this bed, mostly out of anger, and now she'd have to lie in it.

"Go ahead and open the door," Kensuke said. "She knew you were coming."

Yoshi waved to the escorts. "Yakuza stays outside. You know the rules."

Stefan turned the doorknob and opened it. The room beyond was much smaller than he had anticipated. Cluttered from floor to ceiling with all manner of knick-knacks; from potted plants to enormous jars filled with dark liquid to stacks of books, this suite felt more like the home of a packrat than the Madam of the Underworld. The stench of raw fish hung in the air, a consequence of the six aquariums crammed in every corner of the space. Each one was a different shape and size, containing sea life as domestic as a goldfish to the more exotic, like eels, deformed crabs, and a baby shark. None of the aquariums were in the best of shape, the water murky and thick, but the animals still thrived.

One lamp hung from the ceiling over a wooden table. Sitting there, at the center of the room, was a pudgy old woman with leathery pale-orange skin, textured by wrinkles and the furrowed lines in her brow. Her hair was an oily nest of stringy curls, grey with a few strands of black left over from years gone by. On the table was a collection of jars and pots that her hands were busy filling with herbs and stones. Arthritis had set in, her fingers twitching, as she raised her pot-marked hands to welcome her guests.

Her voice crackled from phlegm as she spoke. "Come inside."

Stefan and Kana remained frozen in the doorway, the woman's words heard but not obeyed.

She cleared her throat. "Come inside or go away."

Yoshi nudged Stefan in the back, compelling him to move forward into the dark room. The closer they got to the table, the more the odors of the room overwhelmed Kana. She took a seat at the table where the stench was potent: an earthy musk mixed with rotting eggs. The old woman had to be the source.

The hag eyed them both. "Sit down. You might as well be comfortable during your time here. You all understand English, so we will speak English. Although mine is not perfect."

Skulking in the dark corners of the room were still figures who, until now, were invisible. If it wasn't for their silhouettes moving slowly with each labored breath, and the subtle wheezing, these otherwise lifeless figures would have continued to be unknown—shadows within shadows.

Stefan bowed to the madam before taking his seat. "My name is Shane, and this here is Eliza. It is a pleasure to meet you... what should I call you?"

"I have many names as you know. *Madam. The Shill Mother.* But I think you know me as *Kuroi Majo.*"

"It is a name I've heard, yes."

"Then we are off to a good start. The reputation behind that name will save me the time of having to explain the consequences of wasting my time or disrespecting my home."

Jiang pushed his way past her guards to the table. "Before we get too far along here, I'd like to discuss some manner of compensation." The man apparently didn't hear the words of the old woman about respect. "You see, I met these two at the Black Lotus Ball and facilitated this meeting. And what a find I have brought to you! This woman is tantalizing, to say the least. Surely it is worth a small, humble request."

Kuroi Majo rubbed her weathered hands together, the sound like two pieces of sandpaper sliding against one another. She raised one of her bushy eyebrows to get a better look at this man. "Is that so?"

"Well, I only ask for what is fair, Madam."

"You are Jiang, correct? You have been working for us this last year."

He nodded, leaning on the table. "Yes, that is me."

"And you were a pederast before this. Or should I say, you were *only* a pederast before?"

Lost for words, he avoided eye contact with the old woman and turned his attention back to Kana, flashing his yellow teeth under the lamplight. "I just ask for a taste when it is done. Just something for me to take for myself. Just a small piece if I could."

Even though he danced around being specific, everyone in the room knew what he wanted. His desire was for a piece of Kana's body to take home with him. Whatever piece and for whatever purpose was better left unsaid. He was salivating at the thought, something that didn't escape Kana, Stefan, or Kuroi Majo who turned her focus back to the pots on the table.

The madam wet her lips. "A small piece."

"I think that would be fair."

The old woman continued picking apart the herbs on the table, the pile filled with rosemary and thyme as well as stranger plants Kana didn't know the name of. After picking off a few pieces, Kuroi Majo rolled the leaves and stems between her hands, crushed them with her fist, opened her palm and rolled her knuckles to let the herbs fall into the bowl. "Kensuke, show him what is fair."

Jiang immediately knew he had made a mistake. He raised his hands to plead for his life, but before the words left his lips, Kensuke released his blade and sliced through the side of Jiang's neck. One clean stroke is all it took. Kana and Stefan recoiled in their seats as the decapitated head dropped to the table with a thud, Jiang's face frozen in a state of panic: eyes wide open, mouth ajar, exposing those disgusting yellow teeth.

The hag flicked the back of her hand to her underlings who cleaned the table and collected the head. Kana watched as these poor souls did their madam's bidding, their joints twitching as they worked, a scene she remembered from the performers at the Black Lotus Ball. Kuroi Majo continued picking at the pile of herbs while the mess was cleared away.

"Now perhaps we can speak plainly." She tapped her dirty fingernails against the top of the table. "And speak truthfully."

Stefan pulled himself back to the table, sliding his hand from his mouth. "I'm here to make a deal, Madam. Nothing more than that."

"Of course. But you must be truthful. This is the one time I will allow your lie to be excused. Please do not repeat that mistake." What was she talking about? Did she know their plan? "Your real name is Stefan." Her black pearly eyes rolled up to meet his. "Your brother, Octavius, was known to us. He came here himself trying to barter."

Stefan bowed his head. "It is true. And I do apologize for the deception. We had to use different names. It was necessary to gain access to the Black Lotus Ball."

She picked through the pile of rosemary beside the pot. "I understand young man. I know you. But her..." Kuroi Majo pointed one of her twisted fingers toward Kana "...I do not know. Her, I do not trust. Her, I suspect there's more than what she is showing us."

The witch bounced her finger every time she spoke the word "her", its target the young woman in the red dress at her table. Kana didn't intimidate easily, but this old woman was perhaps the scariest thing she had seen in her life. There was a power here, an ancient power, that ebbed from the hag's pores and radiated throughout the room. It was the same oppressive feeling she had walking down the hallway earlier, now magnified sitting across from its source.

"So, speak girl. Tell me your name."

Mindful of the warning earlier about telling any more lies, and not knowing just how much knowledge such a creature had, Kana told the truth. "I go by Kana."

"Yes, Kana... Cold. Hmmm." The witch inhaled deeply. "Not your given name but it is the name you own. You were willing to sacrifice yourself in order to get close to me?"

"Yes, that's what the plan was. If it came to that I'd have little choice."

"Little choice is correct. If I desired it, your body would join what remains of Jiang in the kitchen."

Stefan put his hand over Kana's. "We thank you for your mercy."

Kuroi Majo corrected him. "I haven't granted you that yet. But we will see. Yes, we will see."

The marionette servants returned to the table from the darkness of the kitchen. They placed a platter at the center of the table filled with pieces of flesh and brain, sorted and organized into separate spaces. Most of the meat was indescribable except for an eyeball and a few jagged pieces of skull, the stench of it wafting toward Kana who didn't know how much longer she could sit here without vomiting.

The witch dove her hands into the pile of brains. "Let me see the book."

Stefan placed the briefcase on the table, unlocked it, and with a sigh lifted the Black Grimoire from inside. The book was heavy in his hands, as if it was reacting to its sister nearby. Kuroi Majo dropped two wet pieces of brain into the largest pot on the table, licked her hands clean, and then snatched the book from Stefan.

"The Black Grimoires," Kuroi Majo said the words as if she were speaking of a beloved child. "So much power. So much mystery around them. I have one in my possession, as I'm sure you know, and for two hundred years I've been trying to unlock its secrets. Some have come willingly but others to this day remain hidden.

"I've enjoyed wealth, longevity, the pleasures of the flesh, and the sorrows of loss that time demands. I was once an *Ame Onna* in the old world. My sisters and I were goddesses, beautiful and loved. Before man took to machines, they needed us to bring rain to their withering crops. But we were all corrupted. From loneliness and sadness, all my sisters were washed away by the very rain they called to mask their sorrows. Only I remained. Truthfully, it was by chance that I found this book."

"It was a blessing, Madam," Kensuke said.

"For a time, yes. I was no longer a simple Ame Onna, destined to lick my skin in the sadness of the storm. I could have real power from the other planes of demons and devils. Oh yes, there are multiple worlds in which we reign. But for all that it has given me, it could never give me what I truly desired."

For the first time, Kuroi Majo looked human. Her head drooped as her lips turned downward. Her days as an Ame Onna, or *rain woman*, lingering in her ill-fated gaze.

Kana laid her palms flat on the table. "Is that why you sacrificed that girl?"

"We sacrifice for many reasons. The body has a strength within it that few understand. Few have lived long enough to see it. Even something as wretched as Jiang here serves a purpose." She took another piece of his remains and crushed it in her fist. "But the beautiful, the young, the spirited, that is something even greater. They taste different. They feel different. So, you must see my conflict here."

Stefan shook his head. "Conflict? You have us at a disadvantage."

Kuroi Majo ignored him and focused on Kana. "You see yourself in me as I see myself in you. Yes, I do. You are bored with what others might consider the *fantasique*, so you needed to find something even more wonderous in this world. And now you see me, someone who has seen it all, someone who has experienced everything." The witch chuckled. "Kana Cold, I am your future, and it terrifies you."

There was truth in the hag's words that ate away at Kana's insides. The mystery of ghosts and spirits had grown tiresome and the search for the Black Grimoires was something else, something deeper than simple spirits and mutant animals. But what after this? What more would there be? What would happen when there was nothing new; no corner of the world to uncover or puzzle to solve? She may not live centuries like the witch, but she could see herself in this weathered woman, tired and empty.

Kuroi Majo tapped at the side of the bowl with her fingernails. "My conflict is not whether to give you my Black Grimoire—I have no more use for it. You would be doing me a favor by removing it. But a price must be paid. Which one of you should I have?" The witch waved her hands over the pot, a thick smoke winding its way up from inside to the overhead lamp. She breathed in the fumes, held her breath for a moment, and exhaled with a perverse sneer, pointing her twitching finger at Stefan. "His lies go deeper than you know, girl. And as I said before, he has already exhausted my patience for lies."

What did she mean? Kana turned to Stefan, his charming smile disarming her as he stroked the back of her hand.

"Ah, there it is." Kuroi Majo growled, closing her hand into a fist as if she was squeezing his neck. "That's the look that made her swoon. Come, boy, show us all how the spider lures the fly."

One of the marionettes returned to the table, this time with the Black Grimoire in hand. It stuttered to a stop and dropped the upper half of its body forward. The witch slid the book from its hands. With its task done, the corpse lumbered back to its dark corner.

"This is what you want, isn't it? The power of demons. The spells that Honorius wrote down, enchantments so terrible that he hid it from humanity. Yes, the prize you desire and lied your way to. I think it would be better in the hands of the girl." Kuroi Majo stroked the front of the grimoires, her fingernails scratching across the runes on the cover. "Yes, I have decided. As for you..."

In a heartbeat, Stefan grabbed Yoshi's gun from his waist, turned it to the old woman, and fired a shot straight for her forehead. The bullet blasted out the back of her skull. Kensuke cursed and lunged for Stefan. Yoshi intercepted him, grabbed him by the neck, and twisted with all his might, killing his superior in the blink of an eye. The third and final guard, Suzuki, charged at the table with a small knife only to be put down by three bullets ripping through his chest and cracking the glass of the aquarium behind him. Stefan stood over Suzuki, watching him choke on his own blood for a moment before plugging one final bullet between his eyes.

"What about them?" Stefan asked Yoshi.

Yoshi glanced into the dark corners of the room at the marionette corpses. "Her slaves? They don't know what's going on. I wouldn't worry about them. Without her spells they are harmless."

Stefan pressed his ear against the door. "Get the book. We have maybe a minute before the Yakuza come in here. They're going to be angry as hell we killed someone under their protection."

Kana hadn't moved an inch since the first gunshot, chewing on her lip as blood oozed from the hole in Kuroi Majo's head, the hag's mouth and eyes wide open. She knew Stefan had a vicious streak in him, but cold-blooded murder was another thing entirely. Was the Black Grimoire worth the cost? "What was she talking about? I can't... I don't know what to think. She was going to let me go."

"She was," Stefan said. "But I'm not."

Until he said that, Kana held on to a shred of hope that there was some other explanation for this, that Stefan was not the monster she was seeing. The second she stood from the table he aimed the gun at her chest.

"This whole time then?" Kana frowned, her hands shaking. "She was right. You are a lying sack of—"

"I did what I had to do," Stefan cut her off. "Don't make this harder than it has to be. Give me the briefcase."

There was a rumbling outside. A chorus of panicked and angry voices chattered on the other side of the door, portending the arrival of the Yakuza. Kana watched the door, waiting for the thugs to come crashing through at any second.

She wasn't going to die here, she couldn't, and certainly not by the hands of this liar. "What will you give me?"

"What?" Stefan's face twisted in confusion.

Kana clutched the briefcase. "I said, what will you give me? I'm not just handing this over to you."

The muzzle of the gun moved up to her face. "I could put a bullet in your head just like the old woman. Don't waste time, Kana."

"Why don't you do it then?" Stefan didn't answer her. Instead, he moved in closer, the smell of burning metal and gunpowder heavy in the air, but Kana didn't budge. "Oh, you need a scapegoat. You need someone to blame her murder on so the Yakuza won't hunt you down and string you up from a streetlight outside."

"Just hand over the briefcase." He blinked long and hard, sucking in his bottom lip. "I swear to God Kana, I will shoot you. Trust me, it's better than what they'll do to you."

Kana clutched the case against her chest. If she held on to it, Stefan couldn't leave. The Yakuza banged away at the door, its hinges rattling, the wood splintering. It wouldn't hold for long. Kana kicked off her high heels and backed away from Stefan.

He kept the gun trained on her face as she slid across the wall to the door.

Stefan's eyes darted back and forth between Kana and the door. "Stop! Don't do it, Kana."

"Shoot her, Stefan! What are you waiting for?" Yoshi barked.

Stefan turned to him for a split second. "Stay out of this!"

It was enough of a distraction for Kana to reach the door and, in one fluid motion, turn the knob and open it. Outside were twenty members of the Yakuza, cursing and gasping the moment they saw the dead bodies of Kuroi Majo and her bodyguards. Stefan made the first move, firing into the crowd of thugs, killing three of them instantly. The rest charged the room, forcing Yoshi and Stefan to look for an exit through the windows.

Kana remained on the ground behind the open door, shielded and unseen by the Yakuza. With them distracted, she snuck through the doorway, down the hall, and into the stairwell near the elevator.

They were several flights up but there was no other choice, she couldn't wait for the elevator. By the time the thugs killed Stefan and realized she was missing, she'd be far away from the hotel.

Her feet pounded against the cold floor of the stairs with nothing but the thin fabric of her stockings covering her soles. It was hard to move even without the high heels, the dress so tight around her legs she stopped to rip a slit in the side. The

Halliburton pulled on her arm, now containing two grimoires that felt as heavy as bowling balls. But there was no stopping, no time for rest. She had to get out of here and get as far away as she could.

Panting from exhaustion, Kana reached the ground floor and pushed her way through the emergency exit. Sure enough, the caravan that had brought her here was still outside. The car keys were with Stefan so one of the Yakuza's trucks or motorbikes would have to do. If she could find a set of keys to one of them, she'd be in the clear. As she looked through the windows of the trucks her attention was called to the other side of the alley by the sound of jingling keys. Those keys belonged to the only member of the gang who stayed behind, the same young woman who mocked Kana when they arrived. The girl held the ring of keys between her index finger in thumb, dangling them in the cold light of the streetlamp above her.

Kana dropped the briefcase to the ground and balled her fists. "Of course, it's you."

FALLING APART

Mimori had a tragic childhood, a troubled youth, and a violent adulthood. She joined the Yakuza at fifteen, one of few females in the region to hold membership in the mafia but proved her worth early on. She loved the power that came from being in the organization and the way people respected her. The Yakuza had become her family, and in a true sense, it was the only family she had ever known. Honor and pride were tantamount. Anyone who dared to insult her family would know a painful death if she had anything to say about it.

And here she was in an alley on a routine escorting job that had just gone south with one of the perpetrators standing right in front of her. The *gaijins* and one of the witch's own guards, an unscrupulous man called Yoshi, had betrayed the old hag and it happened on their watch—on *her* watch. The Yakuza were sworn to protect the Kuroi Majo, so for her to die like a dog in her own home, under the mafia's care, was a grave insult and embarrassment. This foreigner in the red dress, who was too

Western for Mimori's liking anyway, was not getting away without paying for such a dishonorable act.

Kana hoped speaking to her would help. "You don't know what happened. It was the man I was with who killed her. He tried to kill me."

"What's in the briefcase." Mimori casually pulled a blade from her black jacket, admiring it as she waited for an answer.

Kana could see this wasn't going to end peacefully. "It's what we came for. It doesn't concern the Yakuza."

"Everything here concerns the Yakuza!" Mimori screamed. "You foreigners think you can do as you please. Not tonight. Not here. Not with me. Find your courage, girl! I hope for your sake you can fight."

Mimori closed the distance between herself and Kana with lightning speed, her blade aimed for Kana's throat. She missed but continued to slash away. Kana caught her arm, keeping the blade away with her right hand while pushing against Mimori with the left. They continued to struggle, both women's arms tangled together in a knot, the tip of the blade just inches from Kana's face. One slip of the hand, a twitch in her muscles, and the knife would find its way into her windpipe. Mimori snarled as she pushed down on Kana, her clenched teeth reflected in the metal. Mimori looked orgasmic from the struggle as she got closer with each labored breath to plunging the knife into Kana's skin.

Her obsessiveness left her open for Kana to free herself. The Yakuza thug was pressing too hard and throwing her body off balance. Kana let her move a few inches more and once her foot left the ground, Kana twisted to her left, throwing Mimori to the street, untangling their arms. Kana wouldn't let the advantage slip away, grabbing Mimori by the hair and ramming her head into the soda dispenser as hard as she could. The girl looked back at her with a gaping mouth of blood-stained teeth, gawking at her, daring her to do it again. And again, she did, smashing Mimori's face into the machine twice more, drawing blood from her forehead. The thug laughed hysterically as she watched the crimson trickle down her face, smearing the blood with her hands. She charged, her fingers aiming for Kana's throat, only to be sidestepped, punched in the temple, and knocked out cold.

"I... am tired... of people... trying to kill me." Kana doubled over to catch her breath before rifling through the girl's pockets, finding a set of keys. "Thanks... you crazy bitch."

She picked up the Halliburton and strapped it to the back of Mimori's motorbike. One last obstacle to overcome: the dress. The damn thing was still too tight for her to straddle the bike, even with the rip in the side. Kana took the knife that had nearly ended her life a few moments before and cut away at the fabric, fraying it to the point where she could move her legs freely. That solved the problem with her riding the bike but presented another problem as she looked behind her. "My ass is hanging out."

She revved the engine, hunkered down, and sped off towards the railroad tracks nearby. Another four seconds and she would have made it without the Yakuza seeing her, the lot of them exiting the hotel as she made her escape. It didn't matter. She had to make it back to the condo, hope nothing happened to AJ, and find some way out of Japan.

That was easier said than done. Kana had zero familiarity with the layout of Shinjuku, so she relied on the train tracks to lead her back to the other side of the city. She kept the sound of the train to her right, but lost sight of it, forced to use the roadways. An intersection proved to be the first obstacle. She couldn't slow down; the caravan of Yakuza could be heard behind her. She clenched her teeth and blew through the red light hoping to God she didn't get in an accident or draw the attention of the police. No such luck. The police had a problem with the motorbike gangs, the most well-known being the Bosozoku, and the laws were strict around motorbike riders without helmets who ran red lights. She had to get off the streets and quick.

The Yakuza followed, much to the anger of other drivers who honked their horns in protest. The closer the chase got to the heart of the city, the more traffic there was from all the nightclubs and restaurants. That didn't keep one of the Yakuza from firing at her on the open streets. Kana hunkered down and pushed the bike to its limits, the machine shaking as it swerved through cars, past pedestrians, and over uneven asphalt. Her right leg burned. She knew the cause—one of the bullets nicked her leg—but she couldn't take her eyes off the road, she was moving too fast.

The chase quickly became a popular topic on Japanese news stations and social media. Crowds of people in restaurants and homes, cars and cafes, recorded the pursuit on video or streamed it live with their phones.

Kana made a right turn at the next intersection. She had to get back to the railroad tracks. She heard the train's horn blaring off to the left, so she turned down an alley in that direction. Follow the horn and find the train. Unfortunately, the police caught up with the chase, their sirens blaring in the distance. From what she knew about Shinjuku, being captured by the cops would be the same as being caught by the Yakuza.

There was a detour ahead that blocked off traffic from the industrial area on the south side, so she took a chance and crossed the yellow warning signs down the closed roadway. The Yakuza followed, a line of motorbikes aggressively turning down the same corridor. It was a risk that paid off. A Bosozoku street race was about to begin on the same closed street. Kana and the Yakuza were barreling head-on toward a line of three dozen bikers.

No one stopped.

The two gangs collided; curses, bodies, and bikes flying in all directions. In the confusion, Kana disappeared down another alley, using the chaos as cover.

Three blocks later she looked behind her. No one was following. She sighed and checked on the briefcase strapped to the back of the bike, then the wound on her leg. The blood soaked through the fabric, a darker shade of red than the dress itself. She'd have to patch it up herself back at the condo.

Up ahead were the lights of a major roadway. Only a few kilometers to end of the alley. The horn of the train wailed from the same direction.

The instant she hit the end of the alley a car screeched to a halt, blocking her path. It was too late to slow down, too late to turn. She squeezed on the breaks. No good. The motorcycle smashed its front wheel into the side of the car, sending Kana crashing into the street.

The bike's motor sputtered as she tried to sit up straight against the nearby brick wall. Her ears were ringing, she knew her shoulder was separated, and sitting up only made the pain worse. It was then that she recognized the car that blocked her way, the same car she rode in to the Black Lotus Ball.

The bastard had caught up with her.

Through the haze she heard Stefan's voice. "Grab the case." The ringing in her ears wouldn't stop, muffling his words. "Put it in the car. I'll clean this up."

There he was, standing over her like some disapproving parent who had caught his child doing something he told them not to. She didn't want to hear the "I told you so" speech, although the gun in his hand suggested the speech wasn't going to last long.

"I know you don't believe me, but I really don't want to kill you." He waved the gun around as if it wasn't dangerous, like this was a casual conversation between friends. "I don't hate you, Kana, but this is the way it has to go. If you had listened to me though instead of coming up with your own plan, then the worst thing that would have happened tonight was you being left stranded at the Ball while Yoshi and I took care of the old witch. But you insisted."

Kana had words for him, but her body was going into shock. She looked up at Stefan, tears running down her face as she quivered on the dirty street; a bruised woman in a tattered dress with a bullet hole in the side of her leg. A chill ran from the base of her neck down through her legs. The muscles in her abdomen tightened, she heaved and huffed through her nose, her neck straining to hold her head up high. If he was going to kill her, he'd have to do it with her staring right back into his beautiful lying eyes.

Stefan's ended his speech and put his gun away. The flashing red and blue lights of cop cars flashed against the empty office buildings behind him. He was as much a fugitive from the police and the Yakuza as she was. Stefan gently put his hand on Kana's cheek and kissed her forehead. In return, she used every bit of energy she had to spit in his face. He wiped it off casually, laughed for a tick, and spit right back at her.

"*Kinda Cold,*" he mocked, wiping her spit from his face. "*Kinda Conned* is more like it. Enjoy your prison stay before the Yakuza have their way with you. Goodbye, Kana."

He hopped into the car and it sped off. Two cop cars arrived seconds later. One followed Stefan's car while the other stopped, the two officers rushing over to Kana while calling over the radio for backup. It took a few seconds for them to reach her and in that time, she replayed every interaction with Stefan over the last week: the cabin, Israel, the hotel room, oh how she regretted that now! Her sight was fading as the cops circled her, their weapons draw, yelling at her in Japanese to put her hands in the air. The best she could do was raise one hand, the injured shoulder in so much pain that it made her scream when she tried to raise it. She made it to her feet though, the effort sucking up the last bit of energy she had. Her legs buckled and she collapsed, hitting the back of her skull on the curb, knocking herself unconscious.

AN EMBARRASSING HANGOVER

When Kana regained consciousness her head was throbbing, her leg and shoulder felt numb, and she smelled like stale sweat and dead fish. Memories quickly flooded her mind as she remembered what preceded her blackout: Stefan's betrayal, losing the Black Grimoires, being chased by the Yakuza, nearly being murdered four times within a half hour.

Judging by the dusty light creeping through the blinds it must have been morning now. Her first attempt to sit up was met with her body screaming at her to lie back down. She groaned, put her palm to her sweaty forehead, and gingerly laid back down. The only good news was that she wasn't back at the safe house or in jail. This was someone's office, used quite frequently from the stacks of paper on the desk adjacent to her. It was then that she caught a familiar scent, a perfume she couldn't quite place at first, but as soon as she realized who it belonged to, she groaned even louder. "Oh, God no."

Anastasia was sitting at her side, leaning back in a chair with her long legs crossed. "I'm glad to see you're awake now."

As much as it caused her discomfort, Kana twisted onto her side and opened one of her eyes. Yes, it was the blonde, rocking back and forth with a smug look on her face.

"Why? Why me?" Kana huffed.

"I'd think you'd be a little more appreciative than that, Kana. If it wasn't for me, you'd be rotting in a jail cell right now on your way to a Yakuza execution near the ocean. Instant shark food if you know what I mean?"

"Oh, well excuse the hell out of me! You must be loving this."

"Loving what—"

Kana covered her face with her hand. "Yeah, you warned me. Go ahead and get it out of your system. You told me not to get involved in this because I was out of my league. Well, here we are. You had to pull me out of a hot mess I got myself into."

"Kana, I wasn't going to say anything like that. Believe it or not, I'm actually on your side here. No one would blame you for what happened with Stefan."

Kana shot upright on the sofa, whatever pain she felt immaterial to the rage the mere mention of his name brought out in her. "He played me! He made me look like some cheap slut!"

"Kana..."

"No, he did! I was exactly the kind of girl I can't stand. Falling for some bad boy with a foreign accent. How embarrassing is that?"

Anastasia tilted her head and closed one eye. "That's not a broken heart, Kana. That's a bruised ego."

She's right. Kana didn't love Stefan, he was a warm body on a night that she needed it. What he did was, in her mind, far worse. Stefan made a mockery of her. He made her a cliché and proved that she wasn't ready to deal with the big players in the game.

It ate at her.

Kana would have continued her tirade if the pain of her leg, shoulder, and head didn't rush back with a vengeance. She winced and curled back up on the couch, rubbing her temples and clenching her teeth.

"You're getting yourself all worked up. Just try to get some rest for a few more hours. I'll get you some tea or something," Anastasia said.

"Rum," Kana mumbled.

"I think tea would be better—"

"Rum!"

"Okay, okay."

Anastasia left the room and closed the door behind her, not without Kana mumbling another unintelligible insult before she exited. They weren't friends, but they weren't really enemies either. Kana swam in the deep waters, nearly drowned, and was lucky that she was even alive. This wasn't the Anastasia that Kana expected. She was acting more like a big sister than a rival. And like a good big sister she'd take care of her, despite the shower of snide remarks.

AJ startled Anastasia as she left the office. "How's she doing?"

Anastasia closed the door behind her. "Kana is..." She paused for a moment, her head nodding from side to side. "...she's Kana. Go on in and see for yourself."

This office building sat just outside of downtown Tokyo, close enough to the airport. It was also hidden in the middle of the congested commerce section of the city. Hiding in plain sight, as Anastasia called it. On its surface, this was a travel agency owned by Anastasia's father. He allowed her to use it for whatever she needed. Having a billionaire as a father did have its advantages, including a rather sophisticated set of computers that AJ spent the prior night putting to good use.

She left AJ to visit his friend. He went to the office to see his friend, closing the door behind him for privacy.

He spoke softly. "Hey Kana, I just wanted to..." AJ stopped talking once he realized that she was passed out, stretched across the sofa with her injured leg wrapped in bandages. Her hand clutched her necklace, the one she so often lost, but here it was providing some comfort.

It pained him to see her like this. But it wasn't the first time. Usually, this scene was the result of too many drinks the prior evening, and on two occasions before, a broken heart. Today, it was likely a little bit of both.

She always kept that part of her hidden from everyone else except him. AJ saw it as a sign of trust that she would let him help her when she really needed it. By now, he questioned whether they should have taken this job. Look what it had brought them.

"I know you don't like her but Anastasia's alright." He pulled a chair close to the couch and sat down. "You have no idea how scared I was last night. Stefan's people shut down my system and were trying to get to me. I turned it on them though. I had their source signal traced and then sent the police there. It probably bought me enough time to get out of there. Anastasia's people picked me up down the street and brought me here. If it wasn't for them, I'd probably be worse off than..." He struggled to find something to say, letting out a sigh and folding his hands together between his knees.

What a mess. The urge to do something began to gnaw away at him. "You know, when we get home, I think we should take a few weeks off. Just shut the office down and not take any new cases. I doubt we'll be getting paid for any of this and we've spent a pretty penny already just going from place to place. But you've earned a rest. I've earned a rest."

She stirred on the couch, murmuring in her sleep. AJ wondered if she was waking up, but it was a false alarm. Kana rolled her head from side to side and then settled back into slumber. AJ placed his hand gently on the top of her head, stroking her hair to ease whatever nightmare she was having: a flashback to the night before, or maybe it was the Shinigami trying to take advantage of her weakened state, another problem he couldn't help her with. All he could do was sit here by her side.

But was that really all he could do? "This isn't right." There was no way for him to fight, that would be suicide on his part. "But I can't just let him get away with this." He did have other skills though, capabilities that would make this right. He stood up, running his fingers through his blondish-brown curls. "I'm sorry, Kana, I can't let him get away with this."

His mind was made up. Kana was in safe hands with Anastasia, so he could make a move without worrying about her. AJ didn't know exactly where Stefan had run off to, but it wouldn't be too hard to track him down. Before he departed, he removed the necklace from around Kana's neck and pocketed it. She'd be furious with him when she found out, but for the time being it would serve a better purpose with him than with her.

AJ found their host lounging in a chair a few feet from the office. "Anastasia, I need to borrow some cash."

She raised an eyebrow, sipping her tea while she scanned her electronic tablet. "I'd like to help but we'll be leaving once Kana gets up. Why do you need cash?"

"I'm not going with you." AJ grabbed his passport and stuffed it into his bag.

Anastasia put down her tablet. "Wait, where do you think you're going?"

"Don't worry about it. Just whatever you can spare will be fine. I can figure out the rest of the way."

Anastasia followed him as he marched to the front door. "The rest of what way? You can't leave, AJ. Kana needs you here. She certainly doesn't need you doing anything stupid."

"When have you ever known me to do anything stupid? I'm the levelheaded one, remember?"

She clicked her tongue against the roof of her mouth, shaking her head. "I'm sorry, I can't let you leave here."

Anastasia's bodybuilder-sized security guards blocked the exit with their arms crossed.

AJ reached into his pocket for his cell phone. "Mcdunns230."

"What are you talking about now?"

"That's your father's email, right?"

Anastasia blinked rapidly, shrugging her shoulders. "Yes, AJ. That's my father's email. What does that have to do with anything?"

"Remember those pictures you sent me last Christmas when you needed me to hack into one of Cilliotech's account for some case you were working on?"

Her eyes widened. "You wouldn't dare!"

"Yes, I would." AJ held up his phone, the scandalous picture bright and bare on the screen. Anastasia pushed it down so her security guards, who were doing their best to act as if they weren't looking, couldn't see it. "That's low, AJ. That's real low."

"Well, I need to go. I don't want to Anastasia, believe me, but I need to do this."

She sighed heavily, her lips flapping together. "Just tell me that you won't do anything that'll get you killed."

"You know me. I hate violence. I'm not going to charge at him like some muscled up 'roidhead." He glanced over at the security guards and shrugged. "No offense."

"Ah, okay. Alright! Go on. Just contact me however you can in six hours. Six hours, AJ! I mean it."

"Thank you." The green light was given, and he was off.

Anastasia called to him before the doors closed. "She's lucky to have you."

"I know that."

She watched him head out into the street, his bag over his shoulder and a purpose in his step, blending into the throng of pedestrians outside, leaving Anastasia with an even tougher job: how to explain this to Kana.

MY BROTHER'S KEEPER

O vernight flights from Tokyo to Berlin were not easy to get on short notice. Stefan found a way around that, managing to secure a private plane through his various contacts. Yoshi saw his business partner off at the airport where he too needed to catch a flight and leave Japan. The Yakuza would find them if they stayed any longer than a few hours. No matter how good they were this was the Yakuza's territory. They knew better to leave while they could.

The flight would take more than half a day to complete which provided Stefan with enough time to catch up on sleep, brush up on his German, and mull over his plan. Two hours into the flight, the pilot informed him that there would be some turbulence from a massive thunderstorm they'd have to pass over. From above, the gale was a visual fascination instead of an oppressive force of nature that would ruin a sunny day. It seemed so small; the rolling black clouds, their arcs of lighting flashing like jagged coils one second and disappearing the next.

His thoughts turned to Kana as the plane shook and the turbines wailed. He had no qualms about the rouse he played on her. It had been so carefully orchestrated from the very start, and she, being a much younger and far less experienced player in this world, believed in every bit of it. He was sure at this point she was cursing his name a thousand times over and was plotting all the ways she'd avenge herself. And she had every right to do so. But the likelihood of that happening was small.

Kana was a capable woman—relentless and vicious—that much he knew, but being relentless wasn't better than being good, and Stefan was *good* at this. Even the dissension he sewed between her and AJ couldn't have gone any better.

Still, there was a piece of him that admired her and regretted having to betray her trust. Her tough-girl-with-a-soft-heart routine had warmed him and, in another life, the two might have had a chance at being something exquisite. But that wasn't this world. In this world, he needed the Black Grimoires, and she had unfortunately been a necessary tool to obtain them.

The prize was far and beyond worth it. What the Black Grimoires provided couldn't be measured in friendship, love, sex, or even gold. It held a far greater value to him and to those he was working for. Now that two of the three were in his possession he could negotiate from a place of strength.

***

A line of thugs in black suits were waiting for him when he landed in Germany, wearing the same suits as Dieter and his men wore back at his cabin. After gathering his luggage, they escorted him to a classic BMW waiting by the gates that shuttled him off to his next destination.

Nearly twenty-four hours after he left Tokyo, Stefan found himself standing outside the entrance to an unassuming building deep in the woods. It reminded him of his cabin in Bucharest except for the two female secretaries sitting at desks doing a terrible job of hiding the fact they were mercenaries. The security check went through without a hitch, the giant metal door opening, allowing him access to one of the most powerful organizations in the underworld.

"I see you made it." Marcus Godolphin welcomed Stefan as he entered the underground facility. "You look a little worse for wear, Stefan."

"Well, it's hard work doing what I do, Marcus. Not all of us can trade people's livelihoods on a whim from his high towers in Europe, now can we?"

Godolphin scoffed, rubbing at his thick beard. "You say that as if you haven't benefited from it. Remember, if it wasn't for me being your contact in the Society, none of this would be possible. And honestly, it's only because you and your brother have done good work for me in the past that I even considered this."

That much was true. Godolphin had used the services of Stefan and Octavius several times in the past to acquire information and merchandise where others didn't have the knowledge or ability to do so. Always through an intermediary, of course, the aristocrat would never have direct one-on-one contact like this before. Stefan knew who he was, and Marcus was aware that he knew. At this level, there were few identities that remained hidden. The webs of secrecy they all used for commerce were designed by the very same hands.

"We have a room set up for you. The meeting will be in a few hours. You should get some rest until then." Godolphin motioned to the end of the next hallway where a single door sat open, and outside of it, Dieter was waiting. "Oh, of course," Godolphin smirked, "you and Dieter had that little encounter in Bucharest."

Stefan glared at the man outside his room. "Yes. It amazes me how different the members of your little Boy's Club are. That man is not right in the head."

Godolphin took hold of Stefan's arm and pulled him close enough to whisper without being overheard. "He's not the same man who visited your cabin. He's been... enhanced, let's say. I wouldn't cross him. If Dieter was dangerous before, he's psychotically lethal now."

"What happened to him?"

"That's a long story…"

Godolphin did his best to explain to Stefan what Christopher Gallows had done to Dieter, as much as he could. Since that demonstration, Dieter exercised his newly found power in increasingly uncomfortable ways for the brotherhood. They were amid a power struggle within their own ranks and Gallows was using his pet monster project as an enforcer. No one dared to speak against any of his plans or suggestions for fear Dieter would be set loose on them like some rabid attack dog.

"I have to say I'm not all that comfortable staying in that room if he's been in there rifling through it," Stefan admitted.

"It should be safe enough." Godolphin took a step back and squared up to Stefan. "Look, if you find something off in there let me know and we'll find you somewhere else to sleep. But I think he just wants to talk to you, so I'll leave you to it."

Dieter waited for Stefan to get close enough before he spoke. "I thought you'd bring the girl."

Stefan turned his attention to the German Pitbull who was noticeably concealing his left hand in his coat. "The girl doesn't matter. But these…" he raised the briefcase containing the Black Grimoires, "…these books are all that matter right now."

The two stood just a few feet from one another, Stefan waiting for Dieter to clear the path into the room. Dieter casually slid off the doorframe and made way for Stefan to enter, watching him like a snake deciding if it wanted its next meal or not.

The room looked clean, but Stefan checked the lamps, desks, and bed for any listening devices. "If you have something to say little man now would be the time to say it."

Dieter pawed at the doorframe. "You don't have to worry about any of us spying on you. You've come through for us, so we will give you the benefit of the doubt. Normally, anyone not of the Society who made it this far into this place would be shown quite different quarters."

"I'm not a normal guest."

"I wonder, Herr Romano, what would have happened if I had been successful that day at your cabin. Would that mongrel have found the other books? Would we be standing here today having this conversation, or would your body be rotting in a shallow grave?"

Stefan opened and closed the drawers of the dresser, keeping his back to Dieter. "I don't take kindly to threats. I knew after you showed up that I needed to speak to someone. My brother and I have worked for Godolphin's people before. Once I knew what was going on, and how much information you didn't have that Kana did, it wasn't too hard to figure out what needed to happen."

Dieter sucked his teeth. "You still needed our help. Yoshi was quite useful to you dealing with the witch."

"Well, they didn't send you again... to fail."

Dieter's face turned bright red, his chest heaving, but he laughed at the insult. "It is of no matter. The girl is mine anyway. It is only a shame you didn't bring her with you. I could have saved myself the trip."

"There's no need to worry about her. She's irrelevant to this now."

"Oh?" Dieter leaned back against doorway to Stefan's room. "Perhaps you care about her more than you want to admit? Maybe it wasn't the Yakuza that kept you from shooting her?"

"Don't you have somewhere else to be?" Stefan barked.

That was enough for Dieter, his smile now genuine. "I will take my leave then. I do have other places to be right now. And you have a meeting in a few hours yourself."

There was no point in continuing this conversation. It was better to unpack now and tend to far more urgent matters. Dieter closed the door behind him, giving Stefan time alone to think about what he said.

***

Hours later, Stefan awoke and turned on the lamp next to his bed. The room had a rustic decor, from its hand-carved wooden chairs and dresser to the solid oak flooring, but it was still a box with concrete walls and fluorescent lighting—stark and hollow. In the far corner was an opening that led to the bathroom. It was suitable, an enclosed glass shower and sink, just enough for him to wash up from the day of travel.

After drying off Stefan sat on the bed, wrapped in his towel, and stared at the briefcase sitting on the dresser. Something about it felt off. A faint throbbing sound came from the Haliburton. He wondered if the grimoires sensed their sister nearby and wanted desperately to be reunited after so many centuries apart.

He got dressed, exercised for a half hour, and combed his hair before leaving the room. Feeling refreshed and ready to finish this job, he grabbed the briefcase and left his box of a room for a long overdue reunion.

What he didn't notice upon leaving the room was the scorched top of the wooden dresser where the briefcase sat while he slept. It left behind a darkened circle of smoldering embers burned into the wood.

Every corridor of The Hex was monitored by guards, each one eyeing Stefan as he made his way through the labyrinth until he reached his destination. Leaning against the white walls and under the bright lights was Christopher Gallows' lover, dressed in complete contrast to the décor in her dark grey pants suit, bright blonde hair bun, and blood red lipstick.

"Good morning," she said with as little cheer as a person could muster without being dead.

Stefan, seeing a beautiful woman, defaulted into charm-mode, extending his hand and flashing his dimples. "Hello, I'm Stefan. I don't believe we've met before."

"Hannah Schmidt."

She ignored his dimples and his smile, blankly staring at him. There was no desire or attraction here, this Nordic beauty was assessing him as a specimen. For what purpose—either as a threat or a recruit—Stefan couldn't guess. Ice in the middle of the Arctic had more warmth than what she was giving him.

He retracted his hand and straightened his posture. "How is he feeling?"

Hannah looked away from him as she unlocked the door. "You have one hour and then we will need to see you in Christopher's office. Please, do not be late."

She typed a code into the keypad on the wall and walked away, anchored by two guards, leaving Stefan to his visit. Inside the room was the reason for all of this—the lies, the betrayal, the murders—his brother Octavius.

The joy of this reunion was cut short when he saw his brother rambling to himself in a constant state of motion, scurrying around the room with his eyes wide, touching the padded white walls with his palm, retracting, and then scurrying to the opposite wall. Octavius had defaced them with scribblings drawn in crayon and chalk. The markings were so dense that it looked like the work of years instead of months. There were portions that were marked over many times, so much that the thickness of the chalk and crayon cast a small shadow. Other markings were extremely large, stretching from floor to ceiling. The colors of choice were red and black with a few strokes of blue and yellow used to highlight some areas and cross out others.

Stefan called out gently, almost afraid to interact with his brother. "I'm here, Octavius."

He still shuffled and mumbled, completely unaware that Stefan was standing in the doorway of the room.

Stefan spoke up. "Octavius?"

"...and the just will be seen. No, not seen! Punished. Punished! So, the righteous bleed on the floor. But if they don't accept, if they don't see, they won't be cleansed of their purity..." the ramblings continued from Octavius, his focus on his etchings.

"It's me! It's Stefan!"

"...Stefan..." Octavius stopped for a moment. He put his right hand on his face, his fingers gliding down the side of his cheek as he repeated his brother's name thrice. With a snap of his fingers, he shook his head and went back to his rambling, turning his back to Stefan as he feverishly continued his work on the wall.

Stefan's eyes watered. "What did you do, brother? What did you do?"

He wasn't going to cry. Not here. Not now. They had pushed the boundaries in the past when dealing with the dangerous relics of the underworld. Their swagger came from never succumbing to any entity or spell where others had faltered. For years they patted themselves on the back for being so clever, outsmarting ancient workings while reaping the rewards of their ingenuity. That luck had run out for Octavius. Dressed in an old pair of sweatpants and a ratty flannel shirt, neither of which had been washed for days, this was the fate that dealing with the Black Grimoires handed him. A once brilliant man, who had the world as his playground and the underworld as his bank account, now remanded to this jabbering lunatic, struggling to purge the overflow of information that burst at the seams of his mind.

"...and Stefan. Stefan! He will know. Yes, he will know. He can find them. He must find them! He..."

"I'm here, Octavius. I found them." Stefan put his hand on his brother's shoulder. For a moment he feared his brother would strike out at him for breaking his mental trance, but that didn't happen. Instead, Octavius who dropped the crayon from his hand and faced his brother.

Beneath the scruff of his beard, prematurely greying head of hair, and the marks on his face was Stefan's handsome brother. The man who taught him how to woo women, solve mysteries, fire a gun, and con a king, was still somewhere within.

"Stefan?" Octavius repeated, the syllables stretched as he spoke them. "Ste-fan?" He continued doubtfully, then repeated with revelation. "Stefan!"

"Yes, I'm here, Octavius."

"Stefan!"

As if woken from the trance, Octavius hugged his brother tightly. "You found them, you say?"

Stefan lifted the briefcase and placed it on the table in the middle of the room. Octavius went to place his hand on its silver casing but recoiled.

Stefan reassured him. "It's okay. It's safe."

Octavius wagged his finger. "Anything but safe, Stefan. I should never have... I should never have..." He was starting to slip.

"Hey, hold on there." Stefan rubbed his brother's shoulders. "You had a job and you finished it. I should have never walked away from it. I should never have walked away from you. But I'm here now."

"Stefan!" Octavius' face lit up again with a smile. "Open it. I want to see them."

Having exposed himself to one grimoire caused the unbridled mental chaos that decorated this room. Showing him the other two could be catastrophic. Stefan thought it best to limit the exposure.

"Just a quick peek." Stefan entered the combination and undid the latches. With reverence, he lifted the top of the briefcase and revealed the contents to his wild-eyed brother.

There they were, both in pristine condition as if the centuries couldn't weather them. The solid black leather, the intricately etched occult symbols, the geometric shapes decorated with archaic symbols and runes, the fruits of over a decade of research now made real. An unnatural heat emanated from both books, accompanied by a low pulsing hum.

Octavius observed them with delight at first, then confusion, and finally fear. He put his hands to his face and scratched away at his skin, screaming at the top of his lungs.

Stefan shut the briefcase and tended to his brother, rubbing his arms again. "I'm sorry, I'm sorry. I should have known better."

"They have me," Octavius whimpered. "They have me, Stefan. They won't let me go. They won't let me go!"

"Shh. This will all be over soon. I'm going to get you out of here and we'll work on getting you back to the way you were."

It was a good promise. For now, it calmed his brother but was easier said than done. The Thule Society traded in power and information, two things Octavius tried to barter with, and it broke him in the process. He'd have to tread carefully to not wind up the same way while also giving them what they wanted. There was also a lingering concern for what might be unleashed if he were to be successful. He doubted the world would end, but it would absolutely change with the grimoires in the hands of this group. He'd take the necessary precautions and find a haven for himself and his brother should the worst occur.

Octavius's fearful gaze flattened. "We have work to do."

"I have to handle some business first, Octavius."

"With them?" Octavius scoffed as he grabbed a crayon and then went back to his scribblings. It was as if his mind was a paused song that suddenly started playing again right where it had left off.

"I'm not afraid of them," Stefan said. "They need me to finish this. After that, we're getting out of here."

"Right." Octavius was too involved in his writing to care about his brother's plan. "Hurry back. We have much work to do."

Stefan left Octavius to his handiwork. It pained him to witness his once strong, fearless, and remarkably intelligent older brother reduced to a frightened child who couldn't control his thoughts or emotions. Part of him wanted to blame someone, even if it was himself, but that wasn't the truth. Octavius willingly took this job. Maybe if Stefan had stayed then he wouldn't be stuck in a cell babbling to himself. Then again, maybe they'd both be broken if he hadn't left. He'd never know for sure. What he did know was that it was up to him to fix this.

Stefan's next meeting was one he dreaded. Christopher Gallows was a member of The Thule Society he didn't know much about. In fact, he knew almost nothing about the man outside of his relationship with Hannah Schmidt. Whatever his background was remained a closely guarded secret, even within the underworld, where secrets were hard to maintain.

Gallows' office was a simple room with a desk, musty old books of the occult filling a wall of shelves, an antique globe, and a few potted plants. Stefan entered with some trepidation, not knowing quite what to expect from the upstart who sat behind his desk like a king on a throne.

"I guess we should just get down to business," Gallows staid. "There are a few questions I want to ask before you start working on the Black Grimoires." He motioned to the chair in front of his desk.

"About that..." Stefan squinted one eye and pointed to Gallows as he sat down. "What exactly is it that you want me to do with them? My brother is the expert so I'm not sure how much I can contribute."

Christopher laughed and leaned back in his chair. "Games, is it? Listen, so there is no confusion here, I am not a man who likes having his time wasted. I know the Society has been rather flaccid in using its strength for a generation now. Most of them squabble over money and territory as if it were some child's board game. That's not what I am about. I want the legacy of this Society to be restored. So, any stall tactics or negotiation efforts on your part will be wasted on me. I know you are as keen a mind as there is on the Black Grimoires, and much of your brother's knowledge came from your work, not the other way around."

The man had done his homework. It was a good attempt by Stefan to try and see how far he could get with Gallows, even if he saw right through the misdirection. For once, he'd have to play it straight. "My apologies then. What questions do you have for me?"

"That's better." Gallows grabbed a pen and tapped the end of it against the desk. "Right now, we are putting as much security as we can around this project. We're gathering workers from the nearby town as well. It'll take a day for us to get everything in place, but before that happens, I want to know what your price is." Stefan shifted in his seat, watching Christopher's pen tap the wooden desk. "Yes, you want freedom for your brother and immunity from the Society of course. But what is your greatest desire, Stefan? What is it that has driven you for all these years to dig into the earth and extract its secrets and riches? Is it financial gain?"

"It's always about financial gain."

"Yes, of course, but that's not what makes you excited when you are finding an artifact or solving a mystery or even putting a bullet in the head of an old woman." Stefan grimaced at the reference to his actions in Shinjuku. "Afterwards, you enjoy the money and the freedom it provides you. But in the heat of it all, I want to know what makes you thirsty."

What a curious choice of words, Stefan thought. *Thirsty.* He hadn't considered that the sensation he felt when working. A thrill, yes, there was the exhilaration of uncovering a lost relic or solving an ancient riddle. There was also the thrill of the violence that came along with his line of work. He didn't deny it. Why this mattered to Gallows puzzled him more.

"I would say that I like the challenge." Stefan compromised with this answer, not wanting to seem like a sadist. "Octavius and I didn't grow up with much in Italy, but we managed to make a good life for ourselves. A very good life. Our father was Scandinavian, and before he passed, he taught us much of what we knew. When we started working in the underworld there were many that doubted us. They called us Eurotrash and pretty boys playing at being Indiana Jones."

"And you proved them wrong?"

Stefan took a moment to consider the notion. "Yes, I'd say we did. Even these grimoires... for centuries no one even knew they existed. We did the work and made the discoveries, not some stuffed shirt at a university."

"Pride," Gallows muttered with a hint of contempt in his voice. "I'm not entirely surprised by that. A man like yourself who puts so much effort into his outward appearance would clearly be motivated by pride."

This won a laugh from Stefan. "And you are not?"

"Perhaps you could call it pride, but my goals are far deeper. I wondered if yours were as well. No matter. We can speak about compensation in detail now." Gallows tapped the end of the pen one last time and then opened a folder on his desk.

Stefan blinked a twice at how quickly Christopher had changed subjects as if the motivation of pride somehow cut off an avenue of opportunity. This felt more like a job interview than a negotiation. The moment had passed. "Six million U.S. dollars, safe passage to a country of our choosing at which point none of your people are to follow us. We'll know if they do. And neither I nor my brother will ever have dealings with you again."

"Is that all?"

"I can't see there being anything else."

"What about the girl?" Gallows looked up from the folder.

"What girl?"

"This Kana Cold I've heard so much about. It seems you two were... close."

Was he offering Kana as part of this deal or was he asking for her to be eliminated? While there were lingering ties between the two, Stefan knew that ship had sailed the moment he pointed a gun at her. As much as he admired her and delighted in their night together, Stefan had no illusions that there was a future between them outside of her smashing a fist against the side of his face.

"It was part of the game," he said. "She's a young girl. She helped me find the books. That's all."

"So, no feelings for this woman. I hear she's quite extraordinary, not only in looks but in personality, if you find those types of people attractive."

And here was the other part of The Thule Society that made Stefan's skin crawl. Their unabashed racial elitism didn't sit well with him. He was quite sure his olive skin, dark hair, and ethnic features didn't match up to their ideal either. "No. I mean, I have nothing against the girl but there is no affection either. Why do you ask?"

Christopher pushed the folder away, folding his hands together. "We intend to have her eliminated as I'm sure you can understand. She's a loose end. She and that partner of hers are too close to this situation. If she's as capable as I've been told, then that's a problem. Besides, Dieter has his own need to salvage his pride after being bested by an amateur. She was one of Granger's students?"

"One of the later ones. He told me about her some years ago. He said she had a gift for this line of work. I understand what he meant now. By the way, you didn't have anything to do with him…"

"If you're asking whether we killed him, the answer is no. We did not kill Professor Granger."

Stefan waited for more of an explanation, but none came. He tapped the sides of the chair with his fingers, arched his eyebrows, and stood to make his exit.

Christopher stopped him after a few steps. "We are about to embark on a great journey. I hope you know that. We'll keep your names from the history books of course, as you requested. But what we are doing here is going to change the world. Not in a big bang or some shift of the tides, but generations from now what is done here will be known within the most important of circles. I want to see it—this majestic power—that is what drives me. I want to know that it is real. You are making history, Stefan Romano."

Stefan opened the door to the office and stopped after hearing Gallows' words. He had no idea what they would unleash from the Black Grimoires or what power he was about to hand over to The Thule Society. The lot of them were insane. But he was too far along to turn back.

"History will forget my name. And so should you."

BREADCRUMBS

I t was well into the afternoon before Kana woke from her deep sleep. She wasn't in as much pain as earlier in the day, but she still felt like crap. Beside her on a chair was a glass of rum, just as she had requested, and without hesitation, she gulped down a mouthful. The warmth of the shot ran through her body, perking up her spirits instantly.

Her dreams had been filled with unwanted memories, everything from childhood that she tucked away in a corner of her mind to embarrassing moments in her teenage years to the betrayal by Stefan that nearly ended her life. The time for dreaming was over. She needed to find him.

Kana burst through the doors of the office. "Anastasia!"

She didn't have to look far. Anastasia was working on her laptop in the nearby lounge, casually typing away on her keyboard with her long legs looped over the edge of a reclining chair. "I'm glad to see you finally decided to wake up. It's almost 3 o'clock in the afternoon. We need to pack up soon. The Yakuza are organizing, and it won't take them too long to find you here."

"Can you tell me what happened last night. I know, we need to go, but I need to know how I got from the street to here."

Anastasia closed the laptop and sat up properly in the chair. "I might get an actual thank you this time?" Kana's wrinkled forehead told her otherwise. "The police found you on the street unconscious. About three thousand people saw you in that bright red dress—who picked that thing out for you by the way? —buzzing through the streets on a motorcycle with Yakuza shooting at you all over Shinjuku. The Japanese tend to frown on things like that, Kana."

"Yes mom," Kana said. "But why didn't they lock me up?"

"They did. Fortunately, for you, I have contacts in Tokyo who are influential. Before the Yakuza started sniffing around, I had them release you to me. We brought you back here and patched you up."

"What happened to Stefan? Do you know where he is?"

Anastasia turned her attention back to the laptop. "No, I don't."

Kana left Anastasia to search the building, opening closed doors to the smaller offices, peaking into cubicles, and even entering the men's bathroom. "Where is AJ?" she asked, approaching Anastasia again. "I could have sworn I heard his voice last night."

"You did. He sat by your side for a few hours. It's because of him we even knew that you were in trouble. We rescued him too. Stefan set him up at that fancy condo to be killed. If we hadn't arrived and picked him up off the street there's no telling what would have happened to him. I told you not to get him involved."

Kana's upper lip curled. "So, wait you've been watching us this entire time?"

"It's something you're going to have to get used to." The way she said this was like a mother teaching her daughter a lesson. "If you're going to be in this business, you're going to have to know people are always watching you. And the more of a name you make for yourself in the underworld, the more eyeballs are going to be following you. Be thankful they were mine and not someone else's. You've kicked up a lot of dust here in Japan. I'd not come back here for some time if I were you."

"Whatever. Where is AJ now? Why isn't he here?"

Anastasia slunk down in her chair. "He got a dose of macho in him and stormed off after Stefan. He thought the trail would go cold if he didn't, or something like that, so he asked for money and some equipment and took off."

Kana's eyes widened. "He took off?"

"Mm hmm."

"After Stefan."

"Mm hmm."

"And you just let him go? You didn't try to stop him or anything?"

With a groan, Anastasia closed her laptop. "Listen, AJ made his mind up. I told him it wasn't a good idea, but he can be...

convincing when he wants to be. I've never seen him like that before. But I don't think he went out of here for a fight. I think he went after Stefan to make sure he didn't disappear."

"Have you heard from him?"

Anastasia checked her watch. "Not for a few hours, no. He's communicating on backchannels anyway, so I can't call him."

Kana slapped her hands against her thighs. "Well, that's just great. There's one problem with this genius plan you two cooked up: we have no way of finding AJ unless he happens to call us. What if he's in trouble?"

"Again, this wasn't my idea, Kana. I've done quite a bit to help you two out, so if you could drop your attitude for just a minute, maybe you'd see that I'm not the enemy here."

She was right. Kana was letting her emotions make her act like a bratty child who was looking for anyone else to place blame on to distract from their own failures. For AJ's sake, she'd shelve her usual attitude and try to work with another human being for a change. "I'm sorry." The words were like razorblades as they slipped past her lips. "Can you tell me what he said to you the last time you heard from him?"

"It was very short. He's heading to Europe. That's about all that I got out of him. Then he said *tell her I have it.*" Anastasia puffed out her right cheek. "I really do hate the pronoun game."

"The what?"

"The pronoun game: when people use pronouns instead of just telling you what the hell they're talking about. Tell *who* I have *what*? What is *it*? Anyway, I'm assuming he means you. So, yeah, he has *it*."

This really wasn't the time for puzzles. Kana was surprised because AJ never had a fondness for them either.

She went to the kitchen to get another drink, non-alcoholic this time, and snatched a bottle of water from the refrigerator. The aggravation was getting to her again and she slammed the bottle down on the countertop, splashing droplets of water on her chest and neck. "Great," she muttered. As she wiped the water from her neck, she realized that her necklace was missing. She paused for a moment, wiping her neck slower and slower, until she realized what *it* meant.

"The damn necklace." She rushed out of the kitchen back to Anastasia. "You're a computer wizard, right?"

"Uh, I'm okay. Why, what's going on—?"

"Just see if you can—"

"Oh, we're back to Rude Kana that quickly?"

She was really pushing it. Again, Kana bit her lip, took a deep breath, and found a better way to ask the question. "Anastasia, it would be nice if you could help me look at something with your computer."

Anastasia beamed. "Now, how hard was that? What do you need?"

"It's my necklace. AJ took it before he left."

"I see."

"I used to lose the damn thing all the time and he put a tracker on it a while back. It has a camera on it too. I'm not sure what the range is, but you said he was in Europe, so that's something to go on."

"And I assume the tracker software is on the phone that you left at the condo. Well, I can't do anything with that here right now, but we can put something together."

On the other side of the office, Anastasia noticed her bodyguards peering out of the windows and whispering to one another. Even though she didn't want to jump to conclusions it was better to be cautious than careless.

"Get whatever you need from the back. I think we've worn out our welcome at my dad's shop," she said.

One of the bodyguards warned her that one of the Yakuza's spies were seen passing back and forth outside the building. They weren't in any immediate danger, but they didn't want to take any chances. Anastasia's connections in Tokyo wouldn't matter if the Yakuza decided to put her in their crosshairs along with Kana. The other issue would be the police, who were none too kind to gun violence in the country, let alone have a foreigner at the center of it. Anastasia's father had pull, but not *that* much pull. It was time to leave.

***

Anastasia's team ducked out the back of the office into the alley. They took different cars and different routes, keeping as low a profile as possible as they traveled through Tokyo to Haneda International Airport. During the drive, the radio played a news report on Kana's exploits from the night before. The worst moment came when they passed by a large video screen that displayed footage of the chase. Kana wanted to hide as she watched the footage, not because of the violence or the lawlessness, but the infamous red dress did not cover her backside, a fact now supersized for all of Japan to see. At least Anastasia and her bodyguards didn't make a big deal about her embarrassment, although Kana thought she heard one of them utter the words "nice ass" under their breath. That sealed it: never again in her life would she wear a dress.

One thing Kana did appreciate and wouldn't mind taking advantage of again in the future was the extensive network that Anastasia had at her disposal. Much of that was probably due to her father's wealth, but it still required Anastasia to have the wherewithal to know who to contact and exactly what to say to them. The team of bodyguards that were loyal to her, the tech team she was in constant contact with over the phone, and even the private jet and its pilot were employees of hers, not her father. At some point, Kana would pick Anastasia's brain on how in just a few years she managed it all.

"Here," Anastasia yelled to Kana over the roar the jet's engine, "this phone is encrypted and amplifies the tracker for your necklace. No one can crack that. At least that's what they tell me. There's no video though, so either the camera is broken or he's covering it up. But that should be enough for you to find AJ."

Kana turned on the device to see a digitized map of Europe, a flashing red circle, and the route they needed to take. The circle, representing AJ's location, was moving at great speed across the map, suggesting that he was also on a plane.

"You only get three phone calls from that thing so make them count," Anastasia said.

"I thought you'd be coming too."

"Believe it or not Kana I have my own disasters to attend to. But AJ is a good man and I don't want anything bad to happen to him. You should appreciate him a bit more. He's really devoted to you—"

"All right, I get it. Not really the time for a lecture, Anastasia."

The blonde pouted. "I know you guys are partners just... well, anyway, you need to get going. You've got enough fuel to last for a trip to Europe and then some. Pratt is the best pilot I know." She winked and waved to the cockpit. "You're in good hands."

"Right." Kana paused before boarding the jet. "Anastasia, thank you."

This time it was genuine. Anastasia waved in return before her caravan of cars sped off to catch their own flight.

It was a ten-hour flight from Tokyo to Europe. After introducing herself to the pilot, Kana took a seat in the back of the private jet. The liftoff was rough, but once they made it off the island it was a smooth ride over the Yellow Sea and into Chinese airspace. Kana took this time to survey the well-stocked armory at the back of the plane as the well-stocked mini bar next to it.

Tempting as it was, she decided not to drink anymore until this was over. There was no telling what danger AJ was getting himself into. She needed to be clear headed. Her injuries were nagging, the bandage on her leg needed to be changed, and her shoulder still ached. After applying a fresh bandage to her leg, she told Pratt the pilot to inform her when they were near the tracking signal and then settled into a pullout bed in the back of the jet to rest while she still could.

BREAKTHROUGH

A full day had passed since Stefan's meeting with Christopher Gallows and little progress had been made deciphering the Black Grimoires. Fear was the culprit behind the delay. Stefan procrastinated for most of the morning and used the afternoon tending to his brother. He spent a total of one hour investigating the books and in that short amount of time he regretted it. The more he interacted with them, the more changes he felt in his body: his tongue became oily, his scalp itched, his stomach felt as if there was a worm inside trying to get out. Any progress he made was stifled to the point Stefan believed the books were actively working against him, denying him their secrets.

Also weighing on him was his brother's continued mental deterioration. Octavius's condition was deteriorating rapidly which Stefan presumed was because of his proximity to the three grimoires. Between that, and the growing unrest he sensed from The Thule Society who regularly checked in on him with demands for an update on his progress, the pressure was mounting to find a solution.

The problem was he didn't know what he was supposed to find. Having the Black Grimoires together didn't reveal anything, there were no secrets in the binding of the books or pages numbers, the languages used were from several different cultures, a few he didn't even recognize. What he could decipher from the tenebrous pages was random. One page would contain spells for wealth while the next listed half completed equations. It became clear why diving so deep into one of these books bedeviled his brother's mind. Trying to decipher a pattern from all three was madness. As the strange sensations continued throughout his body, he worried something far worse was in store for him if he continued.

In the early evening Stefan returned to his room for a break. Dieter came knocking on his door five minutes after he sat down, the sixth Thule Society member to do so in the last few hours. Stefan opened the door and frowned as he saw the small man on the other side.

Dieter leaned against the side of the door, his favorite position apparently, stroking his chin with his natural hand. "I won't make this any longer than it has to be. You have eight hours Ital. Eight hours to finish your work."

"That's insane. Look, it took years for us to do any significant research on this subject and you want me to crack whatever code, if there is one, in a day or two? I wonder if you aristocrats have any idea what real research is."

"It does not matter. Gallows is growing impatient. To be honest, I also grow impatient."

"Well, he might have to wait a little longer. I'm not any closer to figuring this out than I was yesterday. It might take weeks, months even."

"You don't have that kind of time." Stefan turned his back on Dieter. "Your brother has less."

If it wouldn't mean his certain death, Stefan would have attacked the little imperialist right there and then. He took two steps forward but stopped, noticing Dieter's hand still nestled in his inner coat pocket. "Don't threaten my brother. You've already done enough to him."

"There's nothing we've done to him that he has not done to himself. Those are the conditions."

Stefan balled his fist, waving it at Dieter. "If you harm him then Gallows doesn't get anything from me."

"If you don't produce then we will harm him. Kind of a chicken-and-the-egg situation for you now isn't it? No more wasted time though. You have eight hours. You will not be warned again."

Dieter slammed the door shut. Frustrated, Stefan hurled his dinner tray at the door and screamed. The pressure weighed so heavily that he could feel his mind closing in on itself. Was that anger really his or were the grimoires playing with his mind? He had no way of knowing which only compounded his agony.

Nothing would be accomplished in this room. He'd have to take the books to his brother. Something was missing, and he'd have to risk it to get answers, and maybe Octavius's madness was the key.

Stefan returned to his brother's cell and slammed the books on the table, a wave of heat exploding from them. Octavius observed, for the first time, the complete set of grimoires with a mix of fear and excitement. His face shifted several times between a toothy smile to a trembling frown.

"Don't be scared, Octavius," Stefan said. "I need your help with this. I didn't want to involve you, but we are running out of time. Do you understand?"

Octavius appeared in control for the time being, although his words were slurred. "Time. Yes, there isn't much left. I'm working on it, little brother. I'm working on it."

"I know but..."

What was there to ask? For months Octavius had been scribbling on the walls of this cell and was no closer to finding a solution than Stefan had been in just a day. The Thule Society expected too much. This was a fool's errand.

"I can see it." Octavius broke out into a babbling sing-song as he scribbled on the walls with a crayon. "One. Two. Link them together. How is it? Where is it? Three. Four. Fold them together. I can see it? Not all of it?"

Stefan dragged his palms down his face. "I don't know what you mean. We have to find something."

Another hour went by and neither Octavius's scribblings nor Stefan's reading of the books uncovered answers. Page after page he flipped, through all three books, in desperation to see anything beyond simple spells and minor enhancements, none of which spoke to the *majestic power* that Christopher Gallows was in search of.

Stefan needed another break. Fifteen minutes is all he asked for, just enough to clear his head. Maybe the guards would be helpful and get him something to drink.

On his way to the cell door the revelation struck him like a lightning bolt from the sky. He hadn't noticed it before, and perhaps this was just a coincidence, but the wall with the door to the room was untouched by his brother's writings. Not a mark could be found, even though the adjacent walls were filled right up to the crease.

"Wait a minute." He stepped back into the middle of the room, turning on his heel as he scanned the other three walls, his finger pointing to each. Octavius was reproducing every word, symbol, and glyph of the grimoires faithfully. Three walls. Three books. Damn his fatigue, there was something here. He yelled for the guards to bring him water, not wanting to break this thread he was pulling, so close to an answer. "Three."

His brother heard him. "Yes! That's it. Three. Our dimension. It's connected. I can see it, Stefan! I can almost see it!"

"Three," Stefan repeated.

One of the guards entered the room with a cup of water in his hand. His eyes widened as he witnessed, for the first time, the insanity of Octavius' artwork. Stefan dismissed him with a wave of his hand which the young guard was happy to oblige.

"Three." Stefan went to the books once again and looked over their covers. Only now did the strange shapes look different to him. They weren't shapes at all, but fragments of shapes, broken into three. He stuck his open palm out. "Can I use one of your crayons, Octavius?"

"Yes. Here."

Could it be? With growing confidence, Stefan went to one of the symbols on the wall, a half circle with the dash of a line through its middle. He turned to the books and then looked again at the other two walls. There it was! He filled in the symbol using the corresponding fragments on the other walls, confirming his suspicion by completing those as well.

"Well, I'll be damned. No wonder why you couldn't finish it, Octavius. It's broken into pieces, and you knew that. You tried to put them together but without the other two books, it just confused you. They do connect."

In a moment of clarity, Octavius put his hands on his brother's shoulders. "I can see it now."

An hour later, Stefan sent for Christopher Gallows to meet him in the cell. He managed to beat the clock. This was his time to have some control over the situation and he'd relish in holding court over these smug, self-styled master of the universe.

Christopher Gallows led the brotherhood, flanked by his beloved Hannah. Marcus Godolphin, Timothy Luckless, and Dieter Schneider. Many of them had never seen the inside of Octavius's room. Godolphin and Luckless turned their noses up at the chaos on the walls. It was nothing new to Gallows. He crossed his hands in front of him and stared Stefan down as if to say "show me something".

"We figured it out." Stefan waved them over to the table where the three grimoires lay open.

"I certainly hope so." Gallows picked up a crayon and tossed it aside. "Show us what you have found."

Secondary to his passion for manipulation, Stefan found great joy in teaching. Although his students today were vile and corrupt sociopaths, they could still be taught a lesson. He bounced between the three walls, pointing to the various drawings his brother created while Octavius sat quietly on the floor in the center of the room, rocking back and forth.

"Octavius has been drawing these pictures for months now. At first, it looks like gibberish. He was trying to decode all the symbols using the Vatican codex, but it only took him so far. It wasn't the *complete* codex."

"Complete codex?" asked Luckless.

"Yes. You see, the grimoires on the surface have spells and incantations of course. Most of them are simple spells for trivial things. You can cast a spell for luck or conjure a few minor demons who can cause mischief, but nothing like the *majestic power* Gallows wanted." Christopher thumbed his nose at his line being thrown back at him. "That's because it's real language isn't on the surface." Stefan went back to one of the symbols on the wall. "Each book has pages and pages of runes, right? But they're all incomplete. Or should I say, they're a *third* complete? If you take the same pages—especially the book covers—and match the text, runes, and symbols across all three you get the completed book. Octavius was close but needed the other two grimoires to complete it. Unfortunately, he used one of the spells to try and gain greater knowledge and it turned him mad."

As Stefan continued his seminar, Gallows felt compelled to touch the walls with his bare hands. He traced the lines with his fingers and then looked at the other three walls. The menagerie of madness had an elegance to it, a beauty behind the chaos. "This is fascinating. I imagine it will take some time to translate this into one book?"

Stefan shined a smile and waved the group back to the table. "That's the other part. Honorius was a mathematician. The symbols on the covers form an equation. It's like nothing I've ever seen before."

"So?" asked Dieter.

Stefan turned his back to Dieter, facing the rest of the brotherhood. "So, this text is not from this dimension, but it was written *for* this dimension. The three books represent the three dimensions of our reality. When you put them together..."

Stefan took one of the tomes and gently placed it on top of another. A searing heat radiated from the books forcing Stefan to let go quickly as if he was dropping meat into a steaming pot. The top book merged with the bottom one, the text of this combined grimoire morphing into an entirely different language.

"Dear God," Godolphin said.

Stefan rubbed his hands together as they cooled. "Not God. We're working with the other guy here."

Luckless squinted at the pages. "What language is that?"

Stefan put his hands on his hips. "I'm not quite sure. It may be Hebrew, but an older version of it."

Luckless recoiled from the book. "Hebrew? As in the Jews?"

"What does it say?" Godolphin asked.

"Again, it's only a fragment. I'd have to add the third book to get the full script. I thought I should wait to do that after you saw this."

The rest of the brotherhood looked to Gallows who stood puzzled over the books, tapping his pen on the table. "He was right to not complete the set here. This isn't the place for that. But we have prepared such a place. Dieter, tell our men to ready The Reliquary and set up our security. We will finish this tonight."

Dieter left the cell to complete Gallows' request while the other Society members debated how this discovery would change everything. Godolphin voiced his reservations about moving forward. Stefan's claim that this wasn't the work of God but of Lucifer caused him concern, a warning that was shot down by the rest of the group. To them, demons and angels were one in the same, beings from other dimensions meant to serve them, not to be feared. The Black Grimoires were a form of control and would be used as such.

Stefan pulled Gallows aside from the group with a question of his own. "Not to be too pushy," he said, "but how soon will it be before I can take Octavius out of here? I've convinced him to meditate, and it seems to have calmed him down, but he needs help."

Gallows put his hand on Stefan's shoulder. "You can't leave now." The man's grip was unnaturally strong, sending pins and needles through Stefan's arm. "You need to complete the ceremony and merge the Black Grimoires. You are the man making history, remember? Once the task is done you can leave. You have my word."

Gallows let go of Stefan's shoulder and escorted Hannah out of the cell. Stefan rubbed his neck and arm as he watched The

Thule Society leave, Luckless and Godolphin still debating as the door closed behind them. He knew they didn't trust him and were smart not to. Too smart.

"He might be right, brother." Octavius picked up the crayon Gallows discarded on the floor earlier. "You might not have a choice."

THE NECKLACE

The red dot on the tracker stopped in Germany near a densely wooded area south of Weipelsdorf; a small town not known for anything extraordinary. From the map of the area, AJ was somewhere deep in the woods, miles from any major road, which either meant he found some secret base or that's where his body had been dumped.

Evening was approaching as the jet entered German airspace which meant she'd have to find him, in the middle of the woods, at night. Kana sought advice from the pilot, Pratt, and his co-pilot, Santiago, who spent most of the trip exchanging cheesy jokes and debating American Football. Pratt, from the north, was an ardent New England Patriots fan and even resembled their famous coach in his look: stocky, weathered, and plain. In contrast was Santiago who came from the southern United States and was a diehard fan of the Miami Dolphins despite their lack of championship history. Kana had no interest in their debates over football, but they did have much to tell her about Germany.

"I know this guy, Roscoe," Pratt said as Kana gathered her supplies before leaving the jet.

"Roscoe?" Kana wrinkled her nose. "That's not the name I expected to hear in Germany."

"He's a transplant, moved here six years ago. Not a chatty fellow, that's for sure. He'll take you where you need to go though."

"I've got to go deep into the woods. Can he handle that?"

Pratt nodded to one of the windows. "I'm sure he will."

A small, unassuming beige car rolled quietly across the tarmac to the jet. Pratt waved at the driver who didn't acknowledge him at all. Instead, he waved Kana over to the car, the engine humming.

"Are you sure this guy is okay?" she asked Pratt.

Santiago looked back at her over his shoulder from the co-pilot seat. "He's harmless. He's ugly. Not as ugly as Pratt here, but he's safe."

Pratt aggressively patted Santiago on the shoulder. "Yeah, I'm ugly. Your sister doesn't think so."

"Okay, I'll leave you two whatever this is about. I guess I'll go meet my driver." Kana pushed the door open and lifted her backpack over her shoulders, sliding her arms through the straps.

"Don't forget this." Pratt handed Kana a satellite phone. "If you find him, and need a fast getaway, call us."

Kana thanked him for the phone and continued to the car. Once she was safely in the backseat, they were off, leaving the backside of the airport and toward the rural areas of Germany. Pratt's description of Roscoe was accurate, he didn't speak a word the entire trip, communicating only in grunts and nods. Kana didn't mind. It was time to focus on the task at hand. She was walking into the unknown on what very well could be a one-way trip.

Roscoe pushed the car as far as it could go down the dirt roads of the forest. He stopped a few miles away from the location on the tracker and dropped Kana off along the roadside. She paid him and made her way into the brush, disappearing into the overgrowth.

Dress in black from head to toe would help conceal her from any guards patrolling the area. It wouldn't keep her from being picked up by any sophisticated security system, which an organization like The Thule Society would have hidden throughout the woods, but it would have to do.

"Oh, I see you," she whispered to herself, spotting the lenses in the canopy. The trees ahead were full of cameras pointing in all directions to capture every square inch of land. Even worse, there were tripwires hidden in the carpet of the forest, covered in moss and leaves, disguised as sticks and twigs.

"Let's see how this works." Kana activated an electronic disruptor, a small and expensive gadget she procured from the back of Anastasia's jet. It worked, the three cameras up ahead switched off and the trip wires were disabled. The coast was clear from there. "I might have to thank Anastasia... again."

As she got closer to the location of the red dot, she saw a clearing beyond the trees ahead that led to a sloping hill, covered in moss and overgrowth with a dual road leading up to a lonely cabin at its summit. The tracker signal didn't point to the building but to a location east of it, near the bottom of the hill. Kana crouched down beneath the overgrowth and fog of the forest floor, crawling toward the signal.

Her mind raced with possibilities. Either this meant AJ was dead and they threw his body in some ditch, or he was locked up in a prison, which presented its own set of challenges. Kana wiped those thoughts from her mind. There was no use speculating until she found her friend, alive or dead.

It was only a few hundred yards away now and Kana's heart skipped a beat when she found a storm drain. A large metal grading had been carved into the side of the hill, the runoff from the building flowed out into a stream that cut through the forest floor, snaking its way further off to the east. Kana prepared herself for the worst. When she reached the drain, she found no bodies, no skeletons, no pile of carcasses. The tracker signal ended here, a dead end.

"Damn." She double-checked the device, hoping for more information.

The forest was alive with life—chirping crickets, croaking frogs, the rustling of leaves in the trees above—but nothing human. She searched the area, squinting to see anything out of place or a sign AJ may have left behind. Sure enough, a few feet from the drain was a door intentionally hidden by moss and vines. Beneath the overgrowth something twinkled as it caught the sunlight. She approached slowly, then hurriedly, recognizing the source of the sparkle: her necklace, dangling from the handle of the door.

Kana drew her gun and retrieved the necklace, pocketing it, and turned the handle. The door was unlocked. "Good job, AJ," she whispered. The rusty hinge creaked as she gently pushed the door open and entered. The dimly lit tunnel was empty, droplets of water rhythmically splashing onto the concrete floor. Some of the forest wildlife had slipped inside, spiders hanging their webs on the ceiling and walls, worms and frogs scattering across the floor as she invaded their space. Moss coated the corners of the tunnel, the roots of trees pushed through the ceiling.

Kana put her weapon away and shut the door behind her. This would likely be her only escape route, so she memorized every twist and turn she took through the maze of tunnels.

**

Deep inside the facility under the hill, Dieter stood on a metal platform looking over a loading dock filled with young men running loading crates of equipment into a dozen trucks. Why they needed this equipment Dieter had no idea, but he enjoyed looking down on all these workers.

In case anyone didn't know who was in charge he barked out orders over the bustle. "Come on! We don't have time to waste! Move it!"

One boy tripped over his own feet and tumbled onto the cold concrete, the box he was carrying spilling its contents. No one stopped to help him, fearful of drawing the ire of the already abusive German who stood at the top of a metal staircase screaming as if he was the Fuhrer revisited.

"You there!" Dieter yelled at the boy. "Pick up that mess and get it on the trucks! *Schnell!*"

The young man wasn't moving fast enough for Dieter who marched down the metal ramp to the warehouse floor. The short tyrant smacked him on the back of the head with his normal hand, keeping his deformity hidden, more out of perverse pleasure than an attempt to motivate. The boy took it and, nearly in tears, scrambled as best he could to gather everything that had fallen out of the box.

"Wait a minute. Don't I know you?" Dieter said. At this point, he had only seen the back of the boy's head. Something about him was familiar though. "Stand up!" he instructed.

The boy stood and straightened his clothes. His features were hard to see in the low light under his baseball cap, even this close. Dieter demanded that he stand up straight and push his chin up so his face could be observed.

Ah, there it is. Dieter sneered at the boy. "I thought so. Didn't you show up during recruitment last night in town?"

"Yes sir."

"And weren't you rejected?"

"Yes sir."

Dieter didn't know which angered him more; the fact the kid disobeyed him, his clumsiness, or that the guards were so relaxed that they let this boy inside the facility to begin with. "I should throw you out of here. Why are you so determined to be here?"

The kid wiped away the sweat from his brow, stuttering terribly. "I... I have heard things..."

"What have you heard?"

"That... there was magic here. I just... I just wanted to see. I'm sorry."

Dieter looked the boy up and down, trying to decide whether he wanted this child to stay. The ceremony was scheduled an hour from now which didn't give him enough time to replace the boy and they needed all the help they could get loading the trucks.

"Pick this mess up." Dieter kicked a piece of broken wood and walked back up the ramp.

As the teen desperately tried to gather the spilled materials, Dieter looked around at the rest of the young men loading the truck. He couldn't help but wonder if this child could enter the facility because security had been so pitiful, could there be other unwanted guests? There were too many in the loading dock moving too fast for him to pick out anyone that looked suspicious. Part of him wanted there to be an intruder— someone he could test out his new abilities on. The chances though were slim. Convinced of this, he ordered the guards to keep an eye on the workers and bellowed out to them that any more mistakes would not be tolerated before taking his leave.

From the back of the room, with his hat pulled over his face, AJ lifted boxes into the last truck in the line, the farthest away from Dieter and his tyrannical show of authority. To the other young men working in the loading dock he was just another poor German they picked up from the pubs.

After the final box was loaded, AJ hopped in to the back of the truck. He kept his head down and his mouth shut as they caravan left the loading area. He hoped Kana and Anastasia found the tracking signal and were on their way with an army. If not, he'd be found out sooner or later, and at that point, it would be up to him to stop this madness before it went too far.

THE BLACK GRIMOIRES

T he procession of bodies under the full moon of the forest cast long shadows on the ground from The Hex deeper into the darkness. A line of robed bodies made up the front, their silhouettes passing between the thin trunks of the trees, the headlights of trucks behind them lighting the path.

The Reliquary had gone by many names over the decades since The Thule Society purchased the land. In the 30s and 40s, it resembled more of a temple, modest in size but elegant in its design. Following World War II, the structure was overtaken by a rebellious group within Germany, opposed to the SS and by extension the Society, who organized a razing of the temple shortly thereafter. Led by an ardent Protestant who spread rumors—real or imagined—about the temple's satanic history, he and a few dozen God-fearing Christians marched to the building and burned it down to its skeleton. Through the decades that followed, as The Thule Society reconstituted itself, the building remained in ruin, a painful reminder of the failures of the past. Even today the weathered remnants of the former temple wore scorch marks.

The procession entered the clearing at a methodical, ritualistic pace. The Reliquary was an area about thirty square yards in size, surrounded by strong evergreens on all sides. Standing erect in the middle of this rubble was an altar, flanked by the only two remaining columns of the original structure shooting skyward. The Thule Society formed a circle around the altar while Dieter instructed the workers to unload the trucks and assemble what was needed for the ceremony.

Stefan and Octavius were slow to enter. The sight of these cloaked figures forming a ritualistic circle chilled Stefan to the bone, and in contrast, a heat radiated from the briefcase, the books aroused as he neared the altar.

"I promise you we are going to get out of here safe brother," Stefan whispered to Octavius.

For whatever reason, supernatural or physiological, Octavius had been silent the entire trip from the underground facility to The Reliquary. He placed his hand on Stefan's shoulder as a sign that he understood. As they reached the center of the clearing he stopped, leaving his brother to stand at the altar alone.

He managed one word. "Okay."

Christopher Gallows and Marcus Godolphin were in the middle of their own private discussion. Godolphin kept his voice low. "I'm rather uncomfortable doing this out in the open and in such a rush. It might have been better to study this a bit more."

"Why?" Gallows stood stiff, his lips curling with every word. "Are you scared, Marcus? This is our birthright. You of all should know that our bloodlines were selected for such a night. Our fathers and their fathers held many a night like this one. Don't be afraid of destiny."

"I'm not sure this is destiny."

"Then don't fear eventuality because this is going to happen." Gallows jabbed his finger toward the altar as he spoke. "I realize you are scared, but you will see the power we are about to gain and should have had all this time. When this night is over, you will understand who we are... who we are meant to be."

Godolphin wasn't so sure about that, but he knew it was pointless to argue. Gallows had expertly seized control of the Society, his sentiments shared by the others who either worshiped him like Dieter did, desired to see his vision realized like Schmidt, or simply feared him like Andreas. Holding his tongue was the best option. No more was spoken on the matter. He'd watch like the rest and see if all of Gallows' eccentric desires would be realized.

Christopher placed his hands on the altar's rocky surface, the stone here stained by years of soot and rainwater. There were no words spoken, no grand proclamations of a new era about to dawn or the rise of the Society to its proper place at the head of mankind. Theatrics were not necessary here. Stefan placed the three grimoires, side by side, on the altar. Gallows reclaimed his spot in the circle and watched as the ritual began.

***

Kana chose an alternative path to The Reliquary, following the trail of the Society long enough to see their destination and disappear into the brush without being seen. She found a perch just south of old church. From here, she had an unobstructed view of the altar and a face she hadn't seen since Shinjuku, Stefan.

She remembered his lessons: how to aim, how to hold a gun, when to pull the trigger, every step by step instruction flowed through her mind as she lined up her target, aiming directly at his head. The crosshairs found their mark right between his eyes. She hyperventilated, breathing loudly through her nose and her finger slipped off the trigger. She had slept with this man, kissed his lips, rested her head in the crook of his arm. Happy memories. Memories she didn't want now. She could be just as cunning as he was. The last laugh would be hers.

Just pull the damn trigger.

She gasped, her lungs hurting as she pulled away from the gun sights. It should have been easy, with all the justification she had, killing Stefan was well within her rights. The thought of putting a hole through his head sickened her.

But she had to.

Once again, she turned toward the clearing and aimed her weapon. He was speaking now, reading from the Black Grimoires to the robed figures surrounding him. No more excuses. It had to be now.

She heard heavy breathing behind her. "Fraulein, I must admit I'm impressed." Her stalker had the upper hand and knocked the gun away while simultaneously grabbing her by the throat. It was Dieter, a face she knew she'd see again. He was stronger than before. His hand was like a steel trap, squeezing her windpipe, as he hoisted her off her feet.

"I'd love to kill the bastard myself, but they think he's valuable." The torchlights from The Reliquary and the glow from the full moon cast his face in a clash of reds and blues. "But you..." He turned back to her. "You owe me. It will not be quick, it will not be painless. You need to learn your place. Then, we will be even."

***

When translated in three dimensions, the covers from the three grimoires detailed the ritual that was required to merge them together. Stefan wasn't entirely confident in his translation of Old Hebrew, a version of the language he wasn't familiar with. He'd have to do his best, there was no time, he had to read it.

A hellish heat rose from each book as he opened them, flipping to specific pages detailed in the instructions. With the first part done, and under the watchful eye of Christopher Gallows, Stefan lifted the first book and lined it up with the middle one. The books hummed, the frequency low enough to cause the floor to shake.

Stefan backed away from the altar, his hands singed by the heat as the two books melted into one. Ink slid across the page as if it were fresh, rearranging the symbols on its own.

The torrid heat extended well beyond the altar. The workers murmured, the soldiers clenched their guns tight, even Andreas and Luckless inched away.

Gallows stepped toward Stefan. "Finish the ceremony."

Drenched in his own perspiration, Stefan pushed through the heat and back to the altar. There was no relief. His ears throbbed and his skin cooked. He took hold of the third and final grimoire, read the Hebrew passage, and lifted it into the air. Gunfire crackled through the trees beyond The Reliquary. Stefan dropped the grimoire and backed away.

"Someone's out there in the forest. Over there!" Luckless waved the soldiers to the east.

Godolphin had a clear line of sight to the source. "It's Dieter and some girl."

Stefan squinted, speaking a name he never thought he would again. "Kana."

Gallows slammed his hand against the alter. "Finish the ceremony."

An eruption of gunfire surrounded them. The witnesses of the ceremony ducked, their hands going to their ears as the cracks and pops echoed in the forest beyond. Godolphin and Luckless ordered the guards to head into the woods and find out who was attacking them. They were sitting ducks out in the open with only the broken beams and bricks of The Reliquary offering protection.

"The girl has help!" Luckless yelled. "They're all around us!"

Some of the workers ran off, they were here for the money and not to be shot at. Panic spread as the retreat was disorganized, hired help bumping into troops who were under assault by forces hiding in the woods. One worker wasn't fleeing, in fact, he walked directly to the altar. He shed his baseball cap and denim jacket, put on a pair of thick gloves, and grabbed one of the grimoires.

Stefan's jaw dropped. "AJ!"

The guards soon discovered the shots in the woods were coming from their own weapons, configured to discharge and cause confusion. A few handguns here and a pile of grenades there, enough to make them believe there was a small army ambushing them. AJ figured he had enough time during the chaos to sneak in, snag the books, and disappear into the forrest.

Christopher Gallows pressed the cold steel of his gun against the base of AJ's neck the instant the grabbed the book. "If you shoot me, I'll rip it. Even one page removed will ruin this whole ceremony." AJ had no clue if that was true, but it was a bluff he was willing to gamble with.

***

Kana broke free from Dieter's grip. She went straight for her gun, fired a few shots, but missed entirely. They wrestled over the weapon, but it slipped from her grasp and fell to the forest floor. She balled her fist and struck Dieter between the eyes, breaking his nose and winning a howl.

"Savage!" he barked.

She wasn't done. Kana tackled him, but he countered, wrapping his arm around her neck, preventing her from taking him to the ground. Kana adjusted, wrapping one leg around the back of Dieter's and then pushing up, throwing the German off balance, both now falling to the ground. She still had a hold of him and wasn't letting go. As she went for his arm, this time fully intending to break it, she found something wet and fleshy. Not a hand as she expected, but a coil of tendrils, squirming between her fingers.

They reacted as if they had a mind of their own. The lacey strands of flesh latched on to her arm like the tentacles of a jellyfish, the barbs stinging her. She screamed, a prickling pain shooting up her arm and through her chest. She tried to break free, but the barbs were sunk in deep.

"Oh, you can't get away." Dieter laughed dementedly. "I want to hear you scream again girl. Scream!"

He balled his other hand into a fist and used it like a sledgehammer. Again, and again, he pounded at her ribs and abdomen, winning a cry from her with every measured strike. The delight was intoxicating to him. His eyes were wide, his lips wet, literally salivating at the sight of her anguish. Twice more he struck, his smile growing with every cry and cough.

This was only the beginning. For every second of humiliation he experienced since Israel he would multiply that by ten and return it to her in torture. None of the arts had ever compelled him, but this, his *sadism*, was where his creative mind did its work.

He was so lost in his own sick thoughts it made him predictable. Kana saw an opportunity, an old move taught to her when she trained in Brazilian Jiu Jitsu. Dieter extended his arm so high in the air for every hammering fist that it left his body exposed. Kana clamped her legs around his neck, her right shin looped under his throat and her left leg pressing down on the back of his neck. Dieter's free hand was useless now, flailing around while she squeezed as hard as she could. The pressure pushed his windpipe down on her shin bone, choking him while cracking his bones at the same time. Her left hand then went to the back of his head, increasing the pressure. He squirmed, trying to breathe. Blood trickled from his nose and mouth. His head looked like a balloon inflated to the point of bursting, flush and bulbous.

The thrashing slowed, and his grunts lessened. Defeated, Dieter defiantly shouted his last breath before his windpipe snapped against her shin. She let go and pushed his carcass away, the barbs of his tendrils releasing their grip as he dropped into the dirt and leaves.

Kana took a few moments to catch her breath. She found it strange how a few minutes ago she labored over shooting Stefan but had no remorse whatsoever with the more intimate and violent way she had done away with Dieter. One was out of self-defense and the other would have been cold-blooded murder, or at least that's what she rationalized. She swore she heard the Shinigami's subtle laugh in her head. So be it, she was alive.

Moral complexities aside, she turned her attention to the chaos erupting in the forest. Gunshots and explosions boomed from all directions. Whoever had started the firefight didn't matter. It gave her cover; the guards were preoccupied with defending the grounds instead of protecting their bosses. It was time to move. She brushed the dirt off her jeans, lifted her gun from the ground, and headed toward the altar.

***

Stefan reached out for the grimoire. "AJ, just put the book down."

"You really aren't the person who should be giving me advice right now," AJ said.

"It's business, AJ. Nothing personal. This man is going to blow your brains out. He'll do it, believe me."

The warning sounded genuine to AJ. He didn't doubt the man who held a gun to his head was serious about pulling the trigger. The only thing that kept AJ alive were the pages of the book he had gripped between index finger and thumb, ready to rip.

Octavius broke from his trance and stumbled to the altar. "Stop!" He pulled Gallows' arm down and kept it there.

No longer at gunpoint, AJ turned around, only to be punched in the jaw. Octavius stepped over AJ as he fell on his ass, grabbing the Black Grimoire as he went.

"Octavius!" Stefan yelled.

"I can see it," Octavius said.

Ignoring his sibling's warning, Octavius placed the third book on top of the others, the three becoming one. A blast of heat rushed through the books, a wave of energy so strong it knocked Gallows and AJ back several feet. The ink on the pages shifted again, a blazing red inscription revealed on the black pages. Octavius beamed at his accomplishment, then pulled at his hair and screamed in horror when he realized what he had done.

THE HELLVEIL

―――――∽――――

"What does it say?" Gallows pulled himself to his feet, his face drained of color. "Did he finish the ritual? Is it complete?"

The Black Grimoires sat open on the stone slab, propagating a heat that baked every inch of The Reliquary. Stefan crawled back to the altar but stopped when he saw Octavius convulsing on the ground, clutching at his heart, stomach, and skull. He howled like a wolf, his body arching upward as if God pinched his naval and pulled skyward. He sprung to his feet and stumbled to the center of the ruins, tearing at his hair, and eventually, shedding his flesh into scraps of meat on the ground.

"What on Earth is this, Stefan? What is wrong with him?" Gallows demanded an answer. This wasn't the *majestic power* he sought, this was a living nightmare.

Whispering voices, dark and haunting. surrounded The Reliquary, passing over and between the witnesses to Octavius's unmaking until finally coalescing around him. The voices transferred to him, a language alien to Stefan, forced through his brother's lips in rapid succession. He didn't need to understand the words to catch their meaning—the spirits that possessed Octavius were not here to give enlightenment. A sinister cackle escaped his gaping maw, and on cue, the altar cracked in half. Sinkholes opened around the perimeter of The Reliquary, sucking sections of the old church down into the earth, a deep groan escaping from the newly formed pits.

Whoever remained from the earlier gunshots now left in droves. Most escaped, the less fortunate were victims of the phenomena. Large columns of ethereal mist burst from the ground in ghostly streams of red garnet and hellfire orange. Deformed faces were carried on the streams; a ghoulish menagerie of horned skulls and mangled cherubs, open-mouthed to scoop the fleeing men in their maw. Many were caught, strewn up high into the air, their bodies ripped into pieces and splattered across the treetops.

The *Hellveil* drew enough attention that no one noticed Kana sneaking into The Reliquary—no one except Christopher Gallows, who kept himself from being swept away in the anarchy. The two stood at arm's length, their guns drawn.

Gallows cocked his head. "So, you are the girl."

Kana had no idea who this man was or why he was so fascinated with her. All she knew about him was that he pointed a gun at AJ. Gallows rolled his tongue against the inside of his cheek and lowered his gun. Kana tightened the grip on hers, keeping him in her sights.

"A pleasure to meet you." He turned to his beloved Hannah who was screaming at him from the forest, tipped his forehead to Kana, and joined his woman in retreat.

Kana rushed over to AJ now that the stranger was gone. "Who the hell was that?"

"No idea. Probably the head Thule guy or whatever."

"Are you hurt?"

AJ rubbed the back of his neck. "No. We have to get out of here."

Kana couldn't take her eyes off Stefan. "I'm not finished yet.".

"He's not worth risking our lives over. We need to go. It's finished."

The ghastly streams migrated back to The Reliquary after feasting on the bodies in the forest. They were in search of more, heading straight for Stefan and Octavius.

"Octavius! What can I do?" Stefan pleaded with his brother.

Still spewing a stream of unintelligible words, Octavius rocked back and forth on his knees, ripping ribbons of flesh from bone. He moaned, he laughed, and finally he leaned back on his haunches and loosed a painful howl to the heavens. The din was like nothing Stefan had heard before, inhuman and more monster than beast.

His voice exhausted, Octavius dropped to his hands and knees, vomiting a black liquid that pooled underneath him like hot tar.

"You should have killed her," Octavius spoke, now in English, his voice deep and raspy.

Stefan backed away as the steaming black sludge oozed across the floor. Octavius put his hands to his face, his fingers massaging his forehead, and then dropped them to his sides. Like melted wax his flesh slid off his frame, sticky chunks of pink meat flowing along streams of scarlet, exposing bone and muscle. His oxidized skin glittered in the moonlight. "You should have killed her!"

Stefan cried out for his brother, his hand covering his mouth as the tears streamed down his cheeks, until he saw Kana going for the books. "What are you doing?".

"Did you read this? Why did you put them together?" The ground trembled again, forcing her to shout.

"You know why. It was the job. The Thule Society wanted this power, so I gave it to them. It's what my brother and I have been working on for years."

"Then why didn't you read what was written here?" she asked again, hinting that he missed something important.

"What do you mean? I read it!" Stefan stumbled to the right a few steps as the ground shook again. *"To give man control over the servants of Hell..."*

"No, no, nah-no no no! This is Mishnaic Hebrew. You read it wrong. It reads, *to give man over to the servants of Hell.*"

AJ did a doubletake. "You mean all of this is because he's terrible at translation?"

"Not now, AJ."

Stefan eyed them both, then the books, then Kana again. He slouched in defeat, shaking his head.

Kana's revenge would have to wait. "There must be a way to stop this." She scanned the text, her fingers moving across each word as she read. "The only way to end the ceremony is to detach them. We have to pull the books apart."

"Wait! Stop!" Stefan begged. "If you do that, you'll kill my brother."

The hellfire mist coalesced behind Octavius, shooting up his back like a solid sheet of translucent fire. The Hellveil was alive, the wraith faces hissing as they traveled skyward, each one taking a chunk of Octavius with them as they nipped at his body.

AJ pointed at Stefan's brother. "Look at him! We'd be doing him a favor."

"No! I'll fix this! Get away from there!" Stefan charged the altar, not making it two steps before Kana drew her gun, pointing it between his eyes, a receipt from Shinjuku.

He raised his hands and swallowed hard. "Let me take care of this. Yes, this is all my fault. Yes, I betrayed you, I used you, but it was all to help him. I wasn't out to hurt you and you know that. You're a smart girl. Let me help him the way I know how."

The tremors increased, mini earthquakes growing in magnitude with every iteration. The sinkholes grew, consuming whatever was left behind as the Hellveil disintegrated everything it touch, flinging the remains to the heavens. The Reliquary was ready to collapse.

And Stefan didn't care. "Damn it, Kana! Let me help him!"

"I can't." Kana took a deep breath and grabbed the book with her free hand. She may as well have been touching a hot oven, her hand sizzling the instant she touched it.

Kana shut her eyes from the pain, heard a scuffling to her left, and opened her eyes to see Stefan holding AJ in a choke hold. The bastard was going to force her hand. He was going to barter, she thought, try to exchange AJ's life for his brothers. There was no time for this.

Kana dropped the grimoire, grabbed her gun, aimed, and fired.

The bullet sliced through Stefan's shoulder. He let go of AJ and dropped to his knees, blood bursting between his fingers as he covered the wound.

The wraith voices laughed, coming through Octavius. "You should have killed her." What remained of Stefan's brother was no more than a shambling mass of sinews and blackened bones. The only part of this grotesquery that even resembled the man were his eyes, blue and clear, set in gaping black sockets.

Kana recoiled from the sight of him. He stumbled toward the altar, those blue eyes aimed directly at her with a steely focus.

The streams of hellfire consolidated into a wall of shrieking faces, all flowing skyward, bathing her in its bloodred light, Octavius' stalking silhouette preceded it. With each step, he was gaining in speed, fueled by the curtain of nightmares behind him, hissing and cooing in oily voices.

Kana braced herself for the pain and again took hold of the Black Grimoire. It was like plunging her hands into a scolding hot bath. Her arms boiled from the tips of her fingers to the bend in her elbows. Her nerves, muscles, and bones cooked, screaming at her to let go, but she pressed on. Octavius was a few feet away.

They weren't budging. "Come on! Come on!" Then, some movement, the pages blurring. She could do this. Kana pushed one foot against the cracked rubble of the altar and leaned back. Her muscles were on the verge of tearing, her skin stretched to the point of splitting. With one final scream, she wrenched the book free.

Two of the three tomes split apart and closed, side by side, as if they were simple bindings of leather and paper. Kana spilled off the altar to the floor, the burning gone as she cradled one of the books between her arms. She had no idea how close she was to death until she looked up at the altar to see Octavius frozen in a fearsome pose. His one arm was extended with the sharpened ends of his bony hand unsheathed. She'd have been impaled through the throat if not for falling backward.

AJ avoided the frozen monster as he joined her on the ground. "Are you okay?"

"I'm good, AJ. I'm good."

The *Hellveil* evaporated into a wispy smoke, the demonic voices fading. Octavius' retracted his arm, whimpering as he stumbled away from the altar. He raised his hands in front of his face and, for a moment, the real Octavius had control. His nerve endings screamed from head to toe, sending him into shock, looking for his brother.

Stefan shuffled across the floor, blood pouring from the bullet wound in his arm, to meet his brother at the center of the clearing. He never made it. Octavius' body gave out, slumping to the floor in a smoldering heap.

"Octavius! Octavius!" Stefan cried over his brother's remains. "I'm sorry. I'm so sorry!"

Kana and AJ watched on for a moment as Stefan rubbed his hand over what was left of his brother's head. This wasn't a scene for others to witness. Kana hated him, but she wasn't without compassion. Her revenge on Stefan would wait. Today, she'd leave him to mourn.

AJ collected all three grimoires in the briefcase, locked it shut, and followed Kana away from the clearing.

Stefan's voice followed them. "I should have killed you. I should have."

Kana stopped and glanced over her shoulder. "Your brother was already gone, Stefan. I had nothing to do with it. You did."

"I should have killed you!" The veins in Stefan's neck pushed to the surface, half of his face red with his brother's blood, a string of spit dangling from his lips.

AJ tugged on her sleeve. "Let's go, Kana."

There was nothing left to say. It may have been wiser to put an end to Stefan right there and then. He'd be a monster she'd have to confront down the road, but again, she wasn't a cold-blooded murderer. He'd turn up again someday and she'd be ready for him. For now, she'd give him his dignity. It was the last thing she'd ever give him.

"I SHOULD HAVE KILLED YOU!"

Kana continued walking into the darkened forest. "Maybe you should have."

***

The Thule guards, who had spent much of the last hour searching for the phantom assault team AJ jury-rigged in the forest, now had a new target. Their orders remained the same, even with their superiors absent. Any trespassers were to be eliminated without question or prejudice.

AJ ran a few paces ahead of Kana who's injured leg slowed her down. "How far do you think we are from the main road?" He stopped to let her catch up as bullets cracked the trees nearby.

"It can't be much farther," Kana answered.

He helped her over a log, cinched up his grip on the briefcase, and continued running. "I'd hate to go through all of this and wind up with a bullet in the back."

"You did good, AJ. I know I never say so but..."

"Hey, save the patting each other on the back for when we don't have a platoon of guys hunting us."

Out of breath, Kana wasn't going to argue with him. "Good point."

Kana and AJ were far ahead of the guards whose gunshots thinned out the closer they came to the main road. Another few dozen yards and they would be clear.

The outline of a roadway came into view. AJ reached the roadway first, panting heavily and vowing to himself that he'd take up jogging if they survived this. Kana caught up with him and both raised their hands in the air. A line of the Thule's mercenaries stood between them and the road, weapons drawn. There was no cover, no way to turn around and escape, they were out of options.

AJ laced his hands behind his head. "Can't catch a break, can we?"

A fleet of black SUV's sped toward them and caught the mercenaries off guard. The first vehicle plowed into them, sending their bodies scattering like bowling pins. Those who survived rolled away, opened fire on the trucks, and were shredded by return fire for their efforts.

Kana and AJ ducked but there was no need to, they were not the target. They slowly approached the tinted window of the lead SUV, their hands still laced behind their heads. The passenger side window rolled down and Anastasia stuck her head out and waved them over. "Get in!"

The pair blinked at each other. "I thought you had your own stuff to deal with?" Kana said.

"Are you really going to argue with me right now, Kana? Get your butt in the truck!"

Kana and AJ ran to the car, narrowly avoiding another barrage of bullets coming from the mercenaries in the woods.

Pratt looked back at Kana from the front seat. "I told you we'd get you home safe," he said, stepping on the gas.

The SUV's sped off down the road, leaving the Thule soldiers to watch helplessly as the red break lights faded into the distance.

LOOSE ENDS

wo days later AJ and Kana were back home at their office in Massachusetts. They unlocked the front door, walked into the warehouse, and sighed with relief.

There was work to do of course. Every scrap of information they collected had to be transferred, catalogued, and classified, per procedure as Kana insisted. She felt more relaxed today, and with Case #101 in the books, she slid behind the bar and poured two drinks.

"Tommy Bahama!" Kana raised the bottle so AJ could read the label.

"Who?"

"It's rum. And I don't want to hear any lip from you, AJ. You're having one too."

He scratched the back of his head. "You know, after nearly dying like thirteen times over the last week, one of your drinks seems like the least threatening thing in the world right now."

"That's what I like to hear." She carried both shots to the sofa and handed one to AJ. He looked the glass over tepidly, took a sniff, and wrinkled his nose.

"What the hell is this?"

"Trust me, it's good." She sat down on the couch next to him. "What are we toasting to?"

"That you're in a surprisingly good mood?"

"Shut up, AJ. No, seriously, what should we toast to?"

"I don't know, how about..." His train of thought was cut short by the front door buzzer.

Kana groaned and set her glass on the coffee table before answering the door. It didn't matter who it was, they were closed for the next week. She saw who was standing outside the glass doors and huffed. "It figures."

Tomas Moretti didn't waste any time in tracking them down, dressed in a well-pressed pinstripe suit as he waited patiently outside. They purposely didn't let him know they were in town, wanting at least 24 hours to recuperate, but Kana knew he'd turn up sooner or later. The Black Grimoires were too important to the Church.

"How are you feeling?" asked the man from Rome. "I heard it was a rather eventful trip."

"How did you hear anything about... never mind. Let's get this done," Kana said.

Tomas followed her back to The Bridge. AJ offered him a seat, but he declined.

"First, I want to express our gratitude for all the work you did. You truly lived up to the potential we thought you had. I trust the compensation is adequate."

AJ opened a banking app on his phone and gave Kana a thumbs up. "More than enough. I guess you came to collect."

"Yes, of course." Tomas strutted around the pool table, sliding his finger against the felt corners. "We would have met you at the airport, but these things are better handled with fewer eyes and ears around, no?"

Kana wondered if this is when the other shoe was going to drop and he'd reveal something sinister behind the whole job.

"Here they are." AJ pulled the briefcase from their pile of luggage and opened it on the coffee table. "We had no trouble getting them through customs. They're probably the most dangerous thing on the plane, but TSA doesn't see three old books as a security risk."

Tomas opened the briefcase and stared at the three ancient grimoires nestled next to one another.

Parting with the treasure felt strange to Kana, as if giving them up was a mistake. Then again, what would she do with them? There was no way she'd keep them in the office. Handing them over to Tomas was the best option, no matter how much distrust she had in him or the Vatican.

"What are you going to do with them?" Kana asked. "Those things are dangerous and should be locked away or destroyed if possible."

Tomas closed the briefcase. "The books will be kept safe to be sure. Far out of dangerous hands."

Kana narrowed her eyebrows, taking a step closer to Tomas. "Yeah, but in whose hands?"

"*Them.*"

She cocked an eyebrow, but Tomas didn't flinch. The man wore a mannequin's smile which did nothing to make Kana feel that he was to be trusted.

AJ broke up their staring contest. "Thanks again for the payment, Tomas. Kana and I have work to do—categorizing and all. Can I see you to the door?"

She had to let it go. They had done their part. Whatever was to become of the Black Grimoires was out of her hands and she didn't have the energy, nor the interest at this point, to argue about it. Tomas wasn't going to give her any answers no matter how hard she tried, so she racked the balls on her pool table and left AJ to deal with him.

AJ returned from escorting Tomas. "What was that all about? You think he's up to something?"

"Of course he's up to something, AJ. We need to be up to something too. Our names are out there in the underworld now. First thing tomorrow we need to take that money and secure this place, both the data and the office itself. We're not playing in the minor leagues anymore."

AJ flopped on the couch and kicked his feet up over the arm rest. "I'd be more than happy to take a ghost is in my attic case right now. We can ease into secret societies and skinless demons after a vacation."

"For a while." Kana stuck her lower lip out and nodded in agreement, picking up her drink. "Right now, let's toast to being in the big leagues."

"Fair enough."

AJ handed her a shot glass and braced for the toast. The two paused as if waiting for the other to say something more. Kana could have told AJ how much she appreciated everything he had done, his bravery, his believing in her, and how she might not even be alive if it weren't for him. She also knew he had his own unresolved issues. Was he going to confess his feelings for her or keep them tucked away? God, she hoped he'd keep them tucked away. There was no need to verbalize them now, or ever, if she had her way. Far better to leave this at an awkward toast than ruin the moment.

"To the big leagues," Kana smiled.

"To the big leagues!" AJ repeated.

The two toasted, clinging their glasses together and downing their shots. Kana, of course, took it like a champ while AJ coughed for a minute straight. She laughed as he waved his hand in front of his mouth, trying to cool his burning lips.

She grabbed her pool stick, took her spot behind the table, closed one eye, and lined up the cue ball.

"The big leagues..." She pulled the stick back and took her shot.

LAST CALL

—— ～ ——

Tomas insisted on driving a Bentley on his missions, no matter where he was. Pakistan, Canada, China, Russia, America, it didn't matter, it had to be a Bentley. He refused to drive anything else.

The vintage model, a black and silver 1930s edition, suited him fine with its soft leather interior, the polished wooden console, and monogramed steering wheel. The car was much like him, something elegant in inelegant times.

The vehicle crept to a halt at the next stop light. Tomas watched the pedestrians meander through the crosswalk, imagining what they must of thought at the sight of such a classic machine. Then his far more modern cell phone rang, buzzing against the leather of the passenger seat.

"Yes sir," he answered.

The voice on the other end was obscured by a voice modulator. Tomas listened for a few seconds before answering.

"No sir, they've all been accounted for... The Thule Society hasn't been heard from since, so I don't think we have to worry about them for the time being... yes, sir..."

A child dropped their ice cream cone directly in front of his car. Tomas watched the child's mother try to console the boy. "...the Yakuza have been paid sir, the girl shouldn't be threatened by them... I agree it could be something to use in the future... no, I don't think I've been exposed to anyone but the girl and her partner..." The boy cried louder, reaching out for his mother who scooped him up in her arms and carried him through the rest of the crosswalk.

Tomas tapped with his index and middle finger against the steering wheel. "I'll keep an eye on them... yes, they still think I'm from the Vatican... understood..." The mother and son made it across as the light turned green. Tomas was free to go. He pressed his foot on the gas and continued through the intersection before finishing his call.

"Good, then I will see you in ten hours, Professor Granger."

THE WONDERFULLY WEIRD

Kana's adventures are just beginning...

I hope you enjoyed this first of many full-length stories in the Kana Cold Universe. If you did, I invite you to join our community called "The Wonderfully Weird".

By signing up, you'll get previews of the next Kana Cold novel, a deleted chapter from the Case of the Shinigami novella, and access to my private Facebook group where we talk about all kinds of subjects, not just Kana Cold books. It's a place for people like you who enjoy urban fantasy, paranormal thrillers, and strange and wonderful things from around the world.

Go to: www.AOEStudios.com for more information.

We are also looking for BETA READERS. If you would like to be one, please see the information available on our mailing list or Facebook page.

www.facebook.com/groups/TheWonderfullyWeird

ABOUT THE AUTHOR

KC Hunter is the author of the young adult urban fantasy novel THE BROTHERS LOCKE and the paranormal thriller series KANA COLD.

Since the age of thirteen, KC has lived a creative life as an author, oil painter, landscaper, programmer, as well as many other activities. He now aims to bring many of these visions, characters, and stories to the world at large as a professional author with nearly 45 books planned over the next few years.

Social Media:

www.facebook.com/thekchunter

www.twitter.com/TheKCHunter

WHAT'S NEXT?

Kana knew gaining access to the Paranormal Underground would bring her more fame, more clients, and more travel... she also knew it would bring more problems.

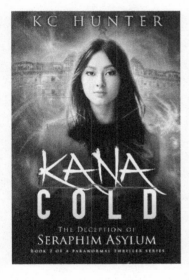

While on a mission with Anastasia in Africa, Kana discovers that not everything is as she thought it would be working in "the big time". She also encounters two new allies, one of which can manipulate reality through what is known as "Art". AJ is forced to confront the sordid history of his family with newest team member Piper, the FBI have taken an interest in Kana's business with their own paranormal problems, and a face from the past looks to seek revenge against all of them.

Kana Cold: The Deception of Seraphim Asylum is the second outrageous adventure in the Kana Cold Universe. Order your copy today through Amazon or download it for free as part of Kindle Unlimited.

Made in the USA
Coppell, TX
08 February 2021

49920673R00184